The Queen of Egypt

Samuel Ebeid

D. X. VAROS

Table of Contents

Prologue
Five Thousand Years Ago

"From Adoria to Egypt," the voice message continued to play, repeating itself over and over. "We are fully prepared to launch our attack on your lands unless you return the heralds safely and deliver the suspects rapidly. If you don't comply, you will endure pain, suffering, destruction, and loss." As per the first commander's order, the aggressive and threatening statement continued to be broadcast from the mothership of the Adorians, commonly knowns among the Egyptians as the People from the Sky or the Celestials.

Only the Egyptian priests, oracles and well-educated elites knew the real story about the Adorians. According to what was written in some ancient scrolls, the Celestials were a highly advanced species who inhabited a medium size planet called Adoria. In the Adorian language, the name meant "the gorgeous lands with magnificent creatures." They were thousands of years more civilized and developed than the Egyptians, or any other nation on Planet Earth or any other inhabited planet in the known universe.

In one of the spiral arms of the Milky Way galaxy, Planet Adoria was located, about one-third of the way to the center. From Earth, it was on the other side of the galaxy. The planet was formed 6 billion years ago, and it was the second planet from twin glowing stars circling each other called the Twins. The planet orbited around their dual suns once every five thousand days, a period which was known as an Adorian year. Also, it had five moons. About half of the planet's surface was covered with water. The remaining half consisted of the five main continents.

Thousands of years ago, and after years of bloody wars between the five continents of Adoria, the celestials finally reached peace. All five united under one kingdom, the Great Realm of Adoria, and under one leader, the Supreme Leader Nexer Chomurista. One of his first commands after rising to power, was uniting the five armies of Adoria under, his most loyal friend, Azan Zalga. Due to the unique location of Adoria in the galaxy and its inimitable orbit around the Twins, the celestials lived thousands of Earth years. Azan, for instance, was over five thousand years old. Compared to his subordinates, five of them stood behind him in the middle of the command center of the mothership, Azan was huge. He towered over all the other Adorians in this preparatory meeting before invading the land of Egypt.

As the Commander-in-Chief of Adoria, Nexer, along with the supreme council consisted of the five elders who represented the five continents, believed that exploring space, using a program in which each continent supplied a critical component was a way to cement the recent peace. This program thrived and in due course it was decided to explore the other planets in the galaxy and to help in nurture other civilizations on the inhabited ones. In time, they reached the Solar System.

Back then, Nexer had assigned his friend Azan to explore Planet Earth. In his report to Nexer, Azan described how they found life. Apparently, a combination of Earth's distance from the Sun, physical properties, and geological history had allowed life to evolve and thrive. Biodiversity had gone through long periods of expansion. Millions of species of plants and animals shared the planet. One of these species, according to Azan's report to the supreme council, called humans had a brain which was believed to be more intelligent in general than that of any other known species on Earth.

Azan also reported a boundless potential for a great civilization that they could nurture to existence in a neck of land between what would be later called the Mediterranean Sea and the Red Sea, which would be called Egypt. For instance, he trusted that a great kingdom on this land was going to have an essential role in geopolitics stems from its strategic position. He believed that it was going to be a hub for trade routes between three continents.

Based on Azan's proposal, the Supreme Council of Adoria, under the leadership of Nexer, decided to invest in Earth through nurturing a great civilization on the banks of the River Nile, the same way they had helped other civilizations in other parts of the galaxy. The council even commissioned Azan to lead the mission.

First, the Adorians guided the primitive tribes that inhabited the deserts of Egypt to settle down in the Nile Valley. Then, they taught the early Egyptians the elements of civilization; agriculture, architecture, and mummification. Right before leaving Planet Earth when Azan's mission was completed, he gifted the first crowned Pharaoh of Egypt with a mysterious substance, called kairemi. The celestials believed that the kairemi would help guarantee stability in the land of Egypt. It was a multi-use substance that allegedly gave wisdom to the rulers, made them appear as half-gods in the eyes of their people, healed them from deadly diseases and injuries, doubled their treasures, served as a weapon of mass destruction against their enemies, and was used to protect the Pharaohs' mummies and tombs.

The early Egyptians illustrated the arrival of the celestials to their lands in their inscription on the walls of the sacred hall in the royal palace in Thebes. One of the walls were decorated with brightly colored emblem of the winged scarab beetle and the eye of Ra, which represented the friendship between the Egyptians and their allies across the galaxy. Another wall showed the ship in which the People from the Sky had arrived. It was a pyramid floating in the air which later inspired the Egyptians to build their tombs with the same shape. Another scene depicted Azan as a slim creature with two antennae, a huge head, three eyes, two wings, two small arms, two short legs, and no fingers or toes. In the same picture, the Celestial creature was handing the kairemi to a crowned Pharaoh.

One more thing the Adorians had done before leaving Planet Earth was that they decided to keep a direct back-channel open with the people of Egypt. They managed to link the most advanced communication devices they had to the gods of Egypt, in case they decided to deliver critical messages to the Egyptians. Back then, the chances of broadcasting a threatening message to the lands of Egypt, like the one was being broadcast now, were very slim. Some of Adorians even believed that establishing such back-channel was an unnecessary step.

For thousands of years, this back-channel between the Adorians and Egyptians existed, yet it had never been used. The relation between the two nations was based on mutual respect, and it was elevated to a comprehensive strategic partnership. Generations after countless generations of Egyptians came to life and then crossed to the afterlife, knowing that they have strong allies on Planet Adoria. Only the current generations shockingly learned that this alliance was about to collapse in ruin.

After thousands of years, the leaders of Adoria had finally found out that leaving this direct back-channel open was a crucial step, particularly after the attack on one of their spaceship, or the floating pyramid as it was known among the Egyptians.

A few weeks ago, communication left Earth and traveled across the galaxy until it reached Adoria. It was a message from the Egyptians that they needed some more kairemi. The message came in conjunction with other reports, which stated that Egypt was witnessing a lot of political turbulence.

The reports described that an Egyptian nobleman, his name was Varis, had led a group of mercenaries from the land of Kush, south of Egypt, attacked the royal palace and killed the royal family, save one young daughter, Princess Merit, who escaped into hiding. As Varis proclaimed himself the new king of Egypt, the hedonistic new royal family had their own struggles, with the king maneuvering to place his daughter, Hamees, on the throne after him, setting aside his own son, Gapi.

Other reports stated that a group of insurgents, called the Free Army which led by a former palace guard named Roma, short of Romaroy, turned defender of Princess Merit. They received a great prophecy and used it to determine Egypt's fate by ensuring the throne, and control of the Kairemi, must go to the rightful Heiress of Egypt. One of the rebels, named Amasis, who happened to be the only son to the former high priest, managed to send the message to the Adorians, requesting more kairemi for Princess Merit.

Even though the Supreme Council of Adoria knew about the tussle over the throne of Egypt, they immediately sent seven Adorians to Earth with an urn full of this magical substance. The council was clear enough in its instruction to the messengers not to get involved in the current Egyptian political unrest. That was why the Adorians arrived in their floating pyramid to Egypt, precisely to the north of a small town, called Badari, located on the border between Upper and Lower Egypt, yet the spaceship did not touch the ground nor open its door until the Pharaoh of Egypt or at least the

5

heir of the throne would arrive. But, the Adorian ship was attacked, the seven heralds were kidnapped, and the kairemi was stolen.

Shortly after, all the statues of the Egyptian Gods, rock and wood alike, in the north and south, in temples and palaces, began at first producing weird noises. When the Egyptians, especially the priests and oracles, frantically approached the rowdily sculptures, they could tell that it was not gibberish. It was a message; an official memo from the People from the Sky. It took the priests some time to make out the words of the message. The first priest put the words together, his eyes suddenly shot open, and his mouth gaped wide. He silently looked at his colleagues for a moment, then he reached for his heart and dropped dead.

When the other priests read the dead priest's interpretation, they saw horrifying ancient Egyptian scripts were put together in a dismaying way; vipers, vultures, crocodiles, snakes, and other disturbing characters which all were put together to compose the Adorian threatening message. The message was clear as a bell. No one could claim that the message was not clear enough. Everyone knew that without the safe return of the heralds, a bloody destiny was waiting for the Egyptians and that the kingdom of Egypt is doomed to extinction; sadly, on the hands of its creators.

"If you don't comply, you will endure pain, suffering, destruction, and loss," the commander of the Adorian troops, Azan Zalga, heard the message rebroadcasting from the mothership to Earth, over and over.

"The Egyptians have always been strong allies," Azan recalled himself trying to talk the supreme council out of the military option against the land of Egypt. "I have just presented to you a strong evident that King Alara of Kush and his priests were behind the assault on our messengers."

"Our ship was broken into on Egyptian lands," the oldest member of the supreme council had fired back at Azan who stood in the middle of a large room, surrounded by the five elderlies and the supreme leader of Adoria. "Our heralds were kidnapped on Egyptian soil. The Kairemi was stolen on Egyptian territory. The Egyptians are responsible for what happened regardless of who did it."

"We have no business or interest in the land of Kush," Azan sadly remembered the council's final decision, after hours of debating. "We helped the Egyptians, and they betrayed our kindness. They should have done everything possible to protect our spaceship, heralds, and Kairemi. You, Azan, are going to lead our troops one more time to Egypt. You either will safely bring the kidnapped Adorians back home; or sadly, you will put an end to a civilization we have started thousands of years ago."

Azan and his subordinates were standing in the middle of a meeting room on board of the mothership. They all were facing a huge transparent screen showing the mothership trajectory across the galaxy to Planet Earth. The curvy route which the ship had been taken for the last couple days showed that it had to make several maneuvers to avoid a few black holes which were in its path.

The mothership, which called Colossal, was square if you look at it from below and tapering to a point like a pyramid if you looked at it from the side. Twelve smaller ships escorted Colossal, three on each side. Behind them came a fleet consisting of more ships; hundreds of them, following the mothership to attack the land of Egypt.

At Azan's signal, his five subordinates, whose feet were not touching the ship's floor the same as Azan himself, mysteriously moved forward, as if they were flying without flapping their wings. They form a circle around their leader. When Azan's three eyes stared up at the screen and then moved them downward where he stood, the whole see-through screen moved down and laid horizontally between the gathered generals, forming a meeting table. The only exception was Azan who stood in the middle of the screen, protruding from its center. As the first commander's small arms raised in the air, the screen turned into a hologram for the galaxy where he stood in its center, as if the galaxy's arms branching out from his body.

Right before Azan's three eyes, the mothership continued to travel on its trajectory. He stared his eyes one more time. This time he gazed at one arm of the galaxy, and it gave a non-verbal command to the hologram technology to zoom in on the Solar System, and then zoom in more on Earth until the hologrammed planet was as big and tall as the first commander himself.

As Azan's eyes kept staring, the system continued zooming in until a map of Egypt appeared in the middle of the gathering, still their leader in the middle of it. The Mediterranean Sea was in front of him and the Red Sea with its two arms on his right hand. The Nile flowed through the center, from the south to the north, passing through Azan's body, between the two deserts. Before Azan's and his subordinates' eyes, the map of Egypt was so anthropomorphic that they could see the big cities like Thebes in the south and Memphis in the north, as well as other smaller cities.

"Here's the plan," Azan sadly told his subordinates.

Chapter 1

Falling Walls

"Hold," Roma shouted, and the voice of his men echoed through the desert, repeating the order, mixed with horses whinnying warning cries. As the commander of the rebels, Roma presided over the frontline. The troops spread out behind him in defensive formation; lines of infantry and archery. All were silently waiting for their leader's order.

Behind Roma now, and behind his troops, there was a great spaceship in the shape of a pyramid floating in the air. A few weeks ago, this floating pyramid suddenly, and out of nowhere, appeared in the Sky, north of a small town, called Badari, located on the border between Upper and Lower Egypt.

Coming from the other side, a large number of the enemy's chariots, cavalry, and footmen, charging forward like a dark cloud on the skyline. Roma knew that the enemy's troops consisted of at least thirty thousand; twenty thousand of them had just arrived from the Kingdom of

Kush to join the ten thousand who were already in Egypt, intending to crush the ten thousand soldiers of the Free Army and reach the People from the Sky.

Roma was twenty-four years old, with short dark hair, dark eyes, olive-toned skin, and a hawk nose. A small white slash of an old scar ran through the outer end of his left eyebrow. He was dressed in a simple dark kilt, a plain collar around his chest, and striped headdress. Roma was one of the few who had managed to escape the royal palace, on the day of Varis' rebellion. Ever since he discovered that Princess Merit was still alive, he pursued one single goal; preparing the road for her arrival.

Roma had to travel to Memphis, in Lower Egypt, and met the high oracle, who had offered him a prophecy, "The short age of the illegal dynasty is drawing fast to a close, and the age of the legitimate heir is dawning."

After convincing some nobles to fund an insurgence, Roma worked on forming, arming, and training a mighty army, called the Free Army, capable of defeating the Kushites and overthrowing Varis. He sent his subordinates across the kingdom, inciting people to join the fight against the usurper. In no time, thousands of people had begun to pour into a secret training camp somewhere in Wadi Hammamat, which was in the mountain area between Thebes and the Red Sea. Varis' mercenaries had combed this area several times, yet they could not find any camps.

The Free Army was composed of less than ten thousand soldiers. Yet, they were well-trained, well-equipped; and above all, they had a cause to support. They believed that an illegal ruler was sitting on the throne of Egypt and that they must help Princess Merit to reclaim her father's stolen crown.

After the Celestials had arrived in the land of Egypt with more Kairemi, this mighty army of the insurgents suddenly poured out of the mountains and headed to the arrival location, surrounding the floating pyramid and preventing anyone from reaching the People from the Sky. They swore that only Princess Merit would meet the Celestials.

"Hold," Roma shouted again, his right fist high in the air, so everyone around could see it. His left-hand was itching to pull one of his two short swords.

In this rocky desert, it was so hot. The sun was beaming high above and there wasn't a cloud in sight. The rays were strong and beat down upon Roma's face. Sweat slid down his back, and for a moment, he raised his forearm to wipe his brow.

As his sight was fixed on the Kushite troops which were rapidly advancing, Roma's heart pounded like a hammer in his chest, but he stood his ground. Slowly, he took his famous defense position. He drew his two swords and held them in a reverse grip; the blades were running parallel to his forearms. Then, he brought both swords behind his back, widened the distance between his feet, and leaned his upper body slightly forward. He wore a blank look on his face. That look had made him well-known among his men as "the unpredictable man," because when he was fighting, his face gave no indication of what he would do next.

"Hold," the leader of the Free Army ordered yet again. As the voice of his men echoed through the desert repeating the order, he took a moment to gather his thought about this eventful day.

About two hours ago, one of his scouts blew the horn and pushed his horse hard to where the Free Army camped. When the scout arrived, he told Roma that a massive army of Kushite Mercenaries was advancing toward them.

Later, and after the arrival of the Kushites, they asked for a pre-battle talk. Roma was shocked that King Varis had led the mercenaries himself despite his deadly injury after the failed attempt to murder him. Along with Zannanza, his military advisor, and Sharek, the man who financed the Free Army, Roma agreed to talk to Varis. However, Princess Merit had suddenly arrived in the middle of the talk. She arrived on the back of her griffin, named The One Who

Tears into Pieces, and avenged her parents' murder by gruesomely killing Varis. The thing that made the whole army of Kushites charge forward.

"Hold," Roma repeated loudly, and his order echoed through the back lines.

Suddenly, a loud roar of the One who Tears into Pieces shifted Roma's focus and distracted his attention. He quickly turned his head to the back and up, where Princess Merit was riding on the back of the griffin, still heading toward the floating pyramid. Just a few moments ago, and after killing Varis and kissing Roma in public for the first time ever revealing that they had a secret romantic relationship, Princess Merit rode her griffin intending to go and meet the Celestials. She planned to meet them and receive their gift, the kairemi.

Princess Merit was only twenty-one years old. Short black hair framed her pretty, oval face. She had an olive complexion, beautiful dark eyes, a celestial nose, full lips, and dimpled chin. She was dressed in a white leather corset and a white skirt. A golden headband like a snake wrapped around her forehead, and a matching belt was around her waist. She was wearing a pair of golden snake armlets around her upper arms. On her feet were sandals with straps that tied around the ankles and calves with gold leaf accents. She had two short swords strapped to her back. Also, she held a bow in her left hand, and a quiver of arrows hung diagonally over her left shoulder.

Carrying the princess on his back was the One Who Tears Into pieces or the king of all the creatures as the Egyptians used to call him because he was one of the most feared creatures in Egypt. He had the body, tail and back legs of a lion; the head and wings of an eagle, and an eagle's talons as its front feet.

Roma's eyes widened when he realized that the loud roar of the king of all the creatures was a warning that something was now chasing them. His jaw even dropped when he saw a winged creature chasing Princess Merit on the back on the One who Tears into Pieces.

What the..., he tried to say, but the words failed him. He could not comprehend what was happening, what was this creature, nor from where it came. It did not take him too long to realize that it was a winged woman, dressed in fine chainmail, which barely covered her female parts, and was holding a bow aimed at the griffin.

"Roma," the voice came from his right, "you need to focus." It was Zannanza, who was standing next to Roma, holding a long sword, a bow was hanged on his left should and quiver was on his back. He was an old man who served as the army commander for Senu III, Princess Merit's infertile uncle, before retiring and becoming Roma's military advisor.

After exchanging a worried look with his military advisor, Roma quickly turned his sight forward to the enemy's troops who were getting closer by the moment.

"Hold," the leader of the Free Army said one more time. He could feel the suspense was consuming his troops. Yet, he knew that they were ready, itching to fight the mercenaries whom Varis and his family had brought from Kush to Egypt to fight for them and their interests across the kingdom. Behind Roma, swords were ready to slash the Kushites' throats, arrows were prepared to pierce their hearts, spears were organized to penetrate their bellies, and shields were arranged to stop them.

"Now," Roma finally shouted once the enemy's front line was close enough, and his captains and generals enthusiastically repeated the order. His eyes shone with excitement as the military tactic was about to be put to the test.

Immediately, a group of tall and muscular fighters, the shortest was at least seven-feet-tall, emerged from the back lines. They were dressed all in black and holding large shields, each was taller than its bearer and made of dense wood. Once they passed Roma and the front line, they used their heavy and tall shields to play their vital role in the battle; blocking the Kushites' way until the rest of the Free Army was ready to perform the next move of Roma's genius plan. These men were called the Blockers whom Roma and his subordinates had carefully chosen and equipped to block the Kushites' way and distract them.

In just a few moments, a wall consisting of hundreds of shields, taller than any of the Kushites, blocked their way to the Free Army's front line. Meanwhile, the spears of the Blockers were going through holes prepared in advance in the shields to penetrate the chests and the bellies of mercenaries in the frontlines of the Kushite army. The screams of the Kushites in the frontlines filled the air, and their blood shot up over the Blockers' shields.

At the same exact moment, the Free Army, behind, started implementing a brilliant plan to defeat the Kushites; it was the plan which Roma cleverly designed with Zannanza's help.

"Falling Walls," Roma shouted, and his order was hurried to be obeyed. Falling Walls was the name which he chose of his plan to defeat the enemy.

As the Blockers were delaying the Kushites from reaching the Free Army, the fighters in the second line quickly began to climb on the back of the soldiers in the first line and stood on their shoulders, forming a high human wall consisting of two lines of fighters. Even before the second line of soldiers was able to steady itself on the shoulders of the warriors of the first line, the third line was climbing the backs of both and rising the human wall one more level to be consisted of three lines, towering over the advanced troops.

"Forward," Roma ordered.

At first, it seemed that the fighters in the bottom line, which each now was carrying two fighters on his or her shoulders, were having a hard time to move forward. However, they eventually made it through and approached the Blockers from behind, towering high over the Kushites frontlines, who were staring up at the human wall before them, not comprehending what was happening nor what was going to happen next.

"Fall," Roma gave the order; and immediately, the human wall collapsed. The fighters of the Free Army jumped over the first few lines of the Kushites, charging with a high-pitched war scream and crashing the mercenaries to the ground. When the soldiers of the Free army stood up, each of them used either their shield or sword to kill the closest Kushite fighter to them.

"It's working," Roma shouted to Zannanza. Tears formed in his eyes. He never doubted his plan, yet watching it succeeding sent chills through his body.

Even before the Kushites soldiers in the back lines could absorb the shock of crushing their front lines in just a few moments, the Blockers moved forward and formed another wooden wall made of their shield, blocking the mercenaries' way and giving a chance for the Free Army make sure to kill everyone was in front lines of the Kushite troops.

As Roma's right sword was slashing the throat of one of the Kushites who was laying on the ground, he cried out, "capture," and his soldiers finished for him, "no one." Their weapons killing whoever was still alive of the Kushites' front lines.

When the sword in the left hand of the leader of Free Army penetrated the chest of another Kushite, he shouted, "show," and his fighters finished for him, "no mercy." Their weapons penetrating and piercing the chests and bellies of whoever stood in their way.

"Forward," Roma and his troops cried out, as they realized that they had already killed every mercenary who was standing a moment ago in the first few lines in the enemy's troops. Coming from behind, the next three lines of the Free army had already formed another high human wall, and they were moving slowly forward toward the enemy, towering over their heads.

"Fall," the order came out of Roma's mouth once the new human wall reached the Blockers from behind, and the wall immediately collapsed, crushing the next few lines of the enemy's troops.

"It's really working," Roma talked to Zannanza, his right sword penetrating the chest of a mercenary which he noticed was still breathing.

Although the Free Army had already managed to break the front lines of the Kushites, more hubbub suddenly broke in the mercenaries' back lines, too. When Roma noticed that, he looked at Zannanza trying to understand; but when the military advisor shrugged his shoulders, Roma found himself running toward a high eminence, especially when he heard one of the fighters next to him saying that it was the mummies of the deceased pharaohs.

When Roma reached the top of the eminence, he quickly turned around to see what had caused the noise in the enemy's back lines. His eyes widened when he saw dozens of mummies of the deceased pharaohs, were attacking the Kushites from behind, riding on the back of living sphinxes, called the Terrifying Ones.

He did it, Roma told himself, thinking of his friend, a young priest called Amasis, who was the son of the former High Priest. Roma watched dozens of the late rulers of Egypt responding to the young priest's call to come back from the afterlife to help the heiress of Egypt. The dead bodies of the deceased pharaohs were wrapped in many layers of pure white wrappings from the head to toes. Each was holding his preferred weapon which he used while was still alive. They came to the battlefield riding on the back of Terrifying Ones which were hybrid creatures with the bodies of lions, and the heads that resembled his king wearing striped, blue and gold headpieces.

Roma's jaw dropped when he saw the giant Terrifying One, which guarded the great pyramid of Giza for hundreds of years, and which he passed by on his way to Memphis to meet the high oracle a couple of months ago. The leader of the Free Army was shocked seeing that the stone statue of the sphinx had turned into a living Terrifying One. Roma watched in awe the gigantic front paw of the Khufu's living sphinx smashing three or four Kushites at a time. Meanwhile, King Khufu himself jumped off the living sphinx, and his long spear was piercing the backs and bellies of the enemy's fighter.

Roma even recognized the mummy of Senu III, Princess Merit's infertile uncle. It was easy to distinguish him because he was fighting using his favorite weapon, the infamous double-bladed sword. Roma served as one of the guards of Merit's uncle, and he saw him multiple times fighting with this weapon. The sword in the hand of Senu III's mummy was slashing the Kushites' throats, decapitating their heads, and cutting off their limps.

When Roma looked a little bit farther, he even saw the mummy of Senu IV, Princess Merit's father. He recognized him because his mummy had no head. Apparently, the beheaded pharaoh had come to the battle, riding with his brother on the back of the Terrifying One. Once they arrived the battle, it seemed that the mummy of Senu IV jumped off, placed his decapitated head on a high rock, and he began showering the Kushites with some kind of invisible arrows that he launched using his royal bow. Roma did not see actual arrows coming out Senu IV's bow; however, he could see the Kushites in the backlines falling and blood seeping from their necks, chest, and bellies. On more than one occasion, Roma noticed that some of the invisible arrows penetrated more than one Kushite who happened to be standing in front of each other. One of the arrows even went through five Kushites, who happened to be standing behind each other in a line, killing them all at once.

Where's Moeris, the question suddenly popped in Roma's head. Once he wondered where his best friend was, his mind quickly produced the answer when he heard more noise coming from the center of the Kushite troops. Roma rapidly turned his head to find out that his friend had managed, somehow, to reach the center of the mercenaries' lines. Using bare hands and intoxicated like hell, Moeris had already cleared a large circle in the middle of the enemy's troops. Beneath Moeris' feet, Roma saw dozens of Kushites who already had fallen, and his friend was standing on their unconscious bodies and were fighting more of them who came up trying to stop him.

Moeris also was one of those few who escaped the royal palace during Varis' rebellion. He was a man of the same age as of Roma, with a pointed face, a nose like a bird's beak, and a neatly trimmed beard. He was the first to join Roma's insurgency after learning that Varis had made up the famine which hit the kingdom to upraise on Senu IV's reign and that a rightful heiress to the throne was still alive.

Roma shook his head in disbelief as he remembered how Moeris, even though had little courage when he was sober, strangely showed exceptional fighting skills when he was intoxicated. Before the battle started the leader of the Free Army had instructed some fighter to not try to sober Moeris up; instead, he ordered them to intoxicate his friend as much as he could get, knowing that Moeris alone was going to cause severe damage in the enemy's lines.

Screaming like a maniac, Moeris cleverly avoided the strike of the enemy's sharp weapons and was able to knock them unconscious. Barehanded, he only used either a powerful punch in their jaws and noses, a mighty kick of his leg into their chests, or even by crashing their heads together, in a way that made the other Kushites get angrier and angrier, trying to stop him.

He still doesn't kill anyone, Roma thought to himself, seeing his friend intentionally had not killed any of the Kushite mercenaries. Roma even recalled that this was not the first time he witnessed Moeris deliberately knocked his opponents unconscious, instead of killing them.

This's amazing, Roma thought, finding a hard time to comprehend what was happening. The battle would have never gone better than this. Even in his best dreams, he had never thought that he would defeat the Kushites that easy. Before his eyes, the Kushite troops were stuck between the hammer of the Free Army and the anvil of the late pharaohs' mummies. Even Moeris, alone, was taking care of the center of the enemy's troops. Maybe he was not killing anyone, but at least he was distracting them and striking fear in their hearts.

Something isn't right here, Roma's mind spontaneously doubted, right at the moment when everything started to turn upside down. The battle that seemed in the beginning almost natural to win was about to turn into complete chaos.

Chapter 2
Celestial Pyramid Down

Flapping two wings as big as the griffin's, Keya flew fast behind the One who Tears into pieces, chasing Princess Merit. A big smile crept on her face when she saw the shock spread on Merit's.

No way could she possibly guess how I became a Paruda, Keya proudly thought to herself. Paruda was an ancient Kushite word which meant, winged creature or avian woman.

Keya was thirty-six-years-old with lavish dark hair that flowed down her back in wide braided locks and dreadlocked ends. She had big black eyes hidden behind thick long lashes and a turned-up nose that perfectly fit her slender elliptical face. She held a unique bow made of gold in her right hand, and a quiver of arrows hung diagonally over her left shoulder. The quiver was full of arrows, dozens of them. The iron-pointed arrows rattled together as she flew fast.

Keya was the daughter of King Alara of Kush. She had been born and raised in Napata, the capital of Kush. About ten years ago, she married Varis, believing that one day this ambitious man was going to rule the great Kingdom of Egypt, and he had done it. Varis' successful rebellion over Senu IV's rule meant that Keya became the second most powerful person of the kingdom of Egypt. Behind her back, people used to call her the Kushites Queen of Egypt.

The source of the new queen of Egypt's power was not only her physical beauty, but also her strong ties to the Kushites, her great wealth, and above all her powerful influence on her late husband, particularly after her brilliant plan which had helped him to kill Senu IV and ascend the throne of Egypt.

Having all this power in Keya's hand helped her to manipulate her husband. Everyone in the kingdom, young or old, poor or rich, noble or peasant, knew that Varis' Kushite wife was behind all these mercenaries that keep pouring into the kingdom. Some people even believed that Varis was just a puppet which danced to the tune of his wife and her father, King Alara of Kush. Not only this, but also that Keya was the one who controls everything behind the scenes.

Keya was behind convincing Varis to relay on mercenaries from her home kingdom. Soon after Varis ascended to the throne, the number of the mercenaries coming from Kush was increasing by the day. Besides the five hundred Kushites whom Varis had used to launch his attack on the royal palace, he had brought over ten thousand Kushites to guard and protect all his interests across the kingdom. With the mercenaries' help, Varis had gained control over Egypt in no time.

Even those Egyptians who at first supported Varis' rebellion over Senu IV's reign eventually began to believe that their new king relied on foreigners, and only foreigners, to protect him. Some even whispered that they felt as if they were under a foreign occupier. Others spoke publicly that they did not see any difference between a kingdom that was ruled by a usurper and a kingdom that is occupied by a foreign power. In both cases, Varis, for them, was no more than a usurper, traitor, and killer.

Even when Varis decided to crush the Free Army which surrounded the arrival location of the Celestials, Keya advised him not to rely on the army of the south, believing that the Egyptian soldiers might refuse to obey his order to fight other Egyptians, even if they were insurgents. She convinced him to rely on Kushites because they would fight whomever he wanted, as long as they got paid. She contacted her father who sent twenty thousand fighters to join the ten thousand who were already in Egypt, forming a massive army capable of crushing the Free Army.

At this point, Keya's plan reached its climax. Her father's army had easily arrived in the heart of Egypt. All they needed to do now was defeat a small army consisted of less than ten thousand rebels; and by the end of this day, the southern half of Egypt was going to be under her father's command.

Tonight, we will celebrate declaring Upper Egypt a district of the Great Kingdom of Kush, Keya thought to herself as she was still chasing Princess Merit. She drew her bow and aimed straight at the griffin, but the arrow missed the target. She grunted in anger, then she vigorously flapped her wings and headed straight behind the One who Tears into Pieces.

Poor princess. She must be wondering why they don't open the door for her, Keya increased her smile, even more, when she saw Princes Merit tap twice on the griffin's neck, ordering him to change his course after realizing that the People from the Sky did not open the door of their floating pyramid for her.

Right after Princess Merit gruesomely killed Varis before his troops, Keya along with her father and a small band of Kushite mercenaries had arrived on top of a high hill on the east side of the battlefield. They came with a huge surprise. It turned out that King Alara had already fucked up the whole situation and screwed everyone over. Only a couple of days after the arrival of the floating pyramid, and before the Free Army had surrounded the arrival location, Keya's father had secretly sent a small band of Kushites there, along with five priests. After securing the area, the priests had used their magic powers to build invisible stairs, which the mercenaries used to reach the floating pyramid, sneak inside, abduct all the Celestials, and seize the kairemi.

Out of gratitude, King Alara of Kush gifted his daughter with the stolen kairemi. After drinking a little bit of the kairemi and using Kushite black magic, Keya turned into a Paruda.

All of a sudden, the One Who Tears into Pieces turned around with a chilling roar and attacked the winged woman who was chasing him. His sharp, long talons tried to tear Keya's chest, and his beak attempted to pierce her face, but she was fast in making some quick maneuvers to avoid getting hurt.

Since Keya's attention was consumed by the fierce aerial combat, which was occurring between her and the griffin, she could not pay a lot of attention to what was going on the ground. However, she would later remember that it was like a split second when the battle of Badari shifted from an inevitable victory for the Free Army to a devastating defeat for both armies, especially among Roma's troops.

What held Keya's attention was the scary, loud roar of the One who Tears into Pieces while he was trying to attack her. Princess Merit, on the back of the griffin, had already reached for her bow and one of the arrows. To be able to shoot at the queen, the princess had to pull the griffin away for a moment. That gave Keya a chance to quickly shoot arrow after arrow at the griffin, but Merit skillfully maneuvered the One who Tears into Pieces to avoid being hit.

Every time the princess got a chance, she quickly turned around and pulled two or three arrows from the quiver and shot them together at the winged creature who was chasing her. Keya skillfully managed to avoid all the arrows, except for one; one arrow which pierced through her left wing. Keya shrieked loudly and stopped chasing the griffin for a moment, glaring at the ugly bloody hole which the arrow had left on her wing. Obviously, killing Princess Merit was not going to be that easy. She needed another technique to win this battle.

Keya looked down for the first time since she flew behind Merit. She heard crashing roars, which forced her to shift her sight to the back of the Kushites' army. In awe, she found the mummies of the deceased pharaohs and their Terrifying Ones leaving the battle in a hurry, as if they were scared of something, or as if they were trying to prevent something from occurring.

What's happening? Keya wondered. *Something significant is going on.*

Hubbub began to swell among the troops. The soldiers had stopped fighting, their heads scanning around, not comprehending what was going on.

I have to stop chasing Merit, Keya decided, especially when she spotted Roma standing on top of the eminence, confused and stunt, not knowing what was occurring nor what to do. The chaos that erupted among his troops was now totally distracting him. Add to this, he was not sure why the mummies and their living sphinxes were suddenly leaving the battlefield.

Keya flew directly toward the leader of the Free Army. She had no intention to stop or slow down. She intended to hit him with all her strength, and she did, screaming loudly. The hit blew Roma from his place and threw him through the air. Then, he crashed to the ground and rolled down heaps of fragments of rocks.

Even though Keya knew that this hit would not kill Roma, she realized that she had something more important to take care of.

I need to save my father's army, she thought.

The damage among the Kushites mercenaries was massive. Hundreds were already killed, many of them got murdered by the Free Army, and the rest were destroyed at the hands of the mummies of the deceased Pharaohs and the Terrifying Ones.

The retreat of the mummies and their beasts was an excellent opportunity to save the Kushites. Keya believed that the captains and generals of her father's army must use this chance to retreat, to save whatever was left of their troops, especially if their backlines were clear to do so. In alignment with her thoughts, the Kushites indeed began to withdraw. Once Keya saw that she flew back to the floating pyramid.

I know how to end this, she thought, her eyes sparkling with an idea.

When Keya was on top of the spaceship. She pulled the kairemi urn, which was attached to her chainmail near the left hip. She quickly opened it and, very carefully, dropped a tiny amount of the kairemi, just one drop, in the air above the floating pyramid. She had heard a lot about using the kairemi as a mass destruction weapon, and it was a perfect time to put all these rumors to the test. She decided to use it to defeat the Free Army and the Celestials themselves.

Last time the Egyptians used the kairemi in a war was over two hundred years ago when the Canaanites tried to invade their lands. A massive army crossed the east border and gained control over the Sinai Peninsula. The Egyptian army used a smart technique to defeat the invaders. They spread rumors that they were going to attack from the west. Immediately, the army of Canaan regrouped and traveled west to face the Egyptians. As the Egyptian generals anticipated, the Canaanites marched through a mountain range. Using black magic, the Egyptian priests were able to control an oversize falcon which carried a small tube containing a tiny amount of the kairemi and drop it on top of the army of Canaan.

Stories suggested that when this mysterious substance fell to the ground, there was a massive explosion, and most of the Canaanites evaporated into the air within the first few moments. The majority had died with severe injuries within the next few hours. Only a few hundred survived this massacre and were able to travel back to their home kingdom and to tell their people of the mass destruction weapon which the Egyptians possessed.

From Keya's point of view now, from above the floating pyramid, the falling kairemi drop looked like the silver medical mercury, except for it was red. Keya's eyes widen when she noticed that the more the drop traveled through the air, heading directly to the top of the spaceship, the bigger in the size it got. The drop's mass was getting doubled by the moment. It kept getting larger and larger. By the time it hit the floating pyramid, its size had exceeded the size of a house. It was a huge red liquid drop that hit the pyramid, and then it was an explosion; a massive explosion like no one ever seen before.

As a huge ball of fire was swallowing the upper section of the pyramid, Keya quickly looked back to where Roma fell down after she had powerfully hit him. She found out that he had finally stood on his feet and was trying to warn his troops, especially those who were in the lines which extended beneath the floating pyramids. Yet, they had no chance.

With wide-open eyes, Keya watched how the explosion was so powerful, sending a devastating wave which instantly vaporized hundreds of the Free Army's fighters who were standing in lines which stretched below and around the spaceship. Meanwhile, the explosion caused the pyramid to split in half, and the two portions immediately began to fall down to the ground.

Before anyone, including Keya, could fathom anything, the shock wave generated a mighty, expanding ring of burning wind which traveled through the air, demolishing everything on its way and setting aflame every single soldier of the Free Army who was close enough to the exploded pyramid.

Keya saw the ring of fire was getting closer to Roma. He was standing there, expecting the approaching fire was going to consume his body the same way it did to most of his fighters. He even closed his eyes, believing that he was not going to open them again. However, just a split moment before the fire reached him, Princess Merit and the griffin had managed to fly down, snatch him and fly to the air.

When Keya saw this, she felt anger boiling inside her. She did not only fail to kill Princess Merit; but also, she was incapable of murdering the leader of the Free Army. Watching the One who Tears into Pieces carrying Roma away, she immediately decided to chase them, again. She followed them for a short period.

The hubbub occurring beneath them on the ground and the screams coming from the dying rebels were enough to distract the princess, so she did not notice that Keya was chasing her. Also, the heavy weight of Roma's body slowed down her griffin. That gave Keya a chance to reach them faster. Shortly, she hit the griffin from the side. The hit was powerful enough that Roma slid from his talons and fell from a very high altitude directly into the middle of the fire which was still consuming whatever was left of his army.

Chapter 3
The Great Looting

"I don't get it," Amasis said, talking to Nefer who, he knew was now standing behind him. He did not look at her; instead, his sight was fixed at the battlefield. "Everything was going as planned. Why have the mummies left? And what was this explosion?"

Not believing his own eyes, Amasis was on top of the mountain which was located on the left side of the Free Army; or whatever was left of it to be accurate. His right hand was holding a staff, while his left hand was covering his gaping mouth.

Amasis was a young, bald priest with sunken eyes. He was dressed in a white kilt, with a leopard-skin sash draped over one shoulder and clasped at the hip with a golden brooch. He was the only son of the former high priest, Ramose, and he was supposed to succeed his father. However, all this had changed following Varis' rebellion. Ramose was killed during the attack on the royal palace right after casting a precautionary, magical spell to protect the kairemi from falling into the wrong hands. When Varis shockingly knew that the kairemi had turned into water, he tried to seduce Amasis by promising him to be the next pilgrim. Although being a pilgrim was the dream of any Egyptian priest (because the honored person would voyage across the galaxy and visit Planet Adoria) Amasis declined the offer and refused to help a usurper, traitor, and killer.

On that day, Amasis not only lost his dream of succeeding his father, but he also was imprisoned. Out of anger, Varis sent him to the dungeon with special orders that he must speak as soon as possible about how to obtain more kairemi as well as revealing Princess Merit's whereabouts. Despite the gruesome torturing, Amasis kept his mouth shut, and he never said a word. Later, he was set free by Roma. When Amasis recovered his strength and his injury's healed, he helped Roma to contact the Celestials for more Kairemi.

Amasis also had another crucial rule in today's battle. He stood on top of this mountain, along with a lovely woman, named Nefer, who held for him a thick, primitive book made of large sheets of papyrus with thick thread binding them together. The book's title was "The Great Ones of Egypt," and it documented all the names of the Pharaohs and their achievements, starting from the first dynasty, all the way to Princess Merit's father, Senu IV. Using magic, Amasis began reading the pharaohs' names. And every time he read a name, the long staff in his hand, which had two carved snakes curled around it, spontaneously moved into the air, pointing in the direction where this Pharaoh's tomb was located.

Apparently, the magical spell which Amasis had cast was a call for all the deceased rulers of Egypt to wake up and help the legal heiress to the throne to reclaim her father's stolen crown. And indeed, the late kings answered Amasis' call.

Earlier that day, Amasis had stood there, watching in awe dozens of the deceased pharaohs, coming to the battlefield, riding on the back of their Terrifying Ones. Even the mummy of Princess Merit's murdered father, who lost his head at the hand of Varis during the rebellion, woke up, carried his decapitated head under one arm and his bow in the other hand, and headed to the battle riding behind his brother's Terrifying One.

Because it was Nefer's first time to see a living sphinx, Amasis, a little bit earlier, had to explain to her how these Terrifying Ones were created. He had witnessed the process of creating these hybrid creatures with his own eyes when he helped his father mummifying the dead body of Senu III. The process was written in a papyrus scroll titled "The Holy Ceremony of Summoning the Terrifying One." The whole method was mystic and eerie, primarily because it was full of ancient, magic. The high priest and the five other elderly priests crossed the river to the Valley of the Kings to summon an ancient spirit from the afterlife, called the Terrifying One. The process included killing a sacrificial lion at the tomb's entrance and replacing its brain with the deceased Pharaoh's brain, which the priests had removed during the mummification process. Then, the high priest cast a magical spell that brought the dead lion to life, but in a shape of a sphinx. Later, the high priest and Amasis made sure that the mummy of the late king carried a small cylinder containing a tiny amount of Kairemi to the afterlife to offer it to an ancient spirit, called The Terrifying One, which in return was going to protect the pharaoh's mummy and tomb.

Amasis even told Nefer that after finishing the funeral ceremony and sealing the tomb, the Terrifying One roared. Then, the beast laid down, his paws stretched out. In awe, Amasis watched the Terrifying One turn into a limestone sphinx statue in front of the tomb's entrance. When this happened, curiosity induced the young priest to extend his arm and touch this magical creature to make sure that he had really turned into a statue. To the young priest's surprise, the Terrifying One indeed had turned into a limestone statue. Disguised in the form of a sphinx, he rested there to protect the deceased Pharaoh's mummy and tomb.

However, this particular Terrifying One who protected the tomb of Senu III in the Valley of the Kings, along with dozens of other sphinxes from across the kingdom, came back to life when Amasis cast his magical spell. They carried the late kings of Egypt to the battlefield and caused severe damage in the Kushite backlines. But for some reason, which Amasis did not comprehend, the mummies and their beasts all of a sudden had stopped fighting and left the battlefield, as if they were afraid of something or they were trying to prevent something from happening.

"I really don't get it," Amasis spoke again in a shocking tone. Yet, he received no response from Nefer. His eyes were scanning the battlefield, particularly where the mummies and their Terrifying Ones, a few moments ago, were hammering the Kushites from behind. He could see only a few Terrifying Ones in the distance roaring and running away.

"Nefer," he called out, "what do you think happened?" Yet, Nefer made no comment. At first, he assumed that she had no answer, the same as him. If he did not know what was happening, how in the world would his junior priestess would.

First time Amasis met Nefer was after Roma freed him from the dungeons of the royal palace. Back then this lovely lady had just quit her job as a whore in a small brothel, called the "House of Roses," which was in a small village north of Thebes, and joined Roma and Moeris in their quest of preparing the way for Princess Merit to come back.

Amasis met Nefer at a small house in an impoverished neighborhood north of Thebes. The moment Amasis' eyes laid on Nefer, he fell in love with her. She was gorgeous and had a perfect, sexy body.

Not only this, but Amasis also much-loved Nefer's intelligence. Only when he complied to her brilliant plan, they escaped unavoidable death. When the Medjay soldiers stormed the house searching for him, Nefer distracted them with her flawless naked body. It was a bold move, yet what happened next was even nervier. Amasis had sex with her for the first time. Matter of fact, it was his first time to have sex in his entire life. Although celibacy was not required to be a priest, he had voluntarily chosen to practice sexual abstinence, believing that sex was the root of all evil. But this belief could not stand a chance in front of Nefer's flawless body and beauty.

After that, Amasis and Nefer started a romantic relationship. He even encouraged her to become the first priestess of Egypt. Just a few days before the battle, she had her hair shaved off in the same way as any of the Egyptian priests. When the fight started, she was standing next to Amasis, dressed only in a leopard skin and holding a book for the young priest which he used to awake and call the mummies of the late pharaohs.

"Nefer," Amasis called again. "Why are you not responding?"

When he received no response from her gain, he had to turn around. He was shocked to find that he was talking to himself all this time. Nefer was not there.

***

Hundreds of miles away, a young man in his late twenties named Caesarion was inside the tomb of Senu III, in the Valley of the Kings. He was dressed in black leather armor with a golden breastplate that covered his chest and shoulders. A huge sword was sheathed on his left side. He was overseeing about a dozen men, who were carrying out the treasures of Senu III out of the tomb and loading them on a huge two-wheeled cart made of wood, which was pulled by two sturdy oxen, one white and the other dark brown.

Caesarion was a nobleman. His older brother was a wealthy and powerful man, named Sheamay, the only brave nobleman who dared to say 'No' to Varis on the day of the rebellion and ended up being killed by two beasts, called the Devourers of the Dead. Later, Sheamay's wife, Nebet, along with her son, Sharek, helped Roma by financing the Free Army, in what appeared in the beginning as avenging the murder of her husband, yet later, it was going to be proven that the mother and the son each had motives of their own.

Sharek, for instance, did not really care about his father's death. All he wanted was to set on the throne of Egypt. When all his dreams were shattered by the return of Princess Merit, he tried to kill her, but Zannanza was faster than he, sending an arrow into the side of his neck.

Roma also did not know that Nebet had an affair with her brother-in-law, Caesarion, and that she was preparing to marry him once her ultimate plan of being the richest noblewoman in the kingdom was completed. That was why she intentionally kept Caesarion out of the scene, preparing him for his fundamental role which he was supposed to play while everyone else was busy with the battle of Badari.

Looting the tombs of the late pharaohs was a dream of Nebet since she was young. For years she wanted to do it, but her late husband refused the idea. He knew that price which they could pay for such a mistake. However, Nebet's greediness blinded her and made her see nothing but looting the late pharaohs' treasures and becoming the richest noblewoman in the kingdom of Egypt.

Nebet was not the first to think of looting the pharaohs' tombs. Dozens of people before her thought in the same thing, yet no one succeeded either because of the lack of planning, resources, or because of the Terrifying Ones who guarded the tombs them against any kind of looters or intruders.

The last person who thought about it was Varis who commissioned his children, Gapi and Hamees, to search for the more kairemi inside the tombs. The difference here was that Nebet did not care about the kairemi. She had no interest in it. All she wanted was the pharaohs' gold, silver, pearls, emeralds, and rubies. To do that, she needed a plan, and her plan was simple.

During the last meeting with Roma, Nebet had convinced him that Amasis, as the last priest who knew the real secrets of the Egyptian priesthood, could call the mummies of the late rulers of Egypt to come back from the afterlife to help the heiress of Egypt. She didn't lie to Roma as this was true and achievable, but what she lied to him about was that this was not only to help the heiress of Egypt but also to give her men the chance to loot the tombs of the late pharaohs while their mummies and Terrifying Ones were busy in the battle.

Led by Caesarion, a small group of looters consisted of a dozen of men headed to the Valley of the Kings, across the Nile from Thebes, during the battle of Badari and started looting the tombs. Meanwhile, dozens of other men were robbing the other tombs of deceased rulers across the kingdom.

As Caesarion's men were carrying out the last items of Senu III's treasures, he walked out of the burial chamber. On his way out, he stepped over the dead body for one of his men, along with dozens of smashed and crushed small, clay statues, called Ushabtis. These statues were funerary figurines which were placed in tombs among the grave goods and were intended to act as servants or minions for the deceased king, should they be called upon to do manual labor in the afterlife. Evidently, the Ushabti statues tried to defend the tomb and the late Pharaoh's treasures by blocking the looters' way, but small, clay statues had no chance in front of powerful men, equipped with heavy, sharp weapons.

When the mummy of Senu III came back to life, answering Amasis' call, and when he began to climb out of the sarcophagus, some of the small clay ushabti statues started to form steps which the mummy stepped onto to reach the floor. More ushabti statues quickly ran to the wall and climbed on each other's backs to reach Senu III's favorite weapon, the double-bladed sword. After stretching his limbs, the mummy extended his right arm toward its weapon, and the sword magically traveled through the air to his hand.

Once the mummy of Senu III left the tomb, the Ushabti statues went back into sleep mode. About four hundred little clay statues surrounded the sarcophagus, waiting for their master to get back to his final home. A couple of hours later, the statues came back to life when they heard some noises outside the tomb. At first, they thought that Senu III had come back, but they shortly discovered that dozens of looters were getting ready to step into the tomb. The Ushabtis knew that the Terrifying One was not there to prevent those thieves from robbing the tomb, so they decided to defend it themselves.

At first, the Ushabti statues tried to carry one of the late Pharaoh's weapons. It was a tremendous battle ax which required king Senu III to deploy it using his two hands. Of course, the weapon was too heavy for the Ushabtis. About a dozen of them failed to just move it for even one foot. Soon enough, they realized that this was not going to work. They thought about something else; the royal dagger of Senu III. It was a smaller and lighter weapon which was made of some sort of dark green metal. Only a few statues were able to carry the dagger, but they knew that it was not enough to stop the looters.

As they felt the looters move fast through the tomb's heavy wooden door, which was left wide open after the departure of the mummies, most of the Ushabti statues quickly formed a defensive line along the entrance of the burial chamber. Meanwhile, the others started to climb on each other's backs until they formed a tall tower. On top of it, they held the dagger.

When the looters arrived at the room, there was a silent moment. They looked at each other, and then at the small clay statues which blocked their way from entering the burial chamber. Next, there was a burst of laughter. The sound of looters' laughter echoed through the maze of corridors deep inside the tomb. When one of them stepped forward to enter the chamber, the Ushabti statues on top of the tower threw the dagger to the man's chest, and he instantly fell down dead to the hard, rocky floor in a thud. The looters had to stop the laughter short and looked at each other again. Carrying their sharp, long weapons high in the air, they charged with a high-pitched war scream. In just a few moments, all the Ushabti statues were smashed and scattered everywhere.

As Caesarion passed this mess of scattered statues, he walked through the corridors until he reached the burial chamber of Senu IV and looked inside it. After the murder of Senu IV, his body was buried secretly in the Valley in the Kings, in a small chamber next to his brother's. The room was totally empty; no treasures nor Ushabti statues; it was only the uncovered sarcophagus. Instead of entering the burial chamber of Senu IV, Caesarion turned around and opened the burial chamber across the corridor. It was the chamber where Queen Tetisheri, Senu IV's late wife and princess Merit's mother, was buried.

After pushing the sarcophagus's lid open, his right hand extended inside and snatched something the mummy was wearing around her neck. It was a beautiful necklace that featured Horus as a falcon with two keys of life attached to his feet.

Caesarion almost jumped off his skin when one of his men suddenly burst into the chamber.

"My lord, they are on their way back?" The man reported in a panicked tone, trying to catch his breath. Only now, Caesarion heard the Terrifying One roaring on his way back to the tomb.

"What?" He barked. "How in the world would they be coming back that fast?" When he received only a shrug from his man, he took a moment thinking. "Go, warn the others," he ordered. "Let's get the hell out of here."

**

Back on the battlefield, Amasis was in shock, not seeing Nefer around.

She was just here, he thought, his eyes scanning around. She was here helping me. *Where did she go?* "Nefer," he called out. "Nefer. Nefer."

The screams coming from the dying rebels forced Amasis to turn around and continue watching, in shock, the massive damage to the Free Army; hundreds of men and women had vaporized as if they had never existed in the first place. The fire had consumed hundreds of them, others were still alive suffering from severe burns, and the shock wave had destroyed the internal organs of other couples of hundred. Only a few hundred, who luckily were in the frontlines and far away from the explosion and the crashing site, had survived the massacre.

When Amasis turned his eyes to the remaining of the Kushite army, he found the captains and general were scrambling to restore orders to their troops. Not only this, but they also were struggling to bring all the troops closer to the center. Amasis had to narrow his eyes to mere slits to get a better look at what was happening in the center of the enemy's army. To his surprise, he noticed that there were two huge chariots, which the Kushites were trying to get as close to as possible.

"King Alara of Kush!" Amasis said in a shocked tone. "What is he doing here?"

Amasis' shock did not stop at the surprise of King Alara's presence on the battlefield, but it went on when he saw the person on the next chariot.

"The high priest of Kush!" He talked to himself. He recognized the old man from the way he was dressed. The high priest of Kush was an old man dressed in a simple kilt and a full-feathered headpiece.

Again, Amasis' shock doubled when he saw seven weird looking creatures, gagged and bound behind King Alara's chariot.

"Celestials!" He said in a shocked tone.

"This is going to spark a war between us and the People from the Sky," Amasis said. He could not fully comprehend how in the world the Kushite managed to put their hands on the celestials, but he was confident of one thing. Regardless of how, it was going to be a big deal.

As Amasis was getting prepared to succeed his father, he learned that the Adorian were a peaceful nation who had powerful allies across the galaxy. Yet, he also knew that the Adorians were featured with a short temper. They never tolerated any kind of betraying their friendship and alliance.

Amasis once read about Planet Loki. It was the first planet the Adorians had explored and nurtured a great civilization there. However, hundreds of years later, there was an accident. Prince Loki IV, the heir to the Lokian throne, kidnapped Princess Adoreen, the first daughter of the Supreme Leader Nexer of Adoria, who had already declined his marriage proposal three times before. The Adorians first tried to resolve this conflict, peacefully, but the Lokians had taken no step to return the princess safely.

Amasis read in an old papyrus scroll, titled "The End of the Lokian Civilization," that the Royal Adorian Space Fleet first surrounded the planet and gave the Lokians a whole Adorian day as a final chance to return the princess. However, the Lokians blew their last chance to solve this conflict peacefully.

Amasis' eyes shot wide when he read that once the deadline had passed, hundreds of the Adorian spaceship entered the Lokians sphere and started launching their devastating green beam, killing everything moving. After three days of mass killing, the Lokians tried to reach a truce to work this out, but it was too late. The Royal Adorian Space

Fleet had one order, wipe out the Lokian civilization root and stem. Amasis' tears rolled down his cheek, and he did nothing to stop them, as he read that Princess Adoreen did not survive the attack either. Within one week, no living creature was still on Loki. For another a few weeks, the Adorian spaceships continued to wipe out all the Lokian buildings to the ground.

"This is going to be a disaster," Amasis talked to Nefer. It took him a moment to remember that she was not there. It was as if she had vanished off the face of the earth or evaporated into the air.

"Nefer," he called out, again, his head scanning around. "Nefer. Nefer." Yet, he did not hear from her or see her. He even tapped twice on his magical staff, waking up the two snakes and sending them to look for her, but they came back later with no answer regarding what had happened to Nefer or her whereabouts.

"Where did she go?" Amasis was stunned. His mind could not fathom what would have happened to her. Yet, his biggest shock of the day was yet to come. "What in the world is happening now?"

All of a sudden, everything grew quiet, the sun hid behind a dark cloud, and the sky darkened momentarily. The earth moved exceedingly, and mountains shook as if they were about to tumble to the ground. Thunder rocked the sky, and wind stormed.

"Lord of the afterlife, please have mercy on us," Amasis prayed, knowing what was coming next. Suddenly, and out of nowhere, dozens of floating pyramids appeared in the sky, above the battlefield.

Silence fell over the entire battlefield, except for the screams and moans of the fallen, injured and burned soldiers. After a moment of silence, the soldiers began to run away in panic, and the spaceships opened fired, launching devastating green beam, targeting everything that was moving down there.

When Amasis turned his sight to the Kushites, he finally understood why the generals and captains were scrambling to get everyone as close as they could to the center, and why the high priest of Kush was there. He had heard rumors before about how talented the Kushite priests were. He even heard that they could make a whole army disappear and then suddenly make it reappear somewhere else. He also heard that the great kingdom of Aksum, south of Kush, had fallen when the Kushite Army suddenly appeared inside the kingdom's walls, after a failed siege for months,

What in the world... Amasis tried to wonder, but his voice failed him as he saw the high priest raising his arms in the air. A considerable bubble emerged from beneath his feet, and it swallowed the priest inside as it continued to grow fast. In no time, the bubble was big enough to cover the whole army of King Alara, and then all the Kushites disappeared as if the earth had opened up and swallowed it. The destructive green beam of the Celestials' ships killed only a few dozen of the Kushites before the entire army vanished in a wisp of smoke before the wind.

Chapter 4

Treaty of Thebes

The last thing Gapi had expected when he arrived Thebes, was finding himself facing two armies; the army of the south under his sister's leadership, and thousands of Kushite mercenaries led by King Alara himself.

"How could this possibly be?" He questioned one of his scouts. He was standing on his chariot. "According to our intelligence, the Kushites should have been dealing with the Free Army now in Badari. How in the world could they have traveled from Badari to Thebes that fast?"

Gapi was in his mid-twenties, with bright hair and fair skin. On his face were scars which could only have been made by the claws of a wild animal. He was dressed in a very simple military uniform; a broad leather band around his waist and a light strap over the right shoulder. He was the only son of Varis. After his father's rebellion, he believed that he should succeed the king on the throne of Egypt.

However, this was nearly impossible because Varis had a different plan.

A few months after Varis's uprising, he had an urgent meeting with his children and commissioned them with a quest which was going to help him decide which one was going to succeed him. Whoever was going to extract the kairemi from the late pharaoh's tombs was going to be his father's successor.

Varis' successor was a sensitive issue in the family, mainly because both Gapi and Hamees, since their father's successful rebellion, were competing against one another over the throne. Add to that, everyone in the kingdom knew that Varis hated his son so much and that Keya was the driving force behind this hatred.

Grudgingly, Gapi had to accept the quest that his father had given to him. He had to accept it to prove to his father that he was worthy of being his successor. He traveled to Memphis in the north, and with the help of the vizier of Lower Egypt, Bek, he tried to break into a few tombs to extract the kairemi. However, every time he did, the statues of the Terrifying One had come to life, attacked and killed the intruders who tried to loot the tombs. At a certain point, Gapi attacked the furious beast, and he was lucky enough to survive after receiving only some scratches that left scars his face.

After that, Gapi received some bad news from Thebes. There was a failed attempt to murder his father, and that his dying father had already proclaimed his daughter, Hamees, to be his co-ruler and successor. Believing that his father and sister had betrayed him, Gapi angrily declared the separation of Lower Egypt from the kingdom and proclaimed himself the Pharaoh of the North.

During a parley with his sister, Gapi managed to deceive her. He made her think that he was not planning to attack soon. Meanwhile, he was in contact with King Fazaz of Libya. Knowing that the Libyans were preparing to launch an attack on Thebes anyway, he wanted to unify the army of the north with the Libyan troops to be able to defeat the Army of the South and claim what he believed was rightfully his, the throne of Egypt. However, when he arrived in Thebes, along with Libyans, he was shocked to find out that he was facing, not only his sister's army, but also the Kushite troops.

Next to Gapi now, King Fazaz of Libya was riding on a white horse. He was a man in his late fifties, well over six-feet, powerfully built and considerably overweight. Threads of gray glistened in his long, black hair. Behind them, a mixture of the army of the north and the Libyan forces stretched for miles and miles.

"Answer me, how could this possibly be?" Gapi questioned his scout one more time. The young man before him seemed trying to collect his thought to be able to answer. He appeared as if he had taken a hard knock to his head. "How in the world could they have traveled from Badari to Thebes that fast?"

"You won't believe it, my lord," the scout finally said in a trembling tone. He was a young man in his early twenties with long brown hair, dark eyes, and light skin. "But I swear to the gods I'm telling you the truth."

"Speak," Gapi ordered the young man before him, his eyes examining the long lines of the southern troops and the Kushites' army, thousands of them, which stood between him and his destination; Thebes.

"I was standing over this eminence," the scout began recounting to Gapi what he saw. His left index pointed to the left. "I was watching the army of the south get prepared for our army's arrival; but all of a sudden, I heard a rushing and peculiar sound, as if hundreds, or maybe thousands, of people, were rapidly cutting through the air, near and around me. At first, my eyes scanned around, but I could see nothing. When I shifted my sight to where the army of the south was located, I found a huge clear bubble emerging from the earth. Then, I heard a loud thud sound as if something had landed heavily on the ground, somewhere in

45

the middle of the bubble; and then, a huge army of the Kushites suddenly appeared as the bubble itself was slowly vanishing. I could immediately tell that these mercenaries were participating in a battle, maybe in the one going on in Badari at that moment, or maybe somewhere else, I'm not sure, because a lot of them were injured and bleeding."

"Do you believe this bullshit?" Gapi asked the woman who drove his chariot, and her response was shaking her head 'No'!

The woman name was Hent, and she had short dark hair, brown eyes, and a muscular body that was toned and shaped by hard training. A few months ago, Hent was the deputy in command of an elite militia called the Medjay force, an elite paramilitary police force that was often used to protect valuable areas, especially areas of royal interest such as capital cities, temples, cemeteries, and the borders of Egypt. Hent became the temporary commander when Gapi, the former commander to this force, had suddenly stepped down and traveled to Lower Egypt. Shortly after however, Hent had to flee Thebes and join Gapi in the north when the royal family accused her of being the mastermind behind the failed attempt to murder Varis.

Some rumors suggested that Gapi had an affair with Hent; a relationship which they kept secret to avoid Varis' anger. Gapi's father had already promised a very wealthy and powerful man in Memphis that Gapi was going to marry one of his twelve ugly daughters. Although Gapi refused to honor his father's promise, he did not dare tell the Pharaoh about Hent. Other rumors even came in alignment with the previous ones, suggesting that Hent had masterminded the failed attempt to murder Varis as a revenge against Gapi's father for trying to set the man she loved aside and pass the throne to Hamees.

"Believe me, my lady," the scout pleaded, speaking to Hent. "I'm telling the truth." Then, he turned his head back to Gapi. "I even heard that your father was there in the battle."

"Are you crazy?" Gapi snapped on him. "What are you talking about now? My father is now laying on his deathbed."

"I'm afraid that we've been blindsided about a lot of things that had recently happened in the kingdom," the scout told his lord. "Apparently, King Alara had sent his best priests who healed the Pharaoh's poisoned body. They also helped in breaking into the floating pyramid, kidnapping all the heralds, and stealing the new kairemi."

Astonished, Gapi turned his head to Hent who appeared baffled by the news, too.

"I knew it," Gapi said to Hent with wide open eyes. "I knew that Keya, and now her father too, were planning something much more important than just replacing me with Hamees. They aimed to sabotage our alliance with the People from the Sky. They know very well that they can't defeat us if the Celestials have our back. I can't believe that my father had let all this happened behind his back. I've always warned him about his new wife, but he never listened to me. Instead, he always accused me that I hated her for no reason. Guess what, Hent. I was right all along." He turned his eyes to the scout and continued. "What other information did you collect?"

"Well, my lord," the scout paused for a moment, swallowing hard before he continued. "I overheard them talking about your father's murder."

Gapi seemed stunned for a moment. He did not know if this was good news or bad. He was not sure if his father's death was what he wanted or not. Yes, his father betrayed him by ignoring the quest and announcing his sister, Hamees, as his heiress and co-ruler. Yet, Varis was still his father.

"He was killed at the hands of Princess Merit," the scout answered the question which had just popped in Gapi question but had no chance to ask it. "Apparently, she arrived before the battle began and killed the pharaoh."

47

"That fucking bitch," Gapi said with bared teeth, squeezing his hand into a fist and holding it inches from his face. "I'm gonna kill her. But first, I need to claim what's rightfully mine." He looked around and cried out, "Prepare for battle."

When Gapi gave the order to his troops, he expected to hear the subordinates behind him repeat the order, but he did not. Half curious and half displeased, he slowly looked behind to find out that all eyes were not on him. Instead, all the warriors, Libyans and Egyptians, were looking at the King Fazaz's hand which clenched into a fist and raised in the air, in a way that meant, Hold.

Libya was the traditional enemy of the kingdom of Egypt. The word "Libyans" decorated the footstool of the throne, along with three other names of the traditional enemies of the kingdom—the Hittites, Kushites, and Assyrians—to symbolize the Pharaoh's power over his enemies.

Over the ages, the Libyan kings never stopped thinking of placing Egypt under their rules. Matter of fact, some Libyans believed that the land of Egypt was historically a part of their great kingdom which they should reclaim these lands and rule them.

When Senu IV ascended the throne of Egypt after the death of his infertile older brother, a mighty Libyan army, consisting of thousands of horses, chariots, and footmen crossed the Western Desert and marched toward Thebes. The Libyans had heard about the impending famine, and they had decided to launch a sudden attack. They believed that the Egyptians were not going to fight for their Pharaoh while they were hungry. Just a week after Senu's coronation, he had led an army of ten thousand infantry, ten thousand cavalries, and five thousand war-chariots into the western desert. The Egyptian military easily crushed the enemy by a combination of brilliant tactics and superlatively trained troops.

However, after the failed attempt to murder Varis, the Libyans thought that the Pharaoh's injury was going to be followed by unrest across the kingdom. They wanted to seize the moment to launch another attack on Egypt. Keya, who ran the kingdom's affairs on behalf of her injured husband, ordered the commander of the Egyptian army to arrest a small Libyan band which dared to cross the border. She even ordered a giant spider called Hairy to kill King Fazaz' messenger who came to Thebes requesting the immediate release of the captured Libyans. That made King Fazaz rush his attack on Egypt.

"From Gapi, the Pharaoh of Lower Egypt, to King Fazaz of Libya," Gapi had written in his message to Fazaz a couple of weeks ago. It was right after discovering that his father betrayed him by proclaiming his sister to be his co-ruler and successor. Also, it was before Gapi's parley with his sister. "We have a common enemy that we must fight together. Help me to claim what is rightful mine, and you will have a true partner and ally sitting on the throne of Egypt."

After listening to Gapi's messenger, King Fazaz had smiled and nodded his head in a way that meant that he agreed. He was sitting in his royal pavilion in the heart of the camp of the Libyan army which had already crossed the border and was heading to Thebes. It was time to change their course. He stood up and walked to a high wooden table where his captain and generals gathered waiting for their king's order. His index finger pointed at a certain point on a map which showed the kingdom of Egypt. The point was located in the middle of the western desert. It was the point where his troops were going to join Gapi's army.

That was why Gapi was stunned when he ordered the army to prepare for battle, yet the king of Libya silently overrode the order by a single soundless gesture.

"What?" Gapi said in a spiteful tone. He was talking to King Fazaz. "Why not?"

"We're gonna talk to them first," The Libyan king replied briefly, signaling to the man behind him to blow a ram's horn three times.

"I thought we had a deal," he argued. Gapi was stunned by King Fazaz's attitude.

"Yes, we have a deal," king of Libya confirmed, "but we're going to listen to them first."

This isn't a good start! Gapi thought to himself, angrily. W*hy is he not leaving me to lead our army, like our deal?* He was hoping that Fazaz would voluntarily explain himself and save his face before all the other captain and generals who gathered to get the commands.

Gapi got even more stunned when Kings Fazaz prodded his white horse to move forward as if he wanted to say, *this talk will happen either with you or without you.*

Gapi quickly motioned to Hent to drive the chariot, and she immediately did, trying to catch up with King Fazaz.

When Gapi looked forward, he could see two chariots, surrounded by over two dozen of Kushites on foot, leaving the frontline for the enemy's troops and were heading to meet them in the middle. It was effortless to tell that one of the chariots was carrying King Alara of Kush; meanwhile, his sister, Hamees, was riding the other one.

Hamees, Hamees, he thought to himself, *what the hell did we do?*

Only now, Gapi began to realize what was happening. On the one hand, the Kingdom of Kush, represented in King Alara, was helping Upper Egypt in this fight. On the other hand, he had called another traditional enemy of the kingdom, the Libyans, to attack Thebes.

What are they going to get in return? The question slowly formed in his head, as they were getting closer and closer to Hamees and King Alara's chariots. *We, my sister and I, had opened the gates wide for foreigner powers to subjugate the great kingdom of Egypt.*

At the signal of King Fazaz, from one side, and King Alara, from the other side, all chariots stopped. King Alara was the first to step down from his chariot and walked forward to meet them. Alara was a huge man with dark skin, wide dark eyes, heavy nose, and pointed beard. He was wearing a crown made of gold and ivory.

From the other side, King Fazaz dismounted his horse and headed to meet the king of Kush.

Gapi's jaw dropped in shock when he found them hugging and laughing as if they were close friends who had been away for a long, long time. Although Alara did not speak Libyan and Fazaz did not know Kushite, it is evident that they knew each other for a long time, and they even had developed a way to communicate which mostly relied on sign language. For an instant, when the Libyan king pointed his right index at the king of Kush, then at himself, and finally pointed at the ground beneath him, Gapi could tell that he was saying, "you and I have made it, here."

Gapi looked at his sister, who was still a mount her chariot, the same as him, and he sensed that she was stunned herself. Hamees was in her early-twenties and was dressed in elegant golden armor. Her scaled skirt fell to her knees. She was strikingly beautiful with fair skin, beautiful long bright hair, brown eyes, small nose, small mouth, and sensual lips. She was beautiful, smart, and above all, a skillful fighter, who had been trained by the best fighters in the kingdom. She was skilled in the use of the sword, spear, and bow.

"What's happening here?" Gapi demanded loudly, addressing King Fazaz and King Alara. He could not hold it anymore.

"Yes, what is happening here?" Hamees shared her brother's concern.

"Shut your mouths, kids," King Alara said in Egyptian with a heavy accent. "When kings talk, princes and princesses don't interrupt."

"What are you talking about?" Gapi snapped, stepping out of his chariot and heading to the two kings. "And how dare you talk to me this way on my land? I'm the Pharaoh of the North."

"Watch your words, boy," King of Kush warned him. "Or, I will have your tongue yanked off your head."

Gapi could not get closer. He had to stop short when some of the Kushites who followed King Alara pointed their sharp spears at his face and chest. His eyes spontaneously shifted to meet King Fazaz's eyes, in a way that meant, *what's happening?*

King of Libya did not say a word. Instead, he just nodded his head with closed eyes to Gapi, in a way that meant, *stand down.*

Although Gapi stood down, Hent's huge sword suddenly, came out of nowhere with a roar, and pierced the throat of one of the Kushites whose spears pointed at Gapi. The sword emerged, dripping, out the back of the Kushite's neck. Before anyone could fully grasp what had just happened, Hent skillfully used her long sword to break a few of the spears which pointed at the face and chest of the person whom she loved with all her heart, and the person whom she would die for. She could not stand idly by while the Kushites were humiliating the Pharaoh of the North.

When King Alara noticed that his fighters were going to lose to this muscular woman, he quickly motioned to one of his men. Immediately, Gapi felt the cold blade of that man on his neck.

"Drop your weapon," King Alara shouted at Hent, "or your prince will die."

When Hent saw the blade on Gapi's throat, she immediately, yet angrily, stopped attacking the Kushites and instantly stepped back.

"Your weapon," King of Kush reminded her, and she dropped her sword, grunting in anger.

"Take her away," King Alara ordered, and his men immediately stormed at her and seized her. Six of them were barely able to capture this powerful woman.

52

"No, please..." Gapi cried out, but he immediately remembered Alara's threat to have his tongue yanked out of his mouth if he was not going to shut up.

"We don't have time for this shit," King Alara talked in a firm tone to everyone. "The People from the Sky have already started their attack. Most probably, they are now coming for us. So, we need to get this done as soon as possible." He looked at King Fazaz, and both nodded their heads in agreement and understanding.

The words left Gapi stunned. He did not know what King Alara was talking about. However, on their way to the royal palace, he overheard King Alara telling King Fazaz of Libya through an interpreter about what had happened during the battle of Badari. Gapi knew some of the Libyan language, not much, but enough to understand that Alara was proudly telling his friend about how he had secretly sent a small band of Kushite mercenaries there, along with five priests, to the arrival location of the Celestial's spaceship. Gapi became more stunned when he knew that after securing the area, the priests had used their magic powers to build invisible stairs, which the mercenaries had used to reach the floating pyramid, sneak inside, abduct all the Celestials, and seize the kairemi.

My scout was right. Alara abducted the Celestials! He surprisingly thought. *And seized the kairemi! This means an open war with the People from the Sky.*

Then, King Alara laughed a lot while he was telling King Fazaz how the Free Army arrived later thinking that they were the first to come to the arrival location, surrounded the floating pyramid, preventing anyone from reaching the Celestials.

Holly shit, Gapi thought when he heard them talking about how, all of a sudden during the battle of Badari, dozens of floating pyramids appeared in the sky and opened fire on everyone down there.

"How did you survive it?" Gapi heard King Fazaz wonder through an interpreter. "And how did you manage

53

to arrive here that fast?" Gapi was eager to listen to Alara's answer, too.

"Well, when you have priests like mine, you can do anything," the king of Kush replied, chuckling. Then, he went ahead, explaining how he ordered his generals and captains to take advantage of the sudden withdrawal of the mummies and the Terrifying Ones to retreat. However, when the celestial spaceships appeared, he ordered the high priest of Kush, Gorulga, to save them.

Gapi heard Alara talk about how Gorulga prayed to Amesemi, the Nubian protective goddess and wife of Apedemak, the lion-god. Amesemi was represented with a crown shaped like a falcon, or with a crescent moon on her head on top of which a falcon was standing. Gorulga's praying to Amesemi included a sacrificial female slave. After watering the sand beneath his feet with the slave's still-warm blood, suddenly a small bubble emerged from the blood. The bubble quickly started to get bigger and bigger by the second until it swallowed the priest inside. As Gorulga continued to pray to the protective goddess, the bubble continued to expand swallowing more people inside, dozens, hundreds and thousands until it covered the whole Kushite army.

When the spaceships of the celestials began shooting their devastating green beams, Gorulga muttered some mysterious words under his breath, and the whole army disappeared as if the earth had opened up and swallowed it. The destructive green beam of the Celestials' ships killed only a few dozen of the Kushites before the entire army vanished in a wisp of smoke before the wind. Shortly after the whole army appeared outside of Thebes walls.

***

Later that night, Gapi found himself sitting with another four people around a long table, in one of the small halls of the royal palace. After the four armies, the army of the south, the northern troops, the Libyans and the Kushites, camped outside of Thebes, the four leaders traveled to the royal palace to talk. King Alara had advised all generals and captains of the four armies to warn troops to stay inside their tents and have no fire past sunset.

Alara's orders came after consulting his right hand, the high priest of Kush, who advised him that the People from the Sky, after they were done with the battle of Badari, were going to launch a siege across the kingdom. They were going to shoot anything that glowed, lit or moved past sunset.

"It has to be completely dark," King Alara ordered his captain and generals. "For your own safety and the safety of your men, it has to be completely dark. Do you understand?"

Still reeling from the shock of what was happening, Gapi was sitting next to King Fazaz, and across the table from Hamees, who sat next to the king of Kush. At the head of the table, sat the Egyptian High Priest, Perneb. Before starting the meeting, King Alara and King Fazaz agreed on allowing Perneb to lead the meeting because he spoke both Kushite and Libyan. He was the only person available to facilitate this multilingual assembly. He was a time-worn man, dressed in leopard skin, with a thin, matted white beard. His thin body was beginning to break down after a rough life. However, his mind was still clear.

Perneb, who followed Amasis's father as the high priest following Varis' ascending the throne of Egypt, had played a critical role in making the new king appear as a half-god in the eyes of his people. As the famine ravaged the land of Egypt, Varis went one day to the Nile and touched the water in front of his people. When the Nile started to rise, Perneb – who in advance arranged everything with his new king – managed to convince the people that Varis was not just a pharaoh but a half-god too. That day, the new king of Egypt appeared to the Egyptians that he was the only one who could redeem them; the only one who could appease Hapi, the God of the Nile, on their behalf; and the only one who could make the river flood again to end the desolation, the drought, and the famine.

Back to the chamber where Perneb was leading this multilingual assembly, the room was immersed in a soft light that came from two fragrant tapers. They all sat around a table on which were wine, food, and garlands of roses.

Gapi noticed that Hamees was trying to avoid locking eyes with him.

She understands what we've done, he thought to himself. *She knows the mistake we've made.*

For a moment, Gapi recalled how his sister had betrayed him. "I pledge loyalty to you," the sound of his voice mixed with Hamees in unison rang inside his head as he recalled themselves reciting the old-fashioned pledge. "I promise to defend you against our enemy. I pledge my heart and soul to you. I'll never cheat or lie to you. No one can turn me against you or you against me. Siblings, forever." *And yet, she betrayed me. She betrayed her older brother.*

Although Gapi's anger was wailing inside his chest, he felt fear, too. Sitting in the same room with King Alara, who had threatened him earlier that day, caused the adrenaline to pump into his bloodstream. Fear clutched his heart that the king of Kush might carry out his threat and order his men, three of them were standing now behind Gapi, to cut off his tongue if he spoke.

The high priest started the meeting by briefing them on what had happened in the Battle of Badari. He spoke first in Kushite, then Libyan, and finally, he talked to Hamees and Gapi in his mother tongue. After the briefing, he took a moment to discuss with King Alara and King Fazaz to clarify the goal of this assembly.

"They want to discuss..." Perneb paused talking to Hamees and Gapi for a moment, swallowing hard. "They want to discuss how you all are going to rule the kingdom of Egypt after the defeat of the Free Army."

"We all!" Gapi barked, but he had to shut up when King Alara stared at him with hard, wild eyes. He did not dare to say anything. He only looked at his sister, in a way that meant, *aren't you gonna say something?* Yet, Hamees again was doing her best to avoid eye contact with him.

"King Alara suggest that you, Prince Gapi, keep the north under your command," the high priest talked to him first, then he turned his head to Hamees, "and you, princess Hamees, keep Upper Egypt under yours."

Prince Gapi! Gapi tried to object, but again, he remembered Alara's warning. *Well, this isn't too bad. At least, nothing changed. I keep the north.* Yet, his relief was relatively short-lived.

"However, Both King Alara and King Fazaz think that you both are," Perneb, again, he paused, swallowing hard, as if he was struggling to find a better way to say it. "They think that you are too young to rule a great kingdom like Egypt."

Hamees wanted to say something, but King Alara gave her no chance by waving to the high priest to finish what he was saying.

"In order to guarantee stability in the land of Egypt," Perneb continued, lowering his eyes sadly, "especially after the attack of the People from the Sky, King Alara wants to appoint his nephew as a high commissioner to help in ruling Upper Egypt, and King Fazaz will appoint one of his men to help you in ruling the North."

Before the high priest finished the kings' demands, Gapi found himself on his feet, glaring at King Alara and then at the king of Libya.

"This isn't what we agreed on, King Fazaz," he snapped in an angry tone.

"Sit down, boy," King Alara cautioned him in a firm voice. "This is your last warning." He gestured to his men in a way that meant, *he's yours if he doesn't comply with my orders.*

"I'm not a boy. I'm the Pharaoh of the North, and you have to treat me better than..." Gapi could not finish his phrase as he found two powerful hands on his shoulder, pushing him down onto his seat. Meanwhile, another two mighty hands forced him to open his mouth wide. It happened too fast that Gapi could not even think of what was happening. With wide open eyes, he only looked at his sister across the table, especially when the third Kushite shoved his filthy hand inside his mouth. Finally, Hamees locked her panicked eyes with her brother's just a moment before the third Kushite yanked Gapi's tongue out of his mouth. Blood splattered all over the table, and the room filled with Gapi's screams.

Chapter 5

Captive, Meal, and Paruda

The wife was only half listening to her husband's plan because her thoughts were already consumed by a sudden concern over the action which they were about to take that night.

"Stay here and wait for our signal," her husband said in a hushed tone. Leaving his wife hiding behind a huge tree, a skinny, tall man in his late twenties quickly took off, darting into the darkness and heading to the royal palace. Even though the Kushite mercenaries well-guarded the palace, this man knew that he had a chance to sneak in through the wall on the eastern side which collapsed a couple of nights ago.

That morning, this man overheard some people in the market talking about how the beautiful metropolitan of Thebes was eventually turning into a ghost city because of the celestials' attack on, not only the city but the entire kingdom, too. Wreckage and debris were everywhere.

Ever since the battle of Badari, the Royal Adorian Space Fleet had put the entire kingdom of Egypt under siege until the safe return of the heralds and the rapid delivery of those who were behind the attack on their floating Pyramid. Every Sunset, and as the sun was on the point of disappearing and the last ray turned a bright green, hundreds of the Celestial spaceship appeared all over the kingdom and started to launch their devastating green beam on anything that moved, glowed or was lit once it was dark.

One night, a floating pyramid hovering over Edfu had set a huge part of a neighborhood on fire when some young men were spotted having a bonfire behind one of the buildings. On another night, a temple in Herakleopolis was blown up because one of the priests forgot to blow all the candles off before sunset. A few nights later, an Adorian spaceship opened fire on a man who was traveling at night north of Thebes, carrying a small lamp to illuminate his way. The man, his donkey and his lamp were vaporized instantly; their bodies converted into gas and desiccated carbon. A week after, a boat traveling in the Nile near Memphis was sank when one of the pyramids of the People from the Sky saw a faint light on board.

The royal palace was not spared either. A couple of days ago, one of the Celestials' ships had spotted one of the guards moving on the eastern wall. Immediately, it had launched its devastating green beam, killing three guards and blowing a large chunk of the wall.

After convincing his wife that this was their moment which they had to seize, the skinny man who was sneaking into the royal palace asked one of his neighbors to watch their three infant children. Then, he and his wife headed to the royal palace. They made sure to not carry any torches to lead their ways. They knew it had to be completely dark.

It was almost midnight, and a full moon hung in the dark sky, shining down on the city. It was tranquil, and the wife could hear no sounds coming from inside the royal palace, except for a faint crack; the unmistakable sound of a neck being broken. A heavy thud followed; the distinct sound of a body hitting the floor.

"Now," the wife quietly told herself once she heard a faint whistle. It was the signal that she was waiting for, and which meant that the way was clear for her to follow her husband inside the palace. She had a curvy body with just a little pouch of a stomach, gorgeous breasts, and big brown eyes.

Hesitantly, the wife darted into the darkness and headed to the collapsed wall, which led to the back courtyard. Once she passed the wall wreckage, her eyes widened in panic, as she saw a Kushite Mercenary lying on the floor, his head twisted grotesquely. She almost froze in fright, her heart pounding relentlessly.

"Right here," she heard her husband whispering to her. He was hiding behind the corner of the granary. "Quickly, over here." He waved for her to hurry up.

The woman scurried, moving fast and quietly, toward her husband.

"I don't think this is a good idea," she talked to him in a hushed tone. "We need to leave before anyone sees us."

"We can't back out now," the husband snapped at her, trying to keep his voice down. He displayed frustration on his face. "We don't have any other option." The source of his frustration was that he had already spent the last few hours trying to convince his wife that they have got to do it.

Although the Nile had already started to flood, and although the water finally reached the fields, the famine was still prominent in the people's mind because the crops would not be ready to start the harvest for another three full moons at least. The granaries were less than half full now, which meant that the kingdom did not have enough food to last through the next harvest season. This led to a surge in the price to a level that this poor man and his wife had failed to feed their kids for the last two days. Their only option now was to sneak into the granary of the royal palace and steal some food for their children.

"I just have a bad feeling about it," the wife said in a pleading tone. "Please let's go back to our kids before it's too late."

"Honey, it's ok," he tried to soothe her, putting his hand on her right cheek. "Trust me. Everything is going to be just fine."

"They are going to kill us," she said, tears rolling down her face and touching her man's hand, "not only for stealing but also for killing. You should not have killed the guard."

"I had to, sweetie," he explained. "He was about to see me. And if he did, we would be dead by now. Believe me, I had no other option."

"But you promised me," she reminded him, more tears rolling down. "You promised me that no one was going to get hurt..."

"Unless I have to," the husband finished for her. "I promised that no one will get hurt unless I have to. And here we are. I had to. Trust me, everything is going to be fine. We just need to move fast before anyone sees us."

Hesitantly, the wife nodded her head in agreement.

"Don't move a muscle," the order suddenly came in Egyptian with an accent.

Both the woman and her husband locked eyes in panic.

I told you, the wife wanted to say, but she did not have to. He already knew that they were finished as the fear was evident in his eyes.

They tried to slowly turn their heads to scan around, searching for the person who had just spoken to them.

"I said don't move a muscle," the order was repeated, and then suddenly they saw three mercenaries emerging from the darkness. They were moving slowly, cautiously, and purposely to surround them from all directions.

"Haven't you heard that there is a new punishment for stealing food?" One of the Kushites talked to the man and his wife in a mocking tone. "You're going to be her next meal." His laughter rang through the backyard.

When the consciousness came back into Roma's body, he uncontrollably coughed his lungs up, spat water out of his stomach and fought for his breath.

"Again," a firm voice came from behind. It was Egyptian with an accent.

Roma instantly tried to kick out once he heard the order, but he got nowhere. It did not take him too long to remember that he was totally restrained. He was lying in a supine position with feet and hands tied to a sloping wooden board; his head lower than the rest of his body. He even tried to move his head, but he could not. Two powerful hands were tightly holding his head from behind, forcing him to look up all the time. Yet, he could not see a lot through the wet, dark cloth which was placed on his face.

Through the cloth mesh, Roma faintly could see the shadow of what seemed to be a large, clay urn. He quickly drew a deep breath, despite the difficulty to do so, anticipating what was going to happen next. For the fifth time that day, Roma saw the very same urn getting closer; and in no time, he felt the sudden chill of the ice-cold water pouring slowly and continuously from the jar onto his face.

The water leisurely seeped through the cloth on Roma's face and began running down his nostrils into his sinuses. He struggled to periodically expel the water by building enough pressure in his lungs, but he quickly realized that this technique failed again. The more water he expelled, the less air he could inhale. Gradually, the water began to fill up his respiratory tract.

Determined to resist, Roma tried to distract his mind by thinking of something positive. He believed that thinking of encouraging thoughts was going to help him survive this torturing technique, which the Kushites widely used against their enemies.

"Keep going," Roma's thoughts were distracted by the order to find that his body was shaking violently.

I'm going to die, he thought to himself in a panic, mainly when the effect of having his sinuses fill with water triggered that feeling that he was drowning. He tried different methods to breathe, none of them worked. As the cold water continued to run through the cloth and down to his nose and mouth, every single in his body was screaming for air.

Suddenly, the water stopped, and finally Roma could breathe.

"You know very well that this will not end," a voice whispered in Roma's ear. "I've got orders from the Regent Queen herself that you must speak. So, guess what! You're going to speak. Why don't you make it easy for all of us?"

When the person said, "the Regent Queen," Roma assumed in his jumbled mind, *The Regent Queen! A new king or a new queen must has ascended the throne. It must be Hamees.* Thinking of Keya made him recall how he needed to get up from being gruesomely tortured in this horrifying way.

Back to the battle of Badari, and when Keya hit the griffin from the side, the hit was powerful enough that Roma slid from his talons. Semi-unconscious, Roma found himself falling from a very high altitude directly into the middle of the fire which was still consuming whatever was left of his army. Although the One who Tears into Pieces roared in anger and immediately flew down to catch Roma before hitting the ground, Keya raced the griffin to reach Roma first. She was faster and cleverer in her maneuvers which helped her to reach Roma first.

When Roma opened his eyes, he found Keya had grabbed him between her arms and flew away. Meanwhile, Princess Merit, riding on the back of the One who Tears into Pieces, chased them, trying to rescue the love of her life. However, Keya was faster and was capable of escaping the griffin's sharp claws and teeth.

As Roma regained some of his energy, he tried to release himself from Keya's arms, but the queen was faster

64

in reaction. Once she noticed that Roma was moving, she sent a powerful kick using her right knee into his groin. Roma gasped, and all the anger of the battle results fused inside him and became a white fire like that of an acetylene torch. Using his right hand, he punched her hard in her face. It was the first time in his life he had ever hit a woman, but he was angry; angry enough to hit anyone, even it was a woman.

Keya got distracted for a moment, and her wings briefly stopped flapping. Yet, she quickly regained her focus when she realized that the One who Tears into Pieces was getting closer to her. She immediately used her wings to fly down; but first, she powerfully slammed her knee one more time into Roma's balls.

Roma howled in pain, and his head fell backward in a way that allowed him to see where they were heading. They were flying straight toward a massive bubble which was getting bigger by the second swallowing thousands of Kushites inside. When Keya - still holding Roma in her arms - penetrated the bubble wall, Roma found that they and the whole army of Kushite mercenaries disappeared from the battlefield and instantly appeared again outside of Thebes walls.

Immediately, Keya dropped Roma to the ground. The pain from the fall was excruciating, and he believed that he passed out for a moment when he hit the ground. When he awoke, he felt very woozy. He sat up very slowly, then the pain jolted him wide awake. The pain was unbearable, he had never felt pain like this before.

Before comprehending what was occurring, he found several Kushite mercenaries seize him. He then heard Keya ordering them in Kushite. Although he did not speak the language of the people of Kush, he understood that she was telling them to take him to the dungeon and that he must talk as soon as possible.

In this dark cell, Roma could not track time. It could be days, weeks, or months. He had no idea. Time seemed prolonged due to the gruesome torturing he received at the mercenaries' hands. He did not know what had happened in Badari nor to his troops after Keya captured him. He even did not know a lot about what had happened to Merit. All he knew that she was alive and that he must tell them about her whereabouts. That was a relief for him, not much but enough to keep some hope inside his mind and heart.

When Roma felt the people torturing him pull the wet piece of cloth away from his face, he was brought immediately back to the present to the dungeon cell. He still could not see. His vision was blurry from the coughing and gasping. He felt short hot breaths hitting his wet, cold face, and the foul breath of his torturer invaded his nostrils.

"All your pain will be over once you tell us where she is?" The voice continues in a soft tone now. "I promise you a quick and painless execution if you tell me where she is."

Roma did not respond. He never had, and he never would. He just closed his eyes and relaxed his muscles, inviting his torturer to shut the hell up and do his job.

And his torturer did so. He first let out a very long sigh of disappointment and then shouted, "Again!"

Quickly, they put back the piece of wet cloth on Roma's face, and the ice-cold water shortly ran through onto his face and down into his nostrils again.

In Roma's scrambled mind, he tried to form some clear thoughts. He wished that they would just kill him, but he knew very well that they would not as long as he did not give them what they are after. They were going to just keep torturing him. Inside his head, he wanted to give up. He knew he was not in control anymore. His instinct told him that he was going to die. His restrained body violently shook a couple of times. Then, the darkness took over him again.

As Roma was losing his awareness, a terrible and dreadful scream rang through the royal palace. Even the bravest of those Kushites who were securing the site got scared and felt the fear rising up within them. Yet, it forced some of them to rush toward the source of the screaming.

Another scream reverberated through the air. The cry was so loud that it could be heard on the other side of the river, sending chills down the spines of the people in their houses, the swarming markets, the holy temples, and the wheat fields.

***

Two stories above Roma's cell, seven powerful mercenaries cautiously stepped into the main royal bedchamber which was completely dark. They nervously scanned the darkness, but they could not see a thing. When their leader barked something in Kushite, one more fighter rushed in with a torch and put it in the nearest iron-holder.

They peered through the faint light given out by the torch and thought it odd to not see the regent queen around. They knew she was there. She had just called for her dinner. The dreadful scream that had rung through the palace was a sure sign that she was hungry and ready for another bloody meal.

"Where is my food?" Keya's voice filled the room, and all eyes searched for the Regent Queen. "I'm famished." She said it in a way that made some of the Kushites at the doorway shiver to the depths of their souls.

Immediately, the same mercenary who asked for the light earlier shakenly muttered out an order. A few of the Kushites instantly went out and came back herding two Egyptians, a woman in her late twenties with a beautiful figure and a skinny man who seemed to be her husband. They were the married couple who had just been arrested after sneaking into the royal palace to steal food. They both were dressed in simple clothes which barely covered their body. They were scared to death, evident in their glaring eyes and trembling legs.

"Out," Keya's voice rumbled the order; and in a blink of an eye, the Egyptian couple was standing alone at the chamber doorway. They quietly tried to step backward.

Although the woman managed to do so, she quickly had to get back to where she was standing a moment ago when the sharp tips of the Kushites' spears pushed her back inside the room. Meanwhile, her man's trembling legs had failed him and found himself on his knees.

"Please, Your Grace," the man begged, in a nasal, frightened tone. "We will never do it again." His head was scanning around. Yet, he could not see the queen.

"We had to," the woman pleaded with a shaky voice. "Our kids are starving, and we had to." Her eyes looked around, trying to spot Keya.

"Please, My Queen," the man gently spoke, hearing a distinct sound of what sounded like approaching steps. However, he still could not see a thing through the faint light. "I beg you."

The woman tried to step backward again, but horrible scream came out of her mouth as one of the spears pushed her harder back inside the room. This time the spear pierced a neat hole in her back from which blood now started to spill.

When the man realized that there was no forgiveness from the queen nor escape from such a bloody fate, it seemed that he decided to die fighting. He looked around one more time. This time he was not looking for the queen. This time he was looking for something with which he was going to fight. He was looking for a weapon. He hoped to see a sword, spear, or even a knife, but he saw none. The crashing sound of his wife falling on her knees, next to him, wincing in pain from her wound, made him cry out in anger and jump to his feet. He finally found it. He found the weapon which he was going to use to defend his wife and himself.

He quickly ran to the iron-holder and picked up the torch. He thrust the torch forward, his shaking hand sending wild flicks of light dancing across the walls, brilliantly illuminating the shadows. He took two small steps forward with his shaky legs toward the bed, thinking that the queen was there, but she was not. Yet, he could still hear her movement through the room. He pushed the torch further and turned around, scanning the room. It was only him, and his wife, no trace of Keya could be found. Yet, they both knew that she was there. They could feel, not only her presence but also that she was approaching them.

They could see only dried blood drenched the floor surrounding what seemed like human bones which scattered across the chamber. It appeared that a fearsome monster had feasted on those people's flesh, and that it was ready for its next fresh meal.

The man had finally remembered that he had heard some rumors about the queen's transformation from a beautiful woman into a winged creature, and later into a dreadful monster.

Full of fear, he slowly raised his head upward, and his eyes widened in shock. A scream uncontrollably leaped out of his mouth as his shaking hand dropped the torch to the floor. His wife could not hold her screams either when she saw the queen was hanging the same way a bat would hang from the ceiling of a cave.

Approaching them from above was Keya who had entirely changed now. Evidently, even the rumors that circled the kingdom since the battle of Badari could not cover even a part of the truth of the transformation that occurred to her. The wings which protruded from Keya's back on the day of the battle was just a beginning which slowly continued through the next following days.

In less than a week after the battle, tiny black feathers had covered her entire body. Even her long hair had fallen out, and feathers replaced it. Her once beautiful eyes had turned into bloody smaller red eyes. Two yellow fangs had protruded from the shrunken gums, and the wrinkled lips leered horribly. Her long nails had turned into long, yellow, and deadly claws. An ugly scar from her aerial battle with princess Merit marked her left wing.

Back in the dungeon, Roma suddenly regained his consciousness on a mix of dreadful screams of horrified people facing a frightful monster. He gasped for breath as he was listening to more cries which were so loud that they reached the dungeon cells where he had just regained his awareness for another round of torturing at the Kushites' hands to speak of Princess Merit's whereabouts.

Chapter 6

Queen of the South

As Hamees was consumed with thinking about her future, a loud gasp of the audience brought her to the present. From her point of view, the great hall of the throne seemed crowded. The place was full to capacity with more people crowding at the gate to enter. The wealthiest noblemen and noblewomen of the kingdom dressed in their finest and had come to celebrate the coronation of their new queen, Hamees, who ascended the throne of Upper Egypt after the death of her father.

The audience's gasps came as a result of the extraordinary entertainer who was performing an impressive aerial show. It was a midget, called the Little Man, who was using two ropes suspended from the ceiling to perform incredible feats of strength, athleticism, aerialism, dancing and lots of acrobatics. The short man was flying through the hall, as he was desperately trying to vie for the attention of another female performer who played a lovely, gorgeous young lady who this midget loved.

The great hall of the throne took up a large portion of the palace, and it had a large, arched entrance. Twenty columns supported the ceiling. The hall was meant to be bare of furnishings to not distract the courtiers from the throne, which was situated opposite the doorway and was elevated by a three-stepped stage. Daylight entered the hall through the window of appearance, and torches and fire pots floodlit the high walls.

Sitting on the throne of Egypt, the new queen of Egypt, Queen Hamees appeared elegant and regal in raiment bedecked with jewels and golden sandals. Her natural beauty made her conspicuous compared to all the elegant women in the hall who used powders and paint, creating an artificial appearance.

The throne was a beautiful masterwork, intended to be a symbol of the ruler's power, authority, and prestige. It was carved out of wood, and it was stunningly overlaid in sheet gold and decorated with valuable stones and gems. The arms were shaped like lions, representing the power of the ruler and his or her ability to govern this great nation. On the back of the throne, there was a natural scene of the Nile, in a gratitude of the river—the most advantageous geographical feature of the Egyptian civilization. The footrest of the throne was made of thick wood that was covered with gold leaves, and which was ornamented with the names of the traditional enemies of Egypt—the Hittites and Assyrians—to symbolize the ruler of Egypt's power over his enemies. A few months earlier, there were two other enemies' names on the footstool, but they were removed due to the change which had happened recently in the kingdom. These two names were; the Kushites and the Libyans.

For Hamees, sitting on the throne of Egypt was like sitting on top of the world. She felt powerful in a way that she had never felt before. She believed that she would need to worship gods no more since she felt like a god herself. She could send as many men as she wanted to their deaths, and she could spare just as many if she so desired.

Sitting on the throne, Hamees was wearing the red Deshret crown of the south on her head.

"My Queen, I'm afraid that you can't wear the Pschent," one of Hamees close consultants had advised her, two days ago during the planning for her coronation day. He was an old man with a completely bent back, white hair, and wrinkled face and hands. Standing before Hamees in her bedchamber, he was holding two papyrus rolls in his left hand.

"Why not?" Hamees had angrily questioned him.

"The Pschent represents the unified Kingdom of Egypt," he had explained in a soothing tone, trying not to piss off his new queen. The Pschent, or the Two Powerful Ones, was the double crown worn by rulers in Egypt. It combined the white Hedjet crown of north and the red Deshret crown of south.

"You might need to read these messages if you would like to understand, My Lady," he had said, bowing his head, slightly.

"Show me what you have got," she had irritably ordered him. She was sitting on a fancy chair made of reed and wood while two maids were braiding her long, bright hair. The first message was from one of their spies in the North who reported that Gapi had been officially coronated as the Pharaoh of the North in a massive ceremony which was attended by the wealthiest noblemen and noblewomen of Lower Egypt. The spy also described in his letter how Gapi embarrassed himself giving his coronation speech using sign language while the vizier of Lower of Lower Egypt interpreted to their guests.

The second papyrus roll was a message from the Pharaoh of the North himself, notifying his sister that he wore the Hedjet and warning her of wearing the Pschent.

"What am I supposed to wear now?" Hamees had demanded an answer, losing her temper.

"I suggest wearing the old, red Deshret Crown of the South," the old man had advised.

For the first time in the last three hundred years, two rulers governed the great kingdom of Egypt. Ironically, these two potentates were a brother and sister, who had to wear the old crowns, rolling the kingdom back to the ages before King Menes of the first dynasty. The last pharaoh to wear the Pschent was their father, King Varis, who had ascended the throne after a manufactured rebellion against Senu IV.

Hamees took a moment recalling how she ended up on, not the Throne of Egypt, instead, the throne of Upper Egypt. She recalled how her father had a special place for her in his heart even though she was his youngest child. He had always believed that she was smarter, braver, and stronger than her older brother. Above all, Hamees resembled her mother more than Gapi. Since she was a little kid, Hamees knew that Varis hated his son so much and that Keya was the driving force behind this hatred.

On the day of the rebellion, for example, Varis had intentionally humiliated Gapi in public. Instead of charging his son with a critical mission, he sent Gapi to check on his new wife. On the other hand, he made his daughter proud of herself when he commissioned her with a crucial diplomatic task; taking care of their new allies, the Kushites.

When Varis wanted to send a highly important and confidential message to King Alara of Kush, he sent Hamees at the head of a heavily armed unit consisting of a hundred chariots. It was a very confidential message that Varis could only trust one of his children to deliver. Above all, it was Keya's advice. On the one hand, the queen wanted her stepdaughter to prove to her father that she could successfully get something like this done. On the other hand, Keya also wanted to make sure that Hamees introduced herself to her step-grandfather, as a possible heiress to the Egyptian throne after her father.

Using her power over Varis, Keya managed to convince him to deny Gapi's birthright to succeed him on the throne of Egypt. Later, he proclaimed his daughter his co-ruler and successor due to his sickness after the failed attempt to murder him. The thing which drove Lower Egypt to declare its separation from the kingdom, and her enraged brother, Gapi, had proclaimed himself the Pharaoh of the north. Not only this but also it drove Gapi to ally with the Libyans to claim what he thought rightfully his.

That was our mistake, Hamees thought inside her head. It was right after the Treaty of Thebes where King Alara of Kush and King Fazaz decided the fate of Egypt after the battle of Badari and after the People of the Sky had begun their siege and attack over the land of Egypt. *We, Gapi and I, have opened the door wide for foreign powers to subjugate Egypt.* She slowly turned her head to the left and looked at the man sitting next to her with disgust in her eyes.

Only that morning, another chair, smaller, lower, and not as luxurious as the throne of Egypt, was added next to it to the left in the great hall. Sitting on that chair was a young Kushite man in his late thirties. The man's name was Shubba. He was dressed like a king but with no crown as much as his wealth permitted. Shubba was King Alara's nephew who had been summoned from Kush after the Treaty of Thebes and was appointed as the Kushite high commissioner to Upper Egypt to help Queen Hamees in ruling Egypt.

Hamees never liked or understood the idea of having someone intervene in her way of ruling her kingdom. When Keya succeeded in clearing Gapi from Hamees's way to success her father, the whole point was to rule the kingdom of Egypt alone. Ironically, Keya's plan was overdone by her father, King Alara, who not only agreed with Gapi over splitting the kingdom into two smaller ones, Lower Egypt in the north and Upper Egypt in the south, he even appointed this silly man who was sitting now next to the new queen of

Egypt, not as an advisor or a counselor to her, but as a high commissioner.

Hamees knew that she was not the only one in the critical position. Her brother, Gapi, who lost his tongue during the discussions of the Treaty of Thebes, was not ruling the north alone as it was supposed to be. Instead, King Fazaz of Libya, as a part of the treaty, had appointed a close advisor to him as the Libyan high commissioner to Lower Egypt.

Hamees' first impression of Shubba was not good at all. Once he arrived, two days ago, he angrily yelled at Hamees's advisor and counselor. He even questioned Hamees about why his chair was not set up yet next to the throne like King Alara had ordered before his departure to Kush. Not only this, but Shubba also insisted on putting the crown on Hamees' head at the beginning of the coronation ceremony. It was supposed to be the high priest's job, but the Shubba told them that he was just following King Alara's orders. For everyone who attended the ceremony, it was a bizarre thing to do, and Hamees herself felt humiliated, especially when Shubba, in his speech, made her coronation and sitting on the throne of Upper Egypt appeared as they would have never happened without the blessing and the help of the Kushites.

A loud round of applause shook the hall when the Little Man finished his performance. The sound of the clapping was loud enough to drag Hamees back to the present, to the great hall of the throne, where the midget was bowing to her at the end of his performance.

Thank the Gods, Hamees thought to herself, nodding her head to the short man and offering him a little smile. Although this talented man managed to stun every single man and woman in the hall with his incredible skills and performance, the new queen of the south was bored to the extreme and wanted this show to end as soon as possible. However, she had to fake a smile to the performer who traveled from his village in the north all the way to Thebes to celebrate Hamees's coronation by performing for her guests. Hamees even had to reward this little man with two thousand deben of copper as appreciation of him.

"Next," Hamees ordered loudly.

From different sides of the hall, the next performers immediately entered as they were called and took up their poses in the middle. With applause, the audience greeted twenty Kushite women with dark skin, strong arms, bare feet, and bare breasts hidden by long hair. A brief, light piece of cloths barely covered their female parts. Their bodies had filled out, with firm, young, well-proportioned breasts, narrow waist, rounded hips, and full-fleshed thighs.

Once the dancers formed a circle in the middle of the hall, loud and rapid music began to play. The performers turned around, their back to the audience, and began shaking their booties.

Immediately, Hamees got excited, knowing that she was going to watch something she had heard about and had waited a long time to see. It was the Bouncing Butts Dance, which she had no chance to see before. She knew that it was a famous dance in the land of Kush where women with big bottoms perform a dance to popular music in a sexually provocative manner involving thrusting hip movements in a low squatting stance.

Before her eyes, twenty women were now performing a very hard, yet sexy, dance which required them to violently shake their booties up and down. At a certain point, the dancers broke the circle and began moving randomly in all directions, performing more twerking movements. Some of them went to the audience and started giving them personal dances in a lascivious manner with the intent to elicit sexual arousal. Others formed a line of five before the throne, their backs to Hamees, showing their skills in vigorously shaking of their gluteus maximi. The more the music got intense, the more the booties bounced.

One of the women in front of Hamees was literally clapping her buttocks. The queen was impressed by her talent and assets. For a moment, she wished that she had a big, curvy, and fleshy ass like these women. She also thought of having one of these women in her bed that night to celebrate her coronation; and thus, she started looking around at them trying to pick one.

One of the things that the people of Egypt had whispered when Varis proclaimed his daughter his successor was her sexuality. This whispering turned into talk when Varis was killed. Now, this talk became questions which the new queen of Upper Egypt must answer.

"I do like men," Hamees had answered her counselor who carefully shared with her the people's concern about her sexual orientation. However, she did not tell him that she had been strongly sexually attracted to women for as long as she could remember.

Hamees' first experience with a woman was with her step-mother. Keya had accidentally walked in on her when she just became a teenager. She was trying to masturbate in her room using a huge cucumber. Her step-mother decided to help her lose her virginity at the ripe old age of thirteen. Being with a woman had always been a fantasy for Hamees. When she tried it, she liked it very much, primarily because her step-mother was sexually experienced.

Not my type, the new queen of Egypt thought, looking at this tall, thick woman at the end of the hall. Her eyes kept moving from one a dancer to another. *Not my type.* Then, her eyes moved to the next performer. *Not my type.* And the following one. *Not my type. Not my type. Not my type.*

I'll pass, Hamees finally decided, thinking of her magical cat. It was one of two cats which she received as a gift from an oracle on her way back one day from Kush. On their master's signal, these two cats would turn into two striking and sexy women with long tails, upright pointed ears, and whiskers around their faces; ready to serve their master in whatever way he or she thought would gratify. Hamees used to have both cats to sexually satisfy her until one day she had to offer one of them to her brother as a gift during a parley before the battle of Badari.

Hamees noticed that the hall was filled with several reactions to Bouncing Booties Dance. Some, mostly men, were so excited, clapping, whistling, and shouting. Others felt uncomfortable, especially those who accompanied their spouses. Some wives were angry and jealous as their husbands were staring at these gluteus maximi. Since the new queen of the south wanted her coronation to be perfect, Hamees decided to stop the show before any trouble would occur. She thanked and rewarded the performers, then she dismissed them.

The next few performances were very boring for Hamees.

This isn't impressive, she disgustingly told herself as she was watching this man who was dislocating different parts of his body while dancing.

This isn't even funny, she thought, listening to some silly jokes from a man who supposed to be funny. However, she faked an amused expression on her face, hoping that no one would notice that she was bored to death.

This's really dumb, she told herself when two men fought, in an acrobatic dance, over a woman in a cage, only to realize that they actually lusted over each other. *I understand the girl-on-girl thing, but guys with each other. Nah.*

Shortly, the crowd in the hall made room for eight powerful men who were pushing a large water bowl, which could fit three people at least inside, into the middle of the hallway. Murmurs filled the hall; people wondering what was next and for what purpose was the bowl.

Hopefully, it's something interesting this time, Hamees wished.

Once the powerful men settled the bowl, the hall fell in a hush, especially when beautiful, romantic music began to softly play.

Hamees, like anyone else in the hall, got surprised when she saw two naked women emerging from the water and began experiencing their love for one another while performing contortions in the bowl.

Now, we're talking, she told herself, watching as the two gorgeous underwater swimmers did little more than moving each other's bodies in an array of sexual positions.

For the first time that night, she found herself enjoying the show. She liked the erotic part. Her eyes were fixed on the dancer with the dark skin. She imagined ending this tedious day with having this gorgeous, sexy woman in her bed tonight. She thought about the moment when she let this dancer touch her nipples, eat her pussy, and finger her butthole.

The loud music brought Hamees back to the hall, where the two naked dancers were concluding their dance in the bowl, amid cheers, whistles, and applause.

Immediately, Hamees waved for the maid next to her, and the maid instantly leaned forward to receive the queen's order.

"Once this is over, I need the one with dark skin in my bed," she whispered in the maid's ear who instantly nodded her head, her eyes fixed at the dancers who were bowing to the audience now.

***

Later that night, Hamees was enjoying the tongue of the dancer with the dark skin licking her clit. The performer gently sucked on it while sticking two fingers in her very wet pussy.

"Am I doing well, My Lady?" The dancer paused, wondering if this was what her queen wanted.

"Yes," Hamees angrily hissed. "Just shut up and eat it."

The performer immediately complied with her queen's order, pushing her tongue deep inside Hamees and looking for her most hidden core.

"Yes," Hamees cried out. "Just like this."

"Do you want me to put that thing on now?" The dancer, again, paused what she was doing to ask. She held in her hand a smoothly carved piece of wood which was explicitly phallic in appearance. This sex toy was attached to what appeared as a leather harness intend to be worn around the waist.

"You know what!" The queen snapped at her. "Out. Get out, now." She was done with this stupid woman who did not stop talking since she got in bed, not giving Hamees a chance to enjoy the sensation go through her body.

"I'm so sorry, My Lady," the woman sincerely apologized. "I won't say another word."

"I said out," Hamees angrily repeated, her loud tone forced two Kushites to enter the chamber and drag the performer out, crying and scared.

Once no one was in the chamber but Hamees, she looked around for something. Something that she knew it was there, yet she was not sure where exactly. Since she was still boiling in anger, she needed that thing so bad to calm herself down. Her head scanned around until her eyes laid upon a cat which was napping on a chair made of reed and wood.

A natural smile appeared on Hamees's face once she saw her cat. Still naked, she sat on the edge of the bed, and her hands instinctively clapped, waking the cat up from her nap. The cat woke up and looked at her master. When the queen winked at the cat, she received a wink in return; and immediately her pet stood up, stretched herself and curled her back into an arch.

As the cat jumped to the floor and headed to bed, the queen could tell that her anger instantly vanished and was replaced by excitement, especially when the cat turned into a striking, naked woman with dark hair, a narrow waist, large breasts, and a curvy butt; yet, she had long tail, upright pointed ears, and whiskers around her pretty face.

Once the woman reached Hamees, she leaned forward and placed a searing, soulful kiss on her lips. The queen immediately laid back on her luxurious bed and closed her eyes. Her moaning filled the room, enjoying the sensation spread through her body.

*

Next morning, a horn loudly blew three times, waking up the new queen of Egypt. She snappishly and frantically pushed away the woman who was sleeping between her arms and sat down. Before about a dozen soldier burst into her royal room, Hamees quickly clapped her hands loudly. In no time, the woman next to her turned back into a cat, laying next Hamees.

"What's happening?" She demanded, standing up and putting a see-through robe around her naked body.

"It's the One who Tears into Pieces," the leader of the soldier firmly replied to the queen. "He's heading here, and we think that two riders are on his back."

Chapter 7
One Smashes and One Chews

Riding behind Princess Merit on the back of the griffin was an exhilarating experience for Moeris. It was the ride of his dreams as he always wondered how a flying bird would see the world from a great height.

From his point of view, the mountains of the Eastern Desert looked like an impression of a giant thumb-print, the Nile appeared as an inconsiderable stream, and the cities and towns seemed like dotted mosaics on the valley of the Nile.

However, Moeris quickly felt sadness tugging at his heart as they approached Thebes, where he could see the devastating aftermath of the Celestial's attack on the city.

Ever since the battle of Badari, the People from the Sky had put the entire kingdom of Egypt under siege as a punishment for what had happened to their heralds. Every night, once the last ray of the sun disappeared, the floating pyramids of the Celestials materialized in the sky across the kingdom and attacked anyone or anything that would dare to move.

From atop the One who Tears into Pieces, Moeris could see the ruins of what used to be palaces, houses, temples, and tombs. The beautiful metropolitan of Thebes had turned into a ghost city where wreckage and debris were everywhere.

The royal palace was not spared either. A couple of days ago, one of the Celestials' ships had spotted one of the guards moving on the eastern wall. Immediately, it had launched its devastating green beam, killing three guards and blowing a large chunk of the wall.

"Moeris, get ready," the princess instructed him loudly. She was leaning to the left and looking downward through a long, hollow rod made of clay.

Moeris knew that Princess Merit was looking through this simple tool to precisely determine their location at such heights.

Once Merit instructed Moeris to get ready, he slowly began to stand up on the back of the One who Tears into Pieces. Between the mighty flapping wings, Moeris was having a hard time maintaining his balance at such high speed and altitude. However, once he was fully standing, he opened his arms wide and raised his head a little as if he was flying.

He was high, as high as hell, evident in the glassy shine of his eyes. He had to chew three full blue lotus flowers right before riding the griffin. Otherwise, he would never dare to approach this beast, ride behind princess Merit, join her in such a risky mission, nor be able to perform the dangerous and crazy move which he was getting ready to execute.

"Now," Merit shouted, and Moeris immediately let his body fall backward. Still opening his arms wide, he just allowed the air to carry his body away from the griffin, while his eyes were staring at the clear blue sky.

As he was freefalling from the sky, he could see Princess Merit take the quiver which was covered with a lid off her back and throw it along with her bow. Then she quickly jumped off the One who Tears into Pieces too, trying to catch up with her companion.

At a certain point, Moeris turned around and took the position that the princess had instructed him to take once he jumped off the griffin.

"When you turn around to face the ground, keep your arms open and higher than your body," he remembered the princess's words. "Your elbows must be straight out of the shoulders, and your hands are at least as far out as the elbows. Also, make sure to bend your legs and leave your lower legs slightly extended into the wind. Spread your knees slightly, so your feet are as wide apart as the elbows." This position, Moeris had known from Merit, was going to help him accomplish any kind of body maneuvers he wanted to do while he was freefalling. Changing the flow of air around his body would help him to do certain and essential movements to position himself exactly where he wanted to land.

When he wanted to turn left, all he had to do was to deflect more air off his right arm than his left. This was done by merely banking like a bird—left arm down slightly, right arm up in proportion. The turn would continue until he resumed the neutral position.

The excitement continued to build inside Moeris as it was only air between him and the earth. He could smell the fresh, crisp, and clean air. He could hear the loud rush of wind, which caused the skin on his neck and face to flap gloriously.

For Moeris, the sensation of freefall was unlike anything else. The feeling was indescribable. Things were happening so fast that his brain did not have time to process anything. The whole experience was windy, adrenaline pumping, and intense. He was not sure if it was real or just a dream.

Although Merit had jumped off the griffin a few moments after Moeris, he quickly saw her catching up with him. Matter of fact, she was faster than him; and in no time, she passed him as she was supposed to reach her destination first according to their plan.

Moeris knew how Merit managed to do so as he recalled her instructions.

"If you want to move forward and faster, you need to deflect more air to the rear," she had told him earlier that day. "Just bring your arms back a little bit and extend your legs. Then, point the tip of your body slightly down, so the air will rush back off your torso and legs, allowing you to slide forward and fast."

Shortly, Moeris noticed that the princess's freefall was getting very close to an end and that she was going to land soon. He watched her rotate in the air a couple of times before getting to a vertical position where her head was up. She strived to make her body as slim and straight as an obelisk. Then, she crossed her arms on her chest in an X and did a full spin as her feet were entering the water of the Nile in a huge splash.

At this point, Moeris' freefalling was coming to an end as well, and he had to get ready to land as soon as possible. However, he was not heading to the river as Merit did a moment ago. Instead, he was heading directly and purposely to the pool which was located in the back courtyard of the royal palace. Also, he did not take the same landing position which the princess used. Instead, he quickly and skillfully aimed to hit the water horizontally in a manner akin to the belly flop.

Moeris believed that this landing position would allow him to dive from the greatest height into the shallow depth of the pool water without sustaining an injury. He alleged that this position would spread the impact over the greatest surface area, and it would achieve the longest time decelerating before hitting the bottom of the pool. Or, at least, this was the theory which he had suggested during preparing for this mission, and which he was going to put to the test to save his best friend.

***

As Merit's head slowly emerged from under the water, she was almost out of breath. Once her nose broke the surface, she sputtered and gasped a gulp for breath. She wiped the water from her eyes and blinked a few times, and then she fixed her eyes on her target; the royal palace.

As her slow emerging continued, it became more evident that she was not using either her arms or legs to break the water surface. Instead, it seemed that something was pushing her up and forward while she was taking a crouching position as if she was ready to run a race.

Without even turning her head or shift her sight, her left arm extended and grabbed the quiver which she threw out before jumping off the griffin. Meanwhile, her right hand reached out and snatched her bow, which was floating on the water surface. After taking the lid off the quiver, she quickly hung it on her back; her eyes still fixed on the royal palace, and her body was still emerging from under the water.

Only when the princess's body was entirely out of the water, she appeared to be crouching on top of a monster creature, its back was covered with longitudinal rows of prominent, bony, keeled scales. The beast was coming out of the water the same way a sunken island would emerge from under the water. It did not take that long for this creature's head to slowly come out of the water. It was long and pointed with the eyes and nostrils located on the top of the head. Teeth were pointed, cone-shaped, and located on the outside of the jaws.

It was one of the two giant crocodiles which the former high priest, Ramos, had summoned to escort the funerary boat during Senu III's funeral. In the same moment, the other colossal crocodile was emerging on the right hand of the Princess. Both crocodiles, one of them carrying Merit on its back, were quietly heading to the east bank of the river Nile, exactly where the royal palace was located.

87

It was well known across the kingdom that these two crocodiles were twin beasts who were born in regular size like any other crocodile lived in the River Nile. However, the former high priest, Ramos, after his return from Adoria as a pilgrim, wanted to show off his new skills which he learned from the Celestials to his pharaoh. He promised Senu III to have water beasts to protect the royal palace from any kind of attack from the riverside, only if needed and when they were summoned.

Rumors suggested that Ramos, one morning, was walking by the Nile bank near the Karnak temple. He had to stop when he heard a baby crocodile's noises. When he got closer to the tree where the sound was coming from behind, he found two crocodile eggs ready to hatch. Apparently, the two little crocodiles were producing some kind of pre-hatching calls.

Ramos first scanned around looking for the crocodile mother, but there was no trace of her. When he sent one of his priests a little bit further in the corn and wheat fields to look for her, his assistant came back later with some bad news. The crocodile was killed during a vicious fight with a hippopotamus. Ramos decided that the two little crocodiles which were about to hatch were the perfect choice to be the protector of the royal palace when they grew up.

That day, Ramos waited by the two eggs through the afternoon until they hatched, and two adorable baby crocodiles were entirely out. Then, he took them to his lounge in the temple. After casting a magical spell which he had learned from the Adorians, he let the two crocodiles into the water. But first, he gave them names. The first was "The One Who Smashes," referring to his powerful tail which later was going to get strong enough that it could smash a whole man with just one hit. The other one was "The One Who Chews," referring to his sharp teeth which later when it was grown up were going to be sharp enough to chew a whole animal in no time.

Next morning, Ramose showed the pharaoh the two baby crocodiles. Senu found it hard to believe that they, each one was now the size of an adult crocodile, were only one day old. Ramose even had to bring the priest who found the dead crocodile mother to testify before the king that he had seen these two beasts coming out of their eggs only the day before. However, Senu did not believe until the next day when he saw "The One Who Chews" and "The One Who Smashes" coming out of the water, each was about ten feet long. The two crocodiles continue to grow fast. In less than a week, each one of them was about forty feet long, the same length of a large boat.

Later, Ramose had given Senu the key to control "The One Who Chews" and "The One Who Smashes." The key was a very simple spell if he or any one of the royal family cast, these two beasts were going to be immediately summoned and protect this person with their lives. As this simple spell was passed to the new pharaoh after the death of Senu III, Merit's father made sure to tell her about this secret in case she needed it one day, the same way she did after jumping from the "One Who Tears into pieces" into River Nile.

Even though Merit was not a good swimmer, she jumped off the griffin, knowing that two beasts were waiting for her down there in the river to save her. As she was still falling free, and right before she broke the water surface, she muttered the following words, "I, Merit, the daughter of Senu IV and the rightful heiress to the Egyptian throne, command The One Who Chews and The One Who Smashes to come out and fight for me."

When the princess hit the water with her feet, she went down very far. Holding her breath, she instantly began swimming up for air. As she was pushing water with both hands and legs, her feet hit something. She quickly stopped and looked down. It was "The One Who Chews" pushing her up. Next to him was "The one who Smashes" swimming up too. When she realized that the two beasts had answered her call, she stopped pushing the water. She just took a crouching position on the back of the beast as if she was ready to run a race, still holding her breath until they broke the water surface.

As they approached the river bank, Princess Merit could tell that her plan was going along just fine so far, especially the distraction part of it, which ultimately relied on Moeris and the One who Tears into Pieces. She noticed that not a lot of Kushites were guarding the walls. Something was happening somewhere near the pool had already drawn all the attention and forced most of the Kushites to leave their position and rush to the back courtyard.

Obviously, Moeris had survived the jump and the freefall, and he was now performing his part of the distraction plan. Merit had heard a lot about Moeris and his extraordinary fighting skills which strangely would not appear unless he was intoxicated.

***

At the exact same moment, the Kushites were pulling Moeris out of the pool. He was slightly shaky and whimpering a little. Evidently, the free fall and the cold water of the pool had sobered him up a little, just a little. All he needed was chewing a couple of blue lotus' petals or drinking a few sips of beer, and he was going to be thoroughly intoxicated again.

As he was coughing, gasping, and gulping air, he noticed that dozens of Kushites were surrounding him. They all had left their position and rushed to the back courtyard when they heard a massive splash in the pool.

Moeris had to look at a huge Kushite with a face covered in a mess of ugly scars; obviously, he was the leader of the Kushites, as he was firmly saying something to his men in Kushite. Although Moeris did not speak their language, he could easily tell that this man was ordering the Kushite to take him to the dungeon. The word dungeon was very similar in both Egyptian and Kushite. He also understood that he ordered them to keep him alive in compliance with someone's orders. Moeris tried to guess, *The Queen Regent, Keya, or the new Queen of the South, Hamees,* he could not tell.

As they were taking him away, Moeris's eyes noticed something hanging out of the belt of one of the mercenaries. He was a tall man, but a bit elfin. He was young and baldheaded. His thick, black eyebrows were drawn together, and his dark eyes glared out at Moeris from under them.

Is this a blue lotus? The question popped in Moeris' mind, narrowing his eyes and tilting his head a little. Hanging from the Kushite's belt was a flower with rich blue petals and a fiery yellow center. It was the Egyptian blue lotus, which grew in the Nile, was also called the "Sunken Happiness" because it opened in the morning, rising to the surface of the water; and then, closed and sank back down into the water at dusk. It was a significant plant in the kingdom of Egypt because chewing it gave people feelings of calm euphoria. For that reason, it was in high demand in the kingdom.

For a brief moment, Moeris recalled when he accompanied Roma to meet the high oracle. On their way back, they visited a small brothel called the "House of Roses." After chewing the petals of five blue lotus, Moeris turned from a coward who ha little courage to a skilled fighter capable of knocking down five Kushites by himself using only his bare hands.

Is this really a blue lotus? The question was repeated in Moeris' mind.

Before Moeris's mind could produce an answer to this question, the tall man approached him and delivered a ferocious punch to his belly. As Moeris was grunting in pain, the leader of the Kushites barked something. Obviously, he was reminding the man who had just hit Moeris that they needed him alive. However, the tall man fiercely shouted something in Kushite. His voice loud and clear, defying his leader by sending another punch to Moeris's abdomen. The leader of the Kushites had to physically release Moeris from the hands of the tall man.

As Kushites were taking Moeris away, he suddenly stopped.

"Wait a moment, please," Moeris pleaded; still grunting in pain. His sudden stop forced the two men who were taking him away to stop too, exchanging looks with their leader.

"I just need to get this from my belt," Moeris continued, smiling. After nodding his head to the Kushite to his right, he slowly pulled his right arm away and reached out to his belt. "Easy, easy," he said in a soothing tone, when all the Kushites around him pointed their swords, spears, and axes at him, thinking that he was pulling a weapon. "It's just a blue lotus."

When the tall man punched Moeris in his abdomen, Moeris did not waste any time. He immediately and cleverly extended his hand and snatched the flower from the man's belt. When the Kushite hit Moeris again, he was able to hide the flower inside his own belt.

Moeris released a sigh of relief when he noticed that none of the Kushites was smart enough to notice that the flower was dry even though he was wet as a dog that's chased ducks into the pond.

"I just want to chew some petals from this beautiful flower," Moeris said in Egyptian, knowing that most of the mercenaries spoke a little Egyptian. He pulled his other arm from the Kushite on his left. He ripped a few petals of the flower and quickly shoved them in his mouth.

The leader said something to his men, chuckling, and most of his men burst in laughter. When Moeris demanded a translation, the Kushite on his left interpreted for him what this leader had just said. He was joking that Moeris was obviously chewing the sunken happiness because he wanted to numb his body, knowing exactly what he was going to experience by the Kushites' hands in the dungeon, but what he was going to do when the blue lotus's effect went

92

away. The Kushites burst in more laughter, and Moeris smiled. He was thankful that the Kushites allowed him to chew the blue lotus; otherwise, he was going to be in deep trouble.

Even though Moeris knew the fate which waited for any was captured by the Kushites, he was not scared or even unnerved. The source of his confidence partly came as a result of being intoxicated; meanwhile, he knew very well Princess Merit's plan, which relied on a huge part on the One Who Tears into Pieces.

All of a sudden, a thunderous sound echoed through the back courtyard. It was a mix between the high-pitched whistling of an eagle and the deep roar of a vicious and gigantic lion.

"Don't be scared. It's just my friend," Moeris mockingly said; still chewing the flower's petals. "It's the One who Tears into Pieces." With amused eyes, he studied how the Kushites were scared to death. Their hands reached for their weapons, and their heads were scanning around, looking for the griffin. Only when they raised their heads to the roof of the royal palace, the Kushites saw the king of all the creatures standing up there; his wings were still spread out and flapping. The griffin roared one more time. It was a roar that even the people who lived in the north part of Thebes were still able to hear it.

"Let me introduce you to the king of all the creatures," Moeris continued, sarcastically. "By the way, have you ever wondered why people call him the One who Tears into Pieces?"

Chapter 8

The Adorian Eyes

When Azan's three eyes stared up at the screen and then moved downward where he stood, the whole see-through screen moved down and laid horizontally between his generals who gathered in a circle around him. The display formed some kind of a table between them, except for Azan who stood in the middle of the screen, protruding from its center. As Azan's small arms raised in the air, the screen turned into a hologram for the royal palace in Thebes.

Eventually, they could recognize a winged creature standing on top of the palace. They knew it was The One who Tears into Pieces who was standing there flapping his huge wings and staring down at several Kushites in the back courtyard. The mercenaries were surrounding a single warrior who evidently just came out or was pulled out of the pool because he was completely wet. When Azan and his generals looked at the western side of the palace, they found two giant crocodiles approaching the riverbank. On the back of one of them rode a female warrior.

Azan was aware that this young lady was Princess Merit, the rightful heiress to the Egyptian throne. He had received a lot of reports which informed him about the princess' struggle to reclaim her father's throne. He even had just received another report a little bit ago that Merit was flying to Thebes in what appeared to be a rescue mission for the man who she loved. That was why Azan had summoned his subordinates to watch live what was happening at the royal palace of Upper Egypt.

However, Azan's attention was distracted when one of his men entered the room. Through some kind of non-verbal communication, the first commander knew that one of their spies, or Eyes, in Egypt had just arrived after summoning her to discuss urgent matters. Azan had to leave his subordinates to continue watching what was happening on the screen, and he went out of the map and headed to a smaller room.

On his way, Azan took a moment to recall how the Adorians had made a deal with the Egyptian rulers to continue studying Earth, the human race, and the land of Egypt. Through the ages, they had recruited hundreds of Egyptians to be their Eyes on Earth and in the land of Egypt. Since the Adorians and people of Egypt were allies, military and political espionage was restricted. Those eyes were recruited only for research purposes.

The People from the Sky placed Eyes in the inns to report about the Egyptians' drinking habits. Others were planted in fields to record everything related to agriculture. More was appointed in courts to study how the elderlies ruled in cases involving small claims and major disputes.

The Adorians also put more Eyes in stables to give detailed reports on the animal and birds who lived in the land of Egypt. More worked on the trade routes to observe what the Egyptians imported and exported. Others were planted in temples to secretly listen to the people's prayers to their Gods. More were placed in the markets to analysis the Egyptian cuisine. Several Eyes were just people traveling around to observe the daily life of the Egyptians and report it to the Celestials.

Even the sexual life in Egypt was one of the things in which the Adorians were interested. Some whores who worked in the sex industry were recruited by the People from the Sky to report about their customers' sexual preferences and habits. The Eye whom Azan was going to meet now was one of those prostitutes who was recruited a long time ago to be one of their spies.

Once the first commander of the Adorian fleet entered a small room, his three eyes stared up at a small screen. Immediately, a hologram video was shown about the Eye whom he was going to meet now. It seemed as if Azan wanted to know as much information about this woman before meeting her. Before his eyes, a toddler girl of no more than four years old was shown on the screen, screaming and crying in a crowded market. It looked like she had lost her parents. She was crying out, calling for her mother and father, but they were not around. She begged people for help, but no one showed her any mercy. She was tired and hungry, and none did her any good.

When Azan used some kind of mental power to fast forward the film a little bit, it was already past sunset, and the market was nearly empty. The little girl was still there walking around, bare feet and dressed in torn clothes. Shortly, the girl heard some weird sounds which she decided to follow, thinking that they might guide her to her parents. When she was out of the town and walked into a cornfield, she saw a small creature. It was one of the Celestials. She did not get scared nor tried to run. Instead, she approached the Adorian who gave her a small loaf of bread, four pieces of dried camel meat, and a goatskin full of water.

Azan fast forwarded the film to see the Adorian take the toddler girl to a secret place located deep in the mountains of the Eastern Desert, where the celestials took care of more orphans. Dozens of boys and girls were brought up in this place and prepared to be the future Eyes of the People from the Sky in the land of Egypt. Later, when these kids grew up, they were sent to the world to help those who saved their lives and took care of them, while no one else did.

As the images continued before Azan's eyes, he saw the toddler girl had grown into a beautiful woman who worked as a whore at a small brothel located north of Thebes, called "House of Roses." In the film, she was now a beautiful lady who dressed in a see-through dress which revealed plenty of her desirable body; her perfect handful breasts with pink nipples, her flat stomach with a diamond stud in her belly button, and her long, toned legs, which peeked through the dress slits.

The prostitute was standing in front of a highly-polished bronze mirror, painting her full lips red and her eyelids black. When she finished, she remained there for a moment. Her eyes inspected the reflection of her gorgeous face in the mirror to make sure everything was perfect; her fair complexion, black hair, an oval face, straight nose, and magnificent dark eyes.

"Nefer, to the Kushites' table, now," Azan heard the Madame and the owner's wife of the brothel ordering the Eye. "Treat them well. They asked for you by name."

At the age of fourteen, and as Nefer was turning into a sexy, gorgeous girl, the Adorians had sent her to this small brothel and instructed her to introduce herself to the owner and ask him for a job. It did not take the owner too much time to hire this new whore, knowing that this stunning girl was going to bring him more money. Nefer's mission inside the brothel was to collect as much information about the Egyptian's sexual habits, behaviors, practices, and orientations.

Shortly, Azan saw Nefer in the display coming back to her room with two men. A young man which he immediately recognized. It was Roma, who later was going to be the leader of the Free Army. The other man was a giant Kushite with a crooked nose and a chunk missing from his left ear. The first commander of the Adorian troops got excited when he saw Roma bringing out a small dagger and putting it on the mercenary's neck. When the Kushite asked for help from Nefer, who was now lying naked on the bed, she shocked him with her answer. She turned around and closed her eyes.

Before Nefer worked as a prostitute in this brothel, the Adorians had taught her the way to send her reports. Every time she slept; she met her recruiter in her dreams where she told him in detail about her customers and all their sexual activities. On that day, when Nefer decided to take a nap while Roma was interrogating the Kushite, she trusted that something important was happening in her room. These two men who supposed to have sex was her, together, turned out to be two enemies who happened that one of them was forcing the other to speak of crucial information.

As Nefer fell asleep, she reported what was happening in her room to her recruiter who instantly advised her to quit her job and join Roma to keep the Adorians aware of the insurgence which was being born in the land of Egypt. It was the best day of Nefer's life. She had always hated this job. Every day she had spent in this brothel, she had thought of quitting at least once. However, she could not betray the Celestials who saved her life and raised her up. Also, she had to stay because working as a whore was the only thing that kept her from being homeless and from starving to death, especially during the famine, which was ravaging Egypt these days.

Azan fast forwarded and now, he watched Nefer waking up after receiving the new instruction from her recruiter. In her dark room, she first quietly watched the Kushite releasing himself, then she followed him to the main room in the brothel to find a considerable fight taking place between Egyptians and Kushites. Immediately, she took a side by helping the two Egyptians, Roma and Moeris. She smashed a vase made of clay over the head of one of the

Kushite, knocking him unconscious. Then, she introduced herself to Roma and Moeris, "My name is Nefer. As you see, I just quit my job here. So, I was wondering if you would let me enjoy your company."

At this point, Azan stopped the film. He had enough information about the Eye whom he was going to meet. Then, through some kind of non-verbal communication with one of his men, he requested the Eye to come in.

When Nefer entered the room, she was entirely different than how she looked in the images. In the last scene she appeared, Azan saw her neatly dressed in a fabulous dress made of white linen. However, she was now entering the meeting room covered only in a leopard skin, the same way the priested dressed. Not only this but she also had her hair shaved off in the same way as any of member of the Egyptian priesthood.

***

Later that day, and when Azan went back to where his subordinates were still gathered around the hologram screen, he found them still watching live what was happening at the royal palace. He did not get back to his position in the middle of the screen. He did not want to interrupt their attention. Instead, he just stood behind them and watched what was going on. Before his eyes, a small battle was happening in the back courtyard where a griffin and an unarmed fighter were handling dozens of Kushite mercenaries. Azan's eyes shone with excitement when he saw Princess Merit arriving as well on the back of one of the two giant crocodiles.

Chapter 9
The One Who Tears into Pieces

"Let me introduce you to the king of all the creatures," Moeris sarcastically told the mercenaries who surrounded him. Intoxicated like he had never been seen before; he was pointing at the griffin who stood on the roof of the royal palace staring down at them. "By the way, have you ever wondered why people call him the One who Tears into Pieces?"

The origins of the griffin were not fully known. Some believed that the former high priest, Ramose, had brought him from Adoria as a gift from the celestials to the Egyptians, and as a seed that eventually would breed himself and produce more of his kind. Others believed that the griffin was one of the nine giant beasts that inhabited the land of Egypt, including serpopards, ammits, giant scorpions, giant spiders, and other beasts.

Those who believed that the griffin was originally from Adoria told stories that When Ramose returned to Egypt as a pilgrim, he introduced the new beast to King Senu III. However, it seemed that the king was not super excited about this creature and did not really utilize it at all. Later, when Senu IV ascended the throne, he was so impressed by the griffin, he gifted him to his only daughter and the heiress to the throne as a bodyguard.

Some stories even went further by telling that the Adorians had studies all the creatures which lived in the land of Egypt. They decided to gift the Egyptians with a creature which combine all the beings found in nature. After so many failed experiments, they finally came up with a better idea. Instead of combining all the creature in a unique breed, they thought of breading the king of the animal, a lion, with the king of the birds, an eagle. The result was the king of all the creature because they believed it would dominate over all the other beings either they were found on the land or in the air.

Meanwhile, those who believed that the One who Tears into Pieces was originally from Earth told other stories that a small band of the Egyptian army was on its way back from the Western Desert. It happened that they lost their way in a desert, where they found themselves face-to-face with a baby griffin. It was the first time ever that an Egyptian found such an adorable, yet vicious, creature.

Although the baby griffin killed some of soldiers, they luckily were accompanied by a priest who was able to cast a spell on this beast to make it sleep peacefully, and the soldiers restrained it tightly. When they brought the griffin to Thebes, they gifted it to the king who assigned a trainer to domesticate it.

Regardless of the griffin's origins, he was now standing on top of the royal palace, his eyes staring downward at the dozens of Kushites. The mercenaries' legs shivered when one more roar reverberated in the air, wondering why people called this giant beast the One who Tears into Pieces.

Still riding on the back of one of the two giant crocodiles, Princess Merit continued her way to attack the royal palace from the river. As she was getting closer, she noiselessly pulled three arrows from the quiver and thrust them forward, together, killing three Kushites who were standing on top of one of the towers. In the blink of an eye, she pulled three more arrows and killed the other three Kushites who guarded the other tower.

Princess Merit was skilled with the bow, and though she hadn't used it for some time, it felt natural in her hands. Her father, even before ascending the throne, saw in his daughter not only a successor but a warrior, too. She was lean, shredded, strong, beautiful, and confident. She was a true and genuine material for a legend warrior.

Senu IV knew that, once he became the king, it was going to be the first time in the history of Egypt that the heir to the throne was not going to be a male. It was going to be his only daughter. He always wondered how the Egyptians were going to take that. Although the Egyptians loved Princess Merit—for her beauty, charm, intelligence, spirit, purity, and innocence—her father knew that the heiress to the Egyptian throne was going to face opposition, merely for being female.

That was why Senu IV did not want to wait for such opposition. Once she became a young woman capable of holding a weapon, Senu IV sent messengers across the kingdom looking for the best trainers who would train the rightful heiress to the Egyptian throne. He wanted her to become a strong warrior who would be able to prove for anyone that she could be a fighter and an heir to the throne like any male.

Within a few weeks, dozens of skillful trainers with great reputations arrived in Thebes, offering their help to make Princess Merit a considerable warrior capable of defending herself and her people when she would sit on the throne. However, none of these trainers had gotten the job because the princess turned them all down. Instead, she convinced her father that she wanted a young man who happened to be one of the pharaoh guards to be her personal trainer. The name of the guard was Roma, short for Romaroy.

From her point of view now, Princess Merit could see the One who Tears into Pieces was still standing on top of the building. According to her plan, the griffin, along with Moeris, was going to play a crucial role to distract the Kushites. After one more roar, the king of all the creatures turned around to face more than two dozen of Kushites who rushed to the roof to fight him.

A big smile grew on Princess Merit's face when she began seeing heads, feet, limbs, hands, and other parts of human bodies flying in the air, and blood splashing everywhere, amid the anguished screams of those who dared to confront this beast who proved once and for all that he was the One who Tears into Pieces.

This was not the first time for the princess to see her griffin do that. A few months ago, she witnessed something similar when Varis and the Kushite mercenaries attacked the royal palace. Ironically, it had occurred in the very same place where it was happening now; the roof of the palace.

During Varis' attack on the palace, Merit was in her royal bedchamber watching from the window which looked out to the front yard. With eyes full of shock and surprise, she was witnessing angry people storming the palace. In a rush, a short and chubby maid helped the princess get dressed. Then, as fast as a deer, the maid helped Merit to strap two short swords to her back. Also, she brought a bow and a quiver full of arrows and handed them to her lady.

The princess and the maid were barely able to breathe through the thick smoke that hung in the air around them. They were coughing desperately, and their eyes were stinging and watering so much that they were could barely see.

With the intention to rush out of her bedchamber to save her parents, the princess was hanging the quiver diagonally over her left shoulder. Her heart fell to her stomach as two guards came in accompanied by the youngest priest in the Egyptian priesthood, Amasis. The relation between heiress to the Egyptian throne and the future high priest of Egypt was based on respect and trust as they had known each other since infancy.

"My Princess, you have to come with me quickly," Amasis talked to Merit in shivering voice. His legs were shaking, and he appeared to be scared as if he saw a demon.

"To where?" She questioned him, grabbing the bow from her maid.

"To the roof," the young priest quickly answered. "I've summoned the One who Tears in to take you away."

"No way," she firmly objected, not believing that she would ever escape, leaving her beloved father and mother behind to face their death. "I have to stay and fight."

"My Lady, you are the heiress to the Egyptian throne," Amasis quickly pleaded, "and your life isn't yours, it's the people's. I'm so sorry, princess. You can't risk your life by staying here. You have to come with me now. Don't worry about the king and the queen, the serpopards and the guards would never let any harm reach your parents. Trust me, My Lady."

After a moment of hesitation, the princess nodded her head in agreement.

"What about me, My Lady?" The maid stopped princess right before leaving the chamber.

"Stay here," Merit instructed her. "I'm sure whoever is attacking would never hurt a maid holding no weapon. Just hide here, and everything will be fine."

"Be safe, Princess," the maid said in a frightened tone.

"You too," the princess said back, turning around and leaving the room, not knowing that the attackers were going to kill this very maid - along with most of the servants and maids who were in the royal palace that day in what was

105

going to be the worst massacre of civilians in the history of the kingdom – and mistakenly were going to take her as Senu IV's daughter.

As the princess' legs flew up the stairs, she looked at the young priest next to her and asked him if he was sure that the king and the queen will be safe.

"Trust me, my lady," Amasis replied, out of breath from climbing the steps. "When was the last time you saw the serpopards let someone near the Pharaoh, and when was the last time the guards let harm reach the queen."

When the princess reached the roof, she saw the One who Tears into pieces surrounded by over two dozen of warriors who were trying to kill him. They were huge, bare-footed men with dark skin, dressed in simple kilts and with what appeared to be feathers in their hair. They were holding axes in their right hands, and there were pieces of cloth covering their noses and mouths. Merit immediately recognized the attackers' origins from the way they were dressed.

Kushites! The recognition suddenly popped up in her head. But, she could not understand why warriors from Kush were attacking the palace of Egypt's Pharaoh.

In awe, the princess watched heads, feet, limbs, hands, and other parts of human bodies flying in the air, and blood splashing everywhere, amid of anguish screams. After the griffin was done with the attackers, he turned around and headed to the princess. He leaned his head down in a way that appeared the he was bowing to her and inviting her to ride on his back in the same time. After exchanging a hesitating look with Amasis, the princess jumped on the back of the griffin, and he immediately flew off.

A sudden, aggressive and prolonged high-pitched cry brought Princess Merit back to present. She was still on the back of the One Who Smashes. She immediately recognized the sound. It was Moeris. Apparently, he restored his intoxication and was fighting whatever was left of the Kushites in the back courtyard.

My way is clear, she told herself, pulling her two swords out of their sheaths and standing up as the two crocodiles reached the bank of the river, ready to rescue Roma from the hands of her enemies.

Merit had to shift her sight to one of the palace's window when she heard a loud, sharp scream which appeared that it came out of an angry monster. A scream that reminded her of the battle of Badari.

It's Keya, the princess told herself, and she immediately saw her.

"Faster," Merit ordered the crocodile beneath her feet, and the beast instantly increased its speed, in synchronization with its twin brother, passing between the armory and bunkhouse. Their way was still clear, as all the Kushites who guarded the palace that day were either busy dealing with the One who Tears into pieces or dealing with Moeris.

Chapter 10

The Mute Warrior

Hent screamed and jumped, waking up with a fright when she heard a monster's roar. Inside her cell, in the royal palace's dungeons, she quickly jumped to her feet and ran to the door's metal bars.

Is it Gapi? She hoped inside her not yet fully awake mind. *Is he finally coming to save me?*

She tried to peer through the darkness, yet she could see no one in the hallway.

What are all these noises? She could hear the sounds of urgent orders, clashing weapons, and dying people. *What's happening? It's an attack on the palace,* she concluded. *Someone is attacking the palace. I hope it's Gapi.*

Hent's head scanned around, trying to grasp the moment. Around her was no more than a small cell which contained no furniture. It was foul with human excrement lay on the ground. Flies, mosquitoes, and all manner of crawling things had infested the cell's walls and floor.

Realizing that she was still confined in this filthy lockup, Hent grabbed on the door's cold metal bars and furiously shook them, groaning in pain with every move. She was frail and in terrible shape. Clearly, she had been cruelly tortured ever since she stood up for the man whom she loved with all her soul, mind, and heart; the man for whom she would die. Her muscular body was bruised and bloodied. The military uniform on her was also covered in dried blood.

Voluntarily, Hent's mind recalled what she suffered since King Alara had ordered his men to arrest her. On that day, she found herself being seized by six powerful men who pulled her away and dragged her through Thebes's gate and streets until they arrived in the royal palace. When they reached the dungeons, they forcefully threw her into one of the cells.

Hent waited there for hours, thinking that Gapi was going to be able to stand for her, the same way she did for him, and be able to free her. Yet night came and went, and her love did not show up. In the morning, some Kushite came to her with some bad news. They were afraid of this powerful, muscular woman, and none of them dared to enter her cell. They just spoke to her through the door's bars.

"We've got you a souvenir from your love," one of the mercenaries said in a mocking tone, throwing something through the bars which landed right between Hent's legs.

It was something which appeared to be like a flesh, a lump of bloody flesh. When Hent narrowed her eyes a little to be able to see in the semi-dark cell, she quickly realized that it was a tongue, human's tongue, which seemed that it was violently yanked out of someone's mouth.

Gapi! She immediately felt her heart stop, and her eyes widen.

Only a mute person, like Hent, would understand the meaning of someone would lose his ability to speak. The only difference was that she was born mute because of an abnormal marriage between relatives. Even though she learned sign language in early childhood, kids and adults alike, mocked her way of communication. Some people even physically harassed her, beating her up and throwing stones at her, thinking that demon spirits acted within her. This made Hent grow up an introvert and made her focus on getting stronger, so she could defend herself.

Through hard training and rough competition, Hent eventually had a muscular, toned, and shaped body. When she joined the Medjay force, and Gapi selected her to be his deputy, she knew some people doubted that she could lead this elite paramilitary force because she was mute, but she proved to everyone that she did not need to speak to be in this position. Her appearance made her fearful and respected among all the other fighters, and she had to maintain this excellent physical shape because of the nature of her position, which required her to be strong and powerful like all the men and women she led, Also, she only needed to give an angry stare, point firmly, signal confidently, or use her bloodcurdling scream to give orders to her soldiers.

However, when Hent knew that Gapi had become mute like her, she instantly felt anger swelling up inside her. Out of rage, she stood up inside the cell and ran to the door. Before any of the Kushites outside could react, her powerful hands traveled through the bars and grabbed one of them by the neck.

Choking and could not breathe, the man found himself rise in the air for a brief moment before his head was violently smashed in the door's bars a couple of times, seeing his own blood splatter everywhere, and then darkness took over him.

Hent didn't release the dead man and retreat until the other mercenaries pulled their sharp weapons and started hitting her arms, yelling, cursing, and shouting. That day she received a nasty cut on the back of her right hand, and the tip of one of the spears made a bloody hole in her left arm.

After the death of one of them at Hent's hands, the Kushites who were responsible for the dungeons were unleashed on her with their cruelest methods of torture. At first, they tried the rack. They brought an oblong, rectangular, wooden frame and slightly raised it from the ground, with a roller at both ends. Hent's feet were fastened to one roller, and her wrists were chained to the other. Although she felt her bones were dislocated with a loud crack, she did not even groan in pain.

When the mercenaries saw that Hent did not cry, scream, or even grunt in agony, they moved to the next torture in their list; the dunking. They tied her to a chair which was elevated by ropes above the river. She was then lowered into the water until completely submerged. The chair was raised only right before she was about to pass out. To intensify this technique, they placed a piece of fruit in her mouth and nose beforehand, so she couldn't get a good breath before being dunked.

Again, when Hent did not show her pain, the Kushites went forward to the next method they had; the brown rat. They completely restrained and tied her to the ground and cut several slits in her stomach. Then they placed rats and trap them with a bowl on her muscular abdomen. A lump of hot coal was placed on top of the bowl, so the rats would get hot, forcing them to escape by tearing out her stomach. However, Hent did not move a muscle. She did not even flinch. Right before the rats went into her belly, the mercenaries took the bowl and the rats away.

For some reason, which Hent did not know, they could not kill her. That encouraged her and gave her hope that Gapi, despite losing his tongue, was coming to save her.

Another roar of the monster who was attacking the royal palace now brought Hent back to her dark cell to find herself still sitting by the door; her hand clutching the bars. She tried to peer through the darkness again, but yet none of the guards were there for some reason. It seemed that whatever was happening up there in the back courtyard had drawn all the attention. She narrowed her eyes and looked into the cell across the hallway from her, she found a young man suspended from the ceiling by robes. She knew that this man was Roma, the leader of the Free Army, who was captured following the battle of Badari.

Maybe it's Princess Merit coming to save him? Hent contemplated, remembering the rumor which she heard once before about seeing Princess Merit sneak out of the palace after midnight and meet Roma in a quiet location near the main dock of Thebes.

Thinking of the relation between Roma and Merit made Hent's own story of being in love with Gapi began trooping down her memory's lane. First, she remembered the day Prince Gapi was introduced to the Medjay soldiers as their new commander after his father's successful rebellion. Hent, back then, was no more than a soldier with a growing reputation as the first and most powerful female fighter joined the Medjay. On that day, Gapi walked through the lines of the Medjay soldiers which stretched for miles outside the walls of Thebes. When his eyes laid on this muscular woman whose body was toned and shaped by hard training, he immediately chose her to be his deputy in command.

Later, Gapi revealed to her that he fell in love with her at first sight and that he promoted her to this position so they could be close to each other. However, he made it clear to her that their relationship must stay down and low because he was not sure of his father's reaction. Despite the secrecy of their relationship, which Hent did not like at first, she fell in love with him, too. She adored his strength and ambition.

It was a shocking moment for Hent when Gapi came to her one day, telling her that he must travel immediately to Memphis. When he told her the details of his father's ridiculous quest regarding extracting the kairemi from the pharaohs' tombs, she almost lost it. She tried to warn him that his father was just distracting him and sending him away, so he could easily pass the throne to Hamees. However, Gapi believed that he must accept the challenge to prove to Varis that he was worthy of being the successor, and he traveled north anyway.

Sitting in her cell, Hent recalled that at the same night when Gapi traveled to Memphis she was summoned by the queen in her royal bedchamber. Varis was not there; and before Hent wondered in her mind where he was, Keya voluntarily explained that the pharaoh was arranging the details of the most important day of his life with the new high priest. Hent knew from some confidential reports which she received, as the deputy commander of the Medjay force, that Varis had built a dam in the south which blocked the river stream and caused drought and famine. This forced the poor people to revolt against Senu III. Gapi later confirmed the story to her. He also told her that Varis was planning, after ascending the throne, that he was going to open the dam and then touch the water in front of his people, so they believe that he ended the famine and that he was a half-god.

The queen then told Hent that she was going to be the temporary commander of the Medjay soldier and that she was responsible for securing the Pharaoh's procession the next day to the main dock in Thebes. Keya went ahead explaining how this day was significant for Varis.

"The king must know how much his people love him," Keya's voice rang in Hent's mind, recalling her orders that night. "But only at the right time. Don't let them get near him before he touches the water. Once he propitiates the God of the Nile on behalf of the Egyptians, you can give the order."

Hent continued to remember the queen's instructions, "The moment the king begins climbing up the stairs, it's your moment. Order your soldiers to clear the way between him and people. Allow them to celebrate their half-god pharaoh. Let them rejoice the end of the famine. Permit them to get closer and touch a god in flesh and get his blessing. Even if the king instructs you against that, just do it. He will thank you later when he sees how much the people love and worship him."

Even though Hent was angry with the King for his continuous humiliation for Gapi, Hent had to accept the temporary position and follow the orders which she just received from the queen. She secured the Pharaoh's procession; and when the river began to rise, she signaled to her soldiers to clear the way between Varis and his people, not knowing that Keya had just deceived her and made her the number one suspect in a failed attempt to assassin the pharaoh of Egypt.

Hent recollected when the chaos erupted at the dock. She thought that the king was going to be proud of her later after seeing how much people loved him. She even smiled at him, thinking that he was happy and enjoying the best day in his life. For a moment, she believed that if she gained his trust, she might be able to convince him later that Gapi was his best choice for his successor. Yet, when an arrow shot Varis from behind, she knew immediately that she was a victim of Keya's scam.

For a moment, Hent thought that what had just taken place was not her fault. Then, it hit her like a flash of lightning. Nobody was going to believe that she was just following the queen's orders. No one was going to think that she did not cause this chaos intentionally to allow the assassin to shoot the Pharaoh. As the chaos continued at the dock, Hent immediately took her horse and fled Thebes.

I hated Varis, and I'm glad he is dead, Hent thought once she heard a scream coming from the back courtyard of the royal palace, *yet I hate Keya even more.* The cry this time was different than the roar she heard earlier. It was a loud, sharp shriek which appeared to come out of an angry monster in the back courtyard of the royal palace

Chapter 11

Liberating Roma

When Moeris heard a loud shriek, he had to stop fighting for a moment and looked up. Coming out of the window, he saw Keya struggling to pass through. Her long wings made things harder than anticipated. Her loud cry made everyone fighting in the back courtyard, even the Kushites, shiver to the narrow their bones.

Seeing this horrible looking creature flying to the roof of the palace made him recall the aerial combat that had occurred between Princess Merit and Keya during the battle of Badari.

The One Who Tears into Pieces will take care of her, he told himself, shifting his focus back to his own battle by sending a powerful kick straight to a Kushite's groin, followed by a mighty blow to the man's jaw, sending him unconscious to the marble floor which surrounded the pool.

Moeris had to duck down, and a spear flew past him, missing his head by only a couple of inches and smacking into a Kushite's chest who was attacking from behind. He did not waste time, as he was standing up, both his hands firmly grabbed the spear, its tip was still protruding from the Kushite's back, and he pulled the Kushite up, forcing him not to fall to the ground. Behind this mercenary, Moeris took cover from more Kushites who were aiming their bows at him at the same time. Over a dozen arrows whistle at him without doing any harm, as a few of them passed him and hit the floor. Meanwhile, the human shield, which Moeris took a moment ago, received the rest of the arrows in his back.

It took the mercenaries a few moments to comprehend how the bare-handed man before their eyes had skillfully survived over a dozen arrows shot at him at the same time. However, these few moments were what Moeris had needed to move on and confront all of them.

Even before the mercenaries' minds were able to comprehend what was happening around them, Moeris dropped the spear, which he used to hold his human shield. The Kushite fell on his knees, and his body leaned forward, but the shaft of the spear prevented the body from falling forward.

Moeris instantly darted forward. His right foot pushed down on the shaft of the spear, and then his left foot did the same on the Kushite's head, sending his body to sail in the air, higher than he should have been able to.

When Moeris landed, he landed with a heavy thud which dragged the Kushites back to reality to find that the fighter who, a moment ago, was shielding behind the falling mercenary, was now, all of a sudden, in the middle of them.

Moeris charged instantly with a high-pitched war scream. He grabbed the heads of two of them and merely smashed them together. As the two mercenaries in his hands were falling down semi-unconscious, he had to lean backward to avoid being hit by an ax, which flew in the air and struck in the head of the Kushite who was on his left. Even when he leaned backward, the back of his head hit another Kushite's mouth behind him, broke several of his front teeth.

Faster than a blink, Moeris' left hand extended and grabbed the ax which had just struck the head of the fighter on his left, as the body was falling to the ground. He hit the man in front of him with the back of the ax-head straight in the jaw. The man took the hit and fell backward to the ground.

Using the back of the ax-head again, Moeris slammed it mightily down over the head of the sixth Kushite, knocking him unconscious. Then he dropped the ax, especially when he had to block a punch from another Kushite. Yet, in a blink of an eye, he landed a one-two combination on the Kushite's face, sending him to the ground.

He stepped on another man's foot, trapping him. Then he knocked him to the ground with a bone-shaking punch. Faster than a stag, he turned around and sent a blow into the eights Kushite's right cheek, and then he stretched out both arms and clamped on the man's ears, discombobulating him.

His fist fractured another Kushite's jaw, followed by a powerful kick from his right leg that cracked a couple of the man's ribs. Another punch to the side of the man's chin caused his head to spin suddenly around and his body to recoil. Moeris did not wait for the Kushite to fall. He quickly sent a heel kick which the man received in his diaphragm before he fell down unconscious.

When he turned around to face the last three Kushites who were left standing in this small battle, he found them dropping their weapons and running for their lives from this crazy warrior who, bare handed, had just knocked down nine mercenaries.

"Come on," Moeris slurred in a frustrated tone. "Where the hell are you going now? I thought we're having fun. Come on." He even started to chase these three Kushites down the pool and toward the garden.

On his way behind the fleeing mercenaries, Moeris raised his eyes for a moment to see the most vicious aerial fight he had ever seen in his entire life. The battle was so tense that, at a certain point, the One who Tears into Pieces savagely pulled the winged creature to the ground, and they rolled and tumbled over each other. After a vicious thrust, Keya had to back away from the king of all the creatures. She vigorously nodded her head, then she flew away.

Moeris was so excited seeing the griffin defeat Keya for the second time in a row, but he had no time to celebrate, as a spear flew through the air, narrowly missing his head. When he looked behind, he found the spear had buried itself in a tree, quivering.

As he was turning his head forward, to where the spear came from, he found over three dozen mercenaries running toward him. He did not stop nor even slow down. Instead, he increased his speed, producing an aggressive prolonged high-pitched cry.

However, Moeris found himself coming to a halt midway when he saw six of these Kushites flying in the air as if something swept them up. He could not believe his eyes when another four mercenaries joined the other fighters in the air as if something else from the other side swept them up. Yet, a big smile appeared on his face when he saw two giant tails sweeping more Kushites and smashing them to the walls. Coming from behind the mercenaries were the two giant crocodiles which Princess Merit had told him earlier that she was going to call them to join them in this mission.

Moeris had to stop watching and charge forward when he saw Princess Merit bravely standing in the middle of the Kushites and skillfully fighting them using her two short swords.

"I got this, princess," Moeris cried out once he got closer to Merit.

"Are you sure?" She demanded, pulling her right sword out of one of the Kushite's throat.

"Yes, I am," he said, flashing her a smile. Then, he jumped high in the air, allowing a crocodile's tail pass beneath him to sweep more Kushites. As he was landing back, he sent a powerful blow to a Kushite who was regaining his consciousness. The man took the hit and rested his head back to the floor, and it was instantly dark again.

"I can see that," Merit proudly talked to Moeris, blocking an ax attack using the sword in her left hand, meanwhile her right sword was slashing the throat of the man who was attacking her. "It won't be too long. Stay alive."

***

After receiving a confirmation nod from Moeris, Princess Merit took off heading into the palace. As she was leaving, she noticed two things. First, she saw the two crocodiles simultaneously moved sideways and inwards, until their bodies slammed against each other, smashing seven mercenaries in between, blood splashed everywhere from the exploded heads and organs. When Merit saw that, she was like, *Damn, Moeris is going to complain that the crocodiles didn't leave for him enough mercenaries to fight.*

The other thing the princess noticed as she was running toward the palace were the three Kushites who followed her, shouting and waving their weapons in the air. She did not stop or slow down. She just ran off. She knew that she did not have enough time. She must reach her destination as soon as possible.

When the three mercenaries who were following Merit turned around the corner where she had just turned a moment ago, they expected to see her still running before them. Yet, she was not there. It was like she had disappeared like a wisp of smoke. They did not stop, they just continued running, thinking that she was just fast enough to turn around the next corner. As they kept running, none of them noticed the hidden door that was noiselessly sliding to shut down a secret passage inside the walls.

The passage was utterly dark, yet Merit was not deterred. She groped her way through the narrow and murky passageway, moving forward to her destination, the dungeons. The princess was born and raised in the palace. She knew all the secret entrances and exits which were designed for emergency situations, and of which the current ruler and Kushites had no knowledge. She had shown this hidden network of passages to Roma who had used them to sneak into the palace once before and release Amasis.

***

A few moments later, Merit quietly reached a long, dark hall, with damp and uneven pavement. Faint light was coming from a single torch on the wall. The torch was all but burned out now and cast only vague shadows around the place. The hall contained two dozen cells, twelve on each side.

"Roma," the princess whispered. She was not sure if any of the mercenaries were still down there. She knew, or at least she hoped, that the hubbub which was occurring right now in the rear courtyard had drawn the attention of all the mercenaries who were guarding the palace.

"Roma," she called in a low tone. "It's me, Merit." Yet, she received no response. "Roma."

Calling her love's name forced a rush of pleasant memories to come clustering around her heart. She recalled the very first time she saw Roma. It was three years ago when she was invited to attend a regular event where the pharaoh had to select the new members of his guards himself. Her Uncle, Senu III, was a great fighter. He loved his niece so much and gifted her the bow she still owned to this day. He was the one who taught her how to shoot multiple arrows at the same time. He wanted her to be strong and able to protect herself. That was why the infertile pharaoh made sure that princess Merit must attend the selection process of the new guards.

On that day, the princess was sitting next to her uncle, bored to death of watching amateur fighters trying their best to be selected as members of the elite band that guarded the royal family. However, when a young man with short black hair, dark eyes, olive-toned skin, and a hawk nose stepped forward to the mock battle, she knew that this fighter was different. She was sure that this man was a very skilled fighter, evident in the small white slash of an old scar which ran through the outer end of his left eyebrow. She liked him from first sight.

Merit had never liked or wished to be a princess. She always believed that her life was not fun or enjoyable. She was never able to speak to boys the same way she grew up seeing maids and servants around her were able to engage in romantic and sexual relations. All of them, except for her. All her movements were reported to her parents. She was guarded around the clock to make sure she was safe. However, when she saw this handsome guy stepping in the mock battle holding two short swords, she immediately decided that this was going to be her man, especially when he defeated both the fighters who dared to challenge him, holding his swords in reverse grip, amid the cheers of the other fighters.

A few weeks later, the princess attended a tournament where the new members of the royal guards, Roma was one of them, participated. When Roma won the tournament, Senu III walked to him and tapped him on his shoulder. The Pharaoh congratulated him and gifted him two short swords.

Later, when the princess's father decided to train his daughter to be a competent fighter, she refused to select from about two dozen skillful trainers who came to Thebes offering their service. Instead, she convinced her father that there was no need to hire a trainer while they already had one. Her father was confused at first, yet he understood later when she reminded him of Roma.

Roma was honored and delighted when he was summoned to the pharaoh's presence and commissioned with a new task, training the heiress to the Egyptian throne. Later, Merit knew from him that he was praying to the gods all the time that he would be picked to personally guard her. It seemed that the gods had not just answered his prayers, they blessed him, too.

Training the princess had given both of them the chance to get together and be able to communicate away from the eyes, which reported all her movements to her parents. Even though Roma took the job very seriously, he was still able to confess his feeling to the princess. He was scared to death and nervous when he talked to her about it the first time, but she quickly comforted him by telling him that she had some feeling for him, too. They decided to keep things quiet because they were not sure about the pharaoh's reaction, especially after she overheard her father talking to the queen that he was planning to marry her to a young, wealthy nobleman from Lower Egypt.

However, the princess eventually had to tell her mother about Roma because the queen received a report that her daughter snuck out of her royal chamber twice in the last week to meet Roma in middle of the night in a secret location on the river bank. The queen liked Roma, and she always talked proudly about how he succeeded in his job of making the princess stronger and more skillful. However, Merit's mother advised them to keep their relationship secret for now until she could figure out a way to tell the pharaoh. This never happened because the queen was killed, along with her husband, ironically on the day she was planning to talk to him about Roma.

As Merit continued her way inside the dungeon, looking for Roma, she recalled the way he kissed her. She like it so much. The first time he kissed her was behind the granary. Knowing that he would never dare to take the initiative, she encouraged him by getting very close in a way that she could feel his short hot breath. When his lips touched hers, she felt a shiver right down through the center of her body. She loved the way he tasted, the slight graze of his chin against hers.

She also liked the way he touched her, always hesitant as if he needed assurance that his caress was welcome, never demanding. It happened a few times that he looked around first to make sure that no one was watching, then he grabbed her hand and swung her around, pressed her against the wall with his muscular body and crushed her lips beneath his. In other occasions, he grabbed her with a fierceness that astounded even him, pulling her body up against his, feeling the shape of her breast beneath the clothing, the tautness of her flat stomach and lean muscles.

What was odd about the relationship was that they never had sex. They fooled around but never had intercourse. Maybe because they had no chance due to all these eyes around them. Or maybe because Roma was very hesitant about it. Merit could tell that in his eyes. He would love to do it, yet he was not sure if he should initiate this or not. She also was not sure either if this would be a good idea or not. After too much thinking as well as consulting her mother, the queen advised her against it because they were not sure about her father's reaction.

A faint voice from one of the cells in which Princess Merit was now searching snapped her back to present. Yet, the sound was no more than a rat running away when it felt her presence. She checked the next cell and found no one there. So, she moved to the next, across the hall, yet no one was there. When she peered through the bars of the following cell, she flinched and shrank within herself. Through the faint light, she saw something horrible that she had never seen before. Before her eyes, she saw a man whom the mercenaries had skinned him like an animal. The man was suspended from the ceiling by a rope; she could see his flesh, veins and nerves.

125

Merit did not know if the man was still alive. He was not moving, so she assumed that he was dead. She wondered what that man had done to deserve a horrible death, and then she remembered that the people who had done this to him would not need a reason for something like that. They were savage, cruel, and maddened creatures who were driven by a hatred for the Egyptians.

"Roma," she called out again, as she was stepping back, her eyes were still fixed at the man in the cell. This time her calling out was a little bit louder, a little bit more urgently. "Roma."

The princess' eyes sprung wide open when she noticed that the skinless man moved a little as if her voice had woken him up from a deep sleep. It took the man a moment to realize that he was still alive and that he had gone through the most horrible experience a man would ever endure. And when he did, his screams filled the place.

Merit froze in her place for a moment, and then she realized that she had to move on. She must find Roma as soon as possible and get the hell out of there. She turned around and moved to the next in the hall to see Roma suspended from the ceiling, too.

Thank the gods, she positively though. She was scared to death of the possibility that the Kushite had skinned Roma alive as they had done to this poor man, behind her, whose screams were still filling the air.

When she got closer to Roma's cell, she could tell that he was still alive. He was moving, and she could see his eyes open through the faint light.

Thank the gods, she thought again. She even was more appreciative when she realized that the door cell was not locked. *Why would they be?* She speculated inside her head. *No one could escape the dungeon unless someone helped them from outside.*

"Roma," she called out, as she was opening the cell's door. This time she was calling in a loud tone, so he could hear her despite the loud shrieks from the dying man behind her.

"My princess," he finally realized what was going on. Obviously, he was unconscious or asleep, and he had just woken on the skinless man's screams. "What are you doing here?"

"I'm here to save your ass," she said, smiling and releasing him, "but don't get used to that." She was moving very fast, realizing that they did not have a lot of time.

As fast as a deer, Merit released Roma, and headed out of the cell. Roma had a hard time walking due to the gruesome torturing he endured. So, she helped him by pushing her shoulder under his arm to boost him up. He moaned several times, but somehow managed to get his feet under him. With her help, he stumbled.

"There's something we have to do first," he suddenly stopped short.

"Do what?" She was confused. "We have to get the hell out of here as soon as possible before anyone comes down."

"There's someone here who we must release, too," he said, groaning.

"Someone?" She echoed. "Who?"

**

A few moments later, Moeris, was rushing to ride on the back of the One who Smashes. Meanwhile, Hent, who had been just freed by Princess Merit from the dungeon, was riding on the back of the other giant crocodile. As the two beasts felt the two riders settled on their backs, they ran toward the river.

At the same time, the One who Tears into Pieces landed next to Princess Merit and Roma. After helping the man who she loved to ride on the griffin's back, she joined him and quickly tapped twice on the neck of the king of all the creatures who immediately flew away. At the same time, the two crocodiles entered the water and swam away, both Hent and Moeris on their backs.

Chapter 12
The Reunion

It was not a secret to anyone in this high-profile meeting that Amasis was half-listening to the heated discussion which had raged through most of the day now. Everyone, sitting in a circle, on this rug made of goat skins, knew that this young priest who was assembling with them had lost his joy since the disappearance of Nefer. He rarely spoke; and if he did, it was in curt tones as if his mind was engaged somewhere else. Some people even whispered that he had lost, not only the person he loved the most, but also his mind.

Across from Amasis, sat princess Merit, her legs folded beneath her. She was dressed in an elegant, short white tunic with golden girdle and fringe. Jewels crafted in gold adorned her dark hair. Her two short swords laid on the ground next to her. Enthusiastically, she was telling them about her plan.

On Amasis right, Roma was sitting. He was dressed in a dark kilt. A headpiece in the same color was on his head. His bruised face had begun to purple already, some parts of these discolorations were barely identifiable now, some others were still hurt, evidently in his groanings, every now and then. Across from Roma, and on Amasis's left, sat Moeris, his legs crossed. Holding a jug of beer in the right hand, he was listening to the princess.

"And this is where Amasis's role comes into play," Merit's words were not enough to bring Amasis back to reality, but it was Roma's powerful hand which shook the young priest's shoulder as if he was trying to wake the young priest up from a troubling nightmare. "You're the one who is going to figure out a way to have the Celestials stop their attack until we figure something out. We need a truce."

"What? What?" Amasis frantically said as if he had just been jolted out of a deep slumber. "Are you talking to me? What? What did you say?"

"Come on, Amasis," Moeris said in a frustrated tone. Obviously, this was not the first time that day where the young priest had lost track of what had been said.

"I'm so sorry," Amasis said in an apologetic tone. "I'm really sorry."

"It's OK, Amasis," the princess said in a soothing tone.

Meanwhile, Roma glared at Moeris and gave him a look that meant, *Don't push him.* Then, he talked to the priest, "There is nothing to apologize for, Amasis. Are you OK? We can talk later if you need to get some rest."

"No. No. No. I'm fine," Amasis confirmed looking directly in Roma's eyes.

"Well, Amasis," Princess Merit talked to the young priest. "We're saying that we might have lost the battle, but we didn't lose the war. We might have lost the Free Army, our Celestial allies, and the mummies of our ancestors and their Terrifying Ones, but there is still hope."

"Yes, Amasis," Roma continued for the princess. "We have to rebuild our forces and get ready for the next battle."

"We think that we have to focus on regaining our old allies' trust," Moeris added. "We have to focus on the

Celestials, our ancestors' mummies, and the Terrifying Ones."

"We have to bring the stolen treasures back to the tombs," Roma explained. "We have to find those behind the biggest looting that happened in the history of this kingdom and bring them to justice. I believe that I can take care of this part. Some rumors suggest that Nebet is behind all of that. I'll do my very best to get to the bottom of things quickly."

"This leaves another problem that we have to handle," the princess continued for Roma. "The Celestials."

"That won't be an easy thing at all," Amasis surprised them that he was aware of what was being said for the first time that day. He even began sharing with them his thoughts. "The heralds were kidnapped in the land of Egypt, and their floating pyramid was destroyed on Egyptian soil. No matter who is behind that action, it will always be our responsibility. They had accepted our invitation to come to our land with more kairemi, and this is what they got in return; kidnapped heralds, destroyed ship, and stolen kairemi."

"We can't fix up everything," Princess Merit responded. "We can't fix the destroyed pyramid, but we can retrieve the kidnapped heralds and deliver the people behind the attack."

"But how are you suggesting that to be done, my lady?" The young priest seemed stunned by the princess' proposal. "No one even knows where the king of Kush is keeping the kidnapped messengers."

"We know where the kairemi is," she answered. "We can start with that one."

"But Keya had already used it," Roma said.

"Used some of it," Amasis corrected him. "Actually, she used a very tiny amount of the stolen kairemi."

"I suggest trapping Keya and retrieving whatever was left of kairemi that she still has in her possession," Moeris intervened, excitedly.

131

"It won't be that easy, my friend," Roma quickly told Moeris, so he would not get too excited for a very difficult task.

"We can start by gathering more information about Keya and the changes she endured after drinking the kairemi," Amasis suggested, and everyone in his presence affirmatively nodded their heads. "Still, I believe that the hardest part is going to be the kidnapped heralds."

"The last thing I've heard was that King Alara of Kush had taken them back to Kush," Moeris recounted to them what he had overheard a few days ago at the market. "Yet, some people say that he keeps them very close to him. He thinks that he can make a deal with the Celestials if they come after him or started attacking his kingdom."

"Well, I think this makes a lot of sense," Roma reflected.

"If this is true, I guess my next destination should be Kush," Princess Merit decided.

"No, you can't..." Roma tried to say, but he quickly realized his mistake. He was still talking to Princess Merit, the legal heiress to the Egyptian throne. Even though she has feelings for him, she was still a princess, and he should follow the protocols when he addressed her. "I mean, my lady. What is your proposal?"

"Well, Roma," she said, giving him a lovely smile. She had one of those smiles that started gently, made men melt, and could be described only as mind-bogglingly enchanting. "I have to travel to Kush and release the heralds. This is the only way to regain the Celestials' trust. Otherwise, their attack on the kingdom is going to continue. Matter of fact, every minute I'm wasting means more innocent Egyptians will be killed, more buildings destroyed, and more fields burned."

"Well, I agree with the second part of your proposal," Roma paused for a moment, trying to figure out if it was a proper way to address the princess of Egypt. "Yet, I have a problem with you traveling to Kush. It's a perilous step. How do you think this is possible? King Alara will never abandon the heralds that easy."

"Of course, it won't be that easy," Princess Merit responded. "I've heard my father and uncle talking about King Alara multiple times, and I know how greedy and stubborn he is."

"That's why you should never meet him," Amasis intervened.

"I guess that is exactly what he was looking for," Moeris added. "Excuse me, my lady. But I think your head would be the best gift for King Alara to his daughter."

"Exactly," Roma exclaimed when Moeris confirmed his concern.

"I'm not planning to either meet or talk to the king of Kush," she said, and silence fell over the room for a few moments. It seemed that everyone in the princess's presence was trying to comprehend what she was saying. "I'm thinking of just releasing the heralds and bring them back safely to Egypt. If we deliver them safely to the Celestials, it would be a great opportunity to regain their trust. Not only this, if we bring King Alara himself to justice by delivering him too to the People from the Sky, I'm sure they will be more satisfied because he is responsible for breaking into the pyramid, kidnapping the heralds, and stealing the kairemi."

"Merit," Roma could not hold it any longer, yet he had to pause again to correct himself, "I mean, My Lady. Excuse me, but this is insane." He had to stop again to correct himself. "I mean this is very dangerous. How in the world do you think you can travel to Kush, release the messengers, arrest a king from his kingdom, and deliver them to the Celestials? That's very dangerous. The most important person in the kingdom can't risk her life by traveling to her enemy's land that way. I'll do this for you."

"What would my people think of me if they see me cower when it comes to defending them," Princess Merit defended her decision. "You already are going to be busy by retrieving the stolen treasures and bringing the people behind this action to justice, so it's me who has to travel to Kush. Plus, did you forget that I have the One who Tears Into pieces."

"My Lady, but…" Roma tried to say, but she did not give him a chance.

"Roma," she said in a lovely tone, while a charming smile crossed her face, "I know you are worried about me, but I must do it. If I won't, I don't deserve claiming my father's throne and crown."

Roma tried to say something, yet he had no chance to speak because Moeris interrupted them this time.

"If you don't mind, My Lady," Moeris said. "It would be a great honor if you allow me to join you on this trip." Then, he looked at Roma. "I think my friend will be more comfortable knowing that you have me there to protect you."

"Still," Roma blurted out. "I know you are a very skilled fighter, Moeris. By the way, we need to have a conversation. We have a lot of things to talk about. Things that I can't forgive myself for not talking to you about all these years."

"Guy stuff?" Merit asked, jokingly.

"Not really," Roma responded. "It's just some stuff that needs to be clarified. Anyway, Moeris," he spoke to his friend again. "I just don't see how you both are going to take such a risky step."

"We will not be traveling alone, Roma," Moeris surprised everyone in the room. They all exchanged looks of confusion.

"What do you mean?" Amasis was the only one in the room able to function to ask this question.

"I mean that we still have the Triple-Sevens," Moeris answered with a gleam in his eyes. Then, he drank all the beer in the jug in a single gulp.

***

As soon as the meeting was coming to some kind of conclusion and was about to terminate, Princess Merit approached the young priest and sat right in front of him.

"Before you leave, Amasis," she put her hand on his arm. "I wanted to thank you for saving my life and for all the things you have done for me."

"You don't have to thank me, My Lady," Amasis said in a friendly tone of voice. "It's my pleasure, honor, and duty."

"Still, I have to personally thank you," she added, smiling.

"I understand, My Lady," he continued, "but you really don't have to."

"No, Amasis," she talked to him in a soothing tone. "If you didn't help me on that day, I would have been dead by now."

"I wish I could have done more," he said in a sad tone. "I should have tried to save the king and the queen, too."

"You can't do everything by yourself," she said. "You have done more than enough. Not to mention that you are the one who figured out how to contact the Celestials."

"I feel this was another mistake of mine," he said, ashamed and looking down at the ground.

"What?" She seemed confused. "Why did you say that? What do you mean?"

"I mean if I didn't contact the Adorians, King Alara would not be able to do what he had done." He answered, still looking down. "The Celestials would not be kidnapped, the kairemi would not be stolen, and the floating pyramid would not be destroyed."

"You are too hard on yourself, Amasis," she said, putting her hand on his arm again. "You did what you had to do. You did not know that all this would have happened. Matter of fact, no one did. In a thousand years, no one would anticipate what happened in the battle of Badari."

"I appreciate your nice words, My Lady," Amasis said, finally raising his head a little and flashing her a smile. "I know you are trying to make me feel better."

"And you will be," she assured him, flashing him a smile, too. She paused for a moment then added, "And she will be fine,"

The smile on his face suddenly retreated and was replaced with a sad look, saying, "I hope so."

"Trust me," she assured him." I'm sure there is a reason behind her sudden disappearance."

"I don't even know if she is still alive," he said, a tear spilling from his eye and running down his cheek.

"There is no need to think she is not," she said in a soothing tone.

He nodded his head in a way that left some doubt.

"I need you to focus, Amasis," she requested. "Can you do this for me?"

He did not answer; instead, he seemed lost again.

"Amasis," she called in a way seemed like she was waking him up, "you have a vital task to take care of."

"I know, My Lady," he finally replied.

"I'm sure you know what to do," she encouraged him.

"Not really to be honest," he surprised her.

"What do you mean?" She was shocked.

"I mean I know what needs to be done," he answered, "yet I still don't know how I will get it done."

"Don't worry, My Lady," Roma intervened. "He said this before, yet he later figured it out." He chuckled in a way that was meant to encourage Amasis that he was able to get it done.

Chapter 13
Princess of Egypt

Ever since their reunion, Princess Merit and Roma did not really get a chance to spend any private time together. The same day she arrived at the battlefield on the back of her griffin to avenge the murder of her parents, Roma was captured and imprisoned in the royal palace's dungeons until two days ago when she managed to free him. That was why, later after the meeting, Moeris and Amasis left, offering the room for the princess and Roma to spend some time together, especially that next morning each one of them was going to travel in a different direction.

The first thing Roma did once his friends left, he headed to the window to make sure everything was OK outside. He pushed aside the reed mat that covered the window and peered out. Other than a few people walking by or dwelling in the neighborhood, Roma did not see any suspicious activities.

"Everything is OK," he talked to the princess, covering the window with the reed mat and turning around to find Merit half sitting half laying down on a straw bed.

"Cool," she playfully said to him, using her index finger to invite him in a very seductive way.

Once he sat next to her on the bed, she sat on his lap. He groaned in pain when she gave him a little kiss on his lips.

"Poor baby," she apologetically spoke, her soft fingers running on his right cheek. She had to stop when he cringed and flinched in pain. "I'm so sorry. What did these bastards do to you?"

"They did a lot," he briefly answered. "Let's not talk about it please, My Lady."

"Roma, nobody is here," she firmly said, yet with a smile on her pretty face. "You don't have to call me," she playfully mimicked his thick voice, "My Lady." She gave him another kiss. This time it was much gentler that he didn't grunt in agony. Actually, he enjoyed it. "I think you know my name. I like that at least someone in the world calls me by name without a title. Say it please." She printed another gentle kiss on his lips, meanwhile her left arm wrapped around him to tenderly get him closer to her.

"You mean Lady Merit or Princess Merit?" He teased her, and she irritably, yet friskily, tried to bite his bottom lip in anger. "Oh, I think I know what you mean. You mean just Merit." Immediately, a lovely smile formed on her beautiful face. This gave Roma a chance to counter, biting her bottom lip and warping his powerful arms around her, in a way that he knew very well that she liked the most. Instantly, Merit felt as if she was melting in his hands. It was fiery, it was passionate, it was the igniting of carnal hunger for which she had been waiting.

Roma's powerful hands suddenly rolled her over, and he was top of her. He first smiled at her and waited until she pulled his hands and placed them on her breasts, inviting him to tease her nipples.

"Too many clothes between us," she joked, as he was caressing her already-hard nipples under the palm of his hands. When he nodded his head, they both quickly stood up. She took her tunic off, tossing it aside and revealing her small, firm breasts. When she noticed that Roma's eyes staring at her taut, rosy nipples and not doing anything, she pushed his hands down, inviting him to help her take off her skirt. Faster than a cheetah, both Roma's powerful hands yanked her skirt free.

Merit closed her eyes when he leaned forward, and his lips touched hers. She pressed her mouth harder against his, then her body followed. For her, this was the moment not meant to have an end. Finally, she realized she needed to breathe, and slowly pulled back, breathing hard.

Yet, they quickly went for round two. Roma had to pause when he heard her gasp. She just felt his hardness pushing against her. To encourage him to continue, she had to reach out and carefully touch his chest. She slowly dragged her hands around to his waist. She looked up at him, placing her body fully against his, and wrapping her arms around him, as she went to kiss him again; her breasts pressed so firmly against his chest, and his hardness pressing against her thighs.

She could not restrain herself any longer; she had to check what the mighty Roma had down there. Her hand slid under the waistband of his skirt, and she felt him shudder. She stopped kissing him to look at him. She found him closed his eyes and raised his head up. She moved her hand farther down and wrapped her fingers nearly around his hard shaft. He gasped loudly.

When she held his skirt and draw it down, Roma's hands pulled her to stand and scooped her into his arms. He laid her down on the bed, and she felt her chest rising & falling as if she had been running.

Roma's hands then went in between her breasts and enveloped them, and she let go of him, releasing gasps and soft cries. He started to move his hands around her small

139

breasts, and she started to feel something uneasy in her body. It was something she had never felt before, but she wanted it so bad. She could not believe all the new, wonderful sensations, and what it felt like to have such desire. She could see herself wanting more of this in her life. She even wanted more. She wanted him to caress her whole body, with his eyes, his hands, and his mouth.

And Roma did.

He leaned down to kiss her breast. Meanwhile, his hand slid down her stomach. When it brushed her pussy, her legs voluntarily spread apart, without even asking her brain for permission. Roma trailed his hands and mouth all over her, until her mind could not even keep pace with all the sensations he created in her. She could not even count all the places he touched, those that had made her twitch, gasp, or moan in a way she never heard herself do before.

The moment his tongue touched her pussy; her legs started to shake. She held tight to the bed and cried out as his tongue moved inside. She never believed she could feel such pleasure, nor endure the fires of such a lust. All her muscles clenched or stretched, and her moans filled the room, enjoying the delightful agony followed by bottomless ecstasy.

Merit widened her eyes when she felt something large, pressing at her entrance. She looked at Roma and then down to see his shaft aimed directly at her pussy. She looked back up, and slowly nodded.

***

Later that day, Merit and Roma laid on their backs, trying to catch their breath.

"That was so good," she told him, with a big smile on her face. "I'd almost convinced myself that sex was something that I could mostly live without. But I've missed it a lot."

"Agree with you," he replied, a similar smile on his lips.

140

"Agree with me about which part?" She teased him. "Having sex for the first time or that you did well today?"

"I guess both," he teased her back.

"You really want me to believe that this was your first time?" She asked, turning around and her legs wrapping around him.

"I swear to the Gods, My Lady," he tried to say.

"Roma!" She almost snapped at him. "First, there is no need to be formal. As you see, no one is here." Her right hand showed him that it was only them in the room. "Second, I'm not going to judge you for anything that happened before meeting me."

"I would have told you if there was anything," he assured her.

"Are you sure?" She winked at him. "No girl ever tried to sleep with the mighty Roma, the best guard in the Pharaoh's personal guards?"

"Never," he sharply and confidently answered.

"How about the other night at the House of Roses?" She winked at him again. "I've heard the story from many sources since I came back."

"Believe me, nothing happened?" He assured her.

"Are you sure?" She teased him again.

"I am getting irritated," he snapped at her, gently pushing her leg away and trying to stand up.

"You are not going anywhere until you answer me," she quickly pushed him down and laid on top of him. "No one leaves princess Merit's presence without her consent, especially if she loves this person."

"But I don't like being questioned this way," he justified his anger.

"I want to make sure that I am going to spend the rest of my life with a faithful person," she explained why she was pushing at him, giving him a gentle kiss on his lips. "I know that nothing really happened that night, yet I want to hear it from you."

Roma had to take a few moments to tell the princess about what had taken place at the "House of Roses." He started by telling her that he and Moeris traveled Memphis to meet the high oracle who gave them a critical prophecy, "The short age of the illegal dynasty is drawing to a fast close, and the age of the legitimate heiress is dawning,"

"On our way back to Thebes, we decided to spend the night at that inn. We were looking for a good bath, a decent meal, and comfy beds." Roma told the princess.

"And a whore or two," she mischievously finished for him.

"Maybe for Moeris," he assured her. "Not for me."

"And?" She encouraged him to continue.

He went ahead telling her that once they entered the inn, the owner asked them to leave their weapons at the door.

"No weapons are allowed here," Roma mimicked the voice of the owner of the inn. "You're going to have to leave them here." Then he continued, "We had to comply because we were starving and stinking."

Roma explained to Merit that once they sat down, he saw seven Kushite mercenaries sitting at the table in the corner, mingling with some whores. After an argument with the owner about serving mercenaries, Roma recognized one of the Kushites.

"He was a giant Kushite with the deformed nose and bitten ear," Roma described the man to Merit. "It did not take too long to realize that he was the same giant mercenary which I had fought at the palace on the day of the rebellion. It was Qamar; the man whom I had broken his nose before pushing him through the window."

"My hero," Merit commented, printing a kiss on his muscled arm.

"What made that night interesting was that I overheard some of the Kushites' discussion," Roma went ahead. "I heard them talking about weird stuff like a flood, Nile, dam, and Kush. Even though the words did not make any sense, they were enough to excite my curiosity to know about what these drunk mercenaries were talking."

"And this where you had to sleep with a whore who was listening to them to tell what was happening," Merit again finished for him.

"That's too much," Roma said, pushing her away and standing up. His naked body appeared lean and sculpted.

"I'm just teasing you," she told him, extending her arm to reach him. "I'm so sorry. I did not mean to piss you off. Please come back."

"Promise me you won't interpret me again," he demanded, very serious.

She did not answer, she only put her hand on her lips in a way that meant, I won't say a word.

"Anyway, when I saw Qamar and one of the whores heading to her room, I decided to do something," Roma said, getting back to bed next to her. "Immediately, I stopped them and asked to join in a threesome." He had to stop when he saw Merit taking away her hand of her mouth and getting ready to say something smart. "Don't even think," he warned her, knowing that she was going to tease him again about having a threesome.

"Thank the Gods, Qamar seemed to be too tipsy to understand what was going on or to recall my face," Roma quickly continued, not giving the princess any chance to make any goofy comments. "Once we got in the room, and Qamar started to get naked, I placed the blade of a dagger which I managed to sneak into the inn against his throat. He tried to ask Nefer for help, but she ignored him."

"Nefer!" Merit echoed after him, seeming stunned.

"Yes, Nefer," he confirmed.

"You mean Amasis's Nefer?" She questioned, not believing it.

"Yes, no one ever mentioned to you that Nefer used to work there?" He was shocked to know that the princess didn't know that.

143

"Wow, that is super interesting," she said in awe. "Continue, please."

"Under pressure, Qamar started to tell me a lot of significant stuff," Roma went ahead, continuing reciting the story to his love. "He told me that the famine was made up."

It was the first time for Merit to know that the King of Kush had helped Varis by building a dam, north of Kush, to block the Nile's stream and cause drought and famine, which eventually Varis used to lead what appeared as a rebellion against her father's reign and steal the Egyptian throne.

"I'm so sorry, baby," Roma tried to make the princess feel better as she knew about how Varis well planned for everything.

"It's not your fault," she said in a sad tone, yet smiling.

"Still," he replied, printing a gentle kiss on her lips. "You know what! Let's talk about something else. Until this moment I have no idea where the One who Tears into Pieces had hid you all this time? Where were you? What were you doing all this time?"

Merit first smiled a little, then she answered him, "Once the griffin took me away that day, he traveled east passing the desert toward the Red Sea coastline. In a fabulous location at the foot of a great hill by the sea, I found myself before a small cave with giant cliffs looming above."

Merit then explained to Roma that the One who Tears into Pieces bowed to her in a way from which she understood that he was inviting her to enter the cave. She trusted this griffin since she was a little kid, and she knew that he would not do anything that would ever hurt her. Thus, she proceeded in, expecting an empty cave, but it was not. Inside the cave, Merit found two adorable baby griffins. Once these babies saw their parent arrived, they happily welcomed him by flying toward him and giving him kisses on the neck and face. Merit was shocked to see that the One who Tears into Pieces had two kids.

144

"Sorry to interrupt you," Roma had to cut in. "How the griffin got two babies? From what I understand that he is one of a kind. So, where did he get a partner to make babies?"

"I wish he could speak to tell us himself," she replied, then she tried to explain. "No one knows for sure the truth behind the origin of the One who Tears into Pieces."

"Even you?" He questioned.

"Even me," she assured him. "Like anyone else, I know two theories. The first is that he is from Adoria and accompanied the last pilgrim on his way home; a theory which the former high priest, Ramose, never confirmed nor denied. In this case, the griffin, according to the rumors, can reproduce without mating."

Roma nodded his head and tightened his eyes in a way that showed he was interested in and following everything she was saying.

"The second theory is that he was found in the desert," she continued. "And in this case, I'm sure there are more griffins somewhere out there, and it looks like that the One who Tears into Pieces has found a mate and..." she naughtily finished with a whistle and by sliding her right index into her curled left hand, laughing and winking at Roma.

"I can't believe you," Roma commented, smiling and shaking his head. "I hope you don't make this gesture when you sit on the throne."

"No, don't worry about that," she said, trying to curb her laughter. "I get goofy only around the people I love, and technically, you are the only one I love after the death of my parents." Talking about her parents made her laughter disappear in a blink of an eye.

"You will be fine," Roma assured her.

"Thank you," she thanked him with a grateful smile.

"Then what?" he encouraged her to continue.

"I thought that the griffin was going to keep me there for a day or two until the danger is passed," she resumed, "but days have passed, and he did not allow me to ride on

145

his back to leave that cave and return home. Every morning, he left and came back later with a goat or a sheep which his kids devoured in a blink of an eye, and some fruits for me. I had a wonderful time with these two adorable babies. We played and had a lot of fun. Yet, I felt like I was isolated. I needed to know what was going on. I did not even know if my parents are still alive or not. I was getting angry by the day at him, and yet he never allowed me to ride on his back."

"One day, I got mad and decided to leave anyway. I walked out of the cave, down the hill and started walking west with the intention to reach Thebes on foot if I had to. He did not try to stop me. He just continued to play with his kids. Later, I discovered that he was quietly following me to make sure that I'm safe. When a lion tried to attack me, the One who Tears into Pieces came out of nowhere and loudly roared. The lion immediately stopped, bowed to his king and left me alone. At this point, he allowed me to ride on his back for the first time since the day he took me away from the place. He did not fly to the west where I went to go; instead, he traveled back to the cave. I was grateful for saving my life, yet mad at him because he would not let me go home."

"I changed my mind about him and knew that he knew what he was doing when one day he came from hunting with no food. Instead, he bowed to me, inviting me to ride on his back. I immediately know that he was trying to make me see something; something which he thought it was important. When I rode on his back, he traveled west. For a moment, I thought that he was taking me home, especially when I realized that we are heading toward Thebes. But we didn't; instead, he flew passing the capital of the south and continued over the Nile to the west. He landed on top of a high hill where I could clearly see the Valley of the Kings. From the top of this peak, I saw a few people carrying two mummies, one for a male and one for a female. Knowing that only kings and queens get buried in this specific tomb, I realized my parents' fate."

Roma had to put his hand on Merit's arm when he saw tears glisten in her eyes.

"A few days later, the griffin took me south," she quickly said, trying to change the subject, "specifically to the borderline between Egypt and Kush. Again, from a high point of view, I saw a massive army of Kushites crossing the border and heading north. I was so confused. I didn't know what had happened and what was going on. On another day, the One who Tears into Pieces took me back to Thebes where he let me freely walk around as if he wanted me to search for answers to the questions which pressed on me."

"I left the griffin behind and headed to a small local inn. It was past sunset and getting dark so fast. That allowed me walk around freely, and none could recognize me. Inside the inn, I sat in a dark corner and waited."

"Waited for what?" Roma cut in, seeming confused.

"Anything," she jokingly answered him. "Waited for anything that would come up. I was desperate for answers. So, I just sat there, waiting for literally anything."

"And did that anything show up?" He inquired.

"Yes," she replied, smiling. "Just a few moments later, I found this old man coming and sitting across the table from me. He was so drunk and, I guess, so horny." She released a short, soft snort, especially when she noticed that Roma got angry.

"Are you upset?" She asked him.

"Should I be?" He answered briefly.

"You seem jealous," she playfully commented just to make him angrier.

"Of course, I am," he angrily replied.

"Don't worry, he wasn't my type," she teased him, and she could see anger coloring his face. "I'm just kidding."

"Then what?" He encouraged her to continue passing this part.

"He bought me a drink, and we had a little chat," she went on. "Obviously, he was trying to get me drunk and take advantage of me later."

"Do you remember the face of this motherfucker?" Roma furiously cut her off again. "Can you recognize him if you see him again?"

"Don't worry about it, Roma," she quickly said, trying to ease him down. "He was an old man, probably with poor sight. He didn't recognize me. Plus, I didn't allow anything to happen. Don't worry. I can take care of myself."

The princess took a brief moment to make sure that Roma was OK. When he nodded his head, she resumed, "Like I said, he was trying to take advantage of me, but I took advantage of him." She chuckled. "Every time I took a sip from my drink, I made sure that he drank a whole cup. Meanwhile, I had him tell me everything that had happened in the kingdom since I escaped the palace. Luckily, he was an old man who enjoyed politics; that made him the best source for the answers for which I was searching."

"He told me about Varis' attack on the palace, the murder of my parents, the disappearance of the kairemi, Varis' quest to his children, Keya's role in all of that, the high oracle's prophecy, and the Free Army. When I tried to get more information about the rebels, especially who was leading them, the old, drunk man passed out. I tried to sober him up a little to answer me, but he was gone."

"And did you know?" Roma asked mischievously.

"Yes, I did," She playfully answered. "As I was leaving the inn, I stopped one of the servers and asked her if she knew anything about the Free Army. A first, the poor server denied knowing anything about the rebels. Yet, when she looked closely at my face, she recognized me. I powerfully held her arm to prevent her from bowing to me in front of all these people. Thankfully, she understood that I didn't want anyone there to know who I was, then she requested that I repeat my question. Again, I demanded an answer about if she knew anything about the Free Army, or at least the name of its leader. The server leaned forward and whisper the name in my ear." Merit mimicked the server's whispering voice, "Roma, short for Romaroy." Once she said that she printed a big kiss on Roma's lips.

"I hope you are proud of me," he wished.

"Very proud," she assured him, flashing him a brief smile.

"So, what bothers you now?" He questioned, realizing that the brief smile turned into a grimace.

"I just remembered my parents," she answered, her eyes watering up, but she quickly blinked the tears away.

"You know what!" He said, jumping out of bed and getting dressed. "Come with me. I know how to change your mood." He extended his hand, inviting her to join him.

"To where?" She wondered, giving him her hand, and he gently pulled her up off the bed.

"You will see," he playfully said. "Just get dressed."

***

"Are you sure about that?" Princess Merit asked. She was a little bit nervous.

"Yes, I am," Roma answered her, standing next to her in front of the house.

"Is that really her?" Merit heard one of the pedestrians asking the man next to him in a frail voice. He was an old man in his late fifties, short but very sturdily built, and wore a gray kilt around his waist, and a colorful collar about his neck, with dark leather sandals made of goatskin on his feet.

"What would Princess Merit be doing in this poor area?" The man next to him answered. He was a little older with mocha skin and a bald head.

Merit saw two women sitting at the door of one of the houses looking at her and whispering something. They were bare breasted, dressed only in torn skirts. Merit immediately assumed that they were wondering if it was her for real or it was just someone who looked like their princess. One of the two women, chubby and glowing with health, ran inside the house and brought her husband.

Obviously, she wanted to confirm that what was she seeing was real. The thin man with a mustache stared at the princess for a moment, then affirmatively nodded his head to his wife.

Merit also saw a few kids, who were playing in the street, had already paused their game. They got together, whispering and pointing at her.

Merit had to look backward and downward when she felt someone holding the end of her skirt.

"Are you Princess Merit?" A young girl of no more than seven or eight years old asked. She had long dirty hair and was dressed in tattered clothes. Although dirt and grime covered her face, she had a delightful smile.

"Hello, sweet heart," Merit said, turning around and kneeling down to talk to this beautiful young girl. "Yes, it's me."

"We love you so much," the girl said, spontaneously hugging her.

Merit first looked at Roma as if she wanted to make sure that this was OK, and he nodded at her with a smile in a way that meant, *don't worry. It's OK.*

Immediately, the princess' arms wrapped around the girl.

"It's Princess Merit," the woman who ran earlier into the house to bring out her husband shouted, announcing that she was right from the very beginning.

When Merit turned her head around, still hugging the young girl, she found the same woman banging on the neighbor's door.

"It's Princess Merit," the woman screamed once a little boy opened the huge wooden door. "Tell your mother Princess Merit is here." The boy looked at the princess for a moment, then he ran inside. Meanwhile, the woman moved to the next door, banging even harder.

"My princess," Merit heard someone calling her. When she turned her head forward, she found a young, beautiful lady who greatly resembled the girl whom she was hugging now. "I'm so sorry. She should not do that," the young lady said, trying to release the princess from her daughter's arms.

"It's OK," Merit assured her. "No worries."

More people around started to shout the princess' name, and more people came out of their houses wondering what was going on. In no time, Merit found herself in the middle of a huge crowd which swarmed toward their beloved princess. In a blink of an eye, the people surrounded her. The majority knelt before their princess. Some kissed her hands. Everyone was happy and celebrating. They burst in cheers. They danced, jumped, clapped their hands, shouted, roared, hugged and kissed.

"Princess Merit," The crowd began to chant. "Princess Merit. Princess Merit. Princess Merit." Meanwhile, a few young men lifted her to their shoulders and started to move around so more people can kiss her hands and kneel before her.

Merit looked behind, searching for Roma. When she saw her love, she smiled at him. Then, she looked up into the sky as the One who Tears into Pieces flying freely above this impoverished neighborhood.

Chapter 14
Curse of the Pharaohs

"Please, My Queen," Nebet pleaded. "You're the only person who could help me." She was kneeling before the throne of Upper Egypt, dressed in a black, floor-length, loose, and shapeless garment. The horrifying look on her face was a shred of evidence that something serious had occurred. "They're coming for me. I'm the only one left."

She was talking to the queen of the south, Hamees, who sat on the throne, wearing the White Hedjet Crown of Upper Egypt and dressed in an elegant chiffon gown in a deep rose color. Next to her, sat the High Commissioner of the South.

"What are you expecting me to do?" Hamees demanded, she looked troubled by Nebet's words. "Even the Queen of Upper Egypt has no power over the curse of the late pharaohs."

Everyone who lived in Egypt knew that the curse of the pharaohs was cast upon any person who disturbed a mummy or broke into a tomb. This curse did not differentiate between thieves and just intruders, and it could cause bad luck, illness, or death.

However, Nebet with the help of her brother-in-law, Caesarion, outlined the great looting of the late pharaohs' tombs on the day of the battle of Badari. They knew in advance that the Free Army, with the help of Amasis, was going to call the mummies of the deceased kings to wake up, ride on the back of their Terrifying Ones and help the rightful heiress to the Egyptian throne against all the domestic and foreign threats. That was why Nebet believed that this was the perfect moment to do what she had dreamt of since she was a little girl. Her marriage to her late husband, Sheamay, had made her rich, but this was not enough. She wanted to be the wealthiest person in the whole kingdom, and she knew how easily she could achieve that.

Nebet had Caesarion hire dozens of men who mostly consisted of thieves, looters, thugs, and other people with criminal backgrounds. A few days before the battle, her brother-in-law divided his men into small groups and sent each to travel to their destination in advance. The night before the Kushite army arrived at the battlefield, each group of Caesarion's men camped near one of the late pharaoh's tomb. They had ordered to wait until it was safe to enter the tombs.

However, Caesarion got mad and lost his temper when he received a message that one of the bands did not listen to his advice of waiting until the right moment. They decided to storm the tomb the night before the battle.

The only survivor told Caesarion that once they began to break the tomb's seal, they heard a thunderous roar of an angry monster. When they turned around, they found the stone statue of the Terrifying One who was crouching a moment ago in front of the tomb had come to life. With frightened eyes, they saw the hybrid creature had already stood up on his feet and had turned around to face them. Another loud roar made some the men flee in horror, but the monster did not let them go anywhere. He quickly attacked and killed them.

The leader of this group had instructed his men not to fear but to maintain order to be able to survive this beast. At his signal, they all threw their spears at the beast at the same time. To their astonishment, just a second before any of the spears hit the Terrifying One, he turned into a limestone statue, and all the spears struck the stone and shattered into pieces. Then, the statue came to life again and continued attacking them, his fangs sinking into throats and his claws garbling faces.

At a certain point, the only survivor of this massacre attacked the furious beast, and he was lucky enough to survive after receiving only some scratches to his face. Then, he fled surreptitiously while the Terrifying One was devouring the rest of his men.

Out of rage, Caesarion slapped the only survivor on his injured face. Then, he had to split his own group into two halves and send one of them to the other tomb with strict orders not to storm the tomb until the Terrifying Ones were gone.

The next morning, Caesarion watched in awe when the sizeable circular stone which covered the tomb's entrance, moved to the side as if some mysterious power had pushed it away. The wax seal on the tomb's door suddenly exploded, and the door flew open. He also almost lost his mind when he saw the mummies of Senu III and his brother, Senu IV, leaving the tomb. Then, the Terrifying One came back to life, got to his paws, and roared loudly. The two mummies climbed onto the back of the Terrifying One, and the beast roared one more time, before taking off in a run, heading to the battlefield.

Only at that moment, Caesarion signaled to his men to move forward into the tombs.

Some of them tried to back out when they saw a warning at the tomb's entrance, which read, "For any man who shall enter my tomb, there will be a judgment."

155

Caesarion quickly talked these men out of the idea of backing out. He convinced them that it was very safe as long as the Terrifying One was gone.

However, a few moments later another few men got scared and tried to run away when they saw another inscription on the wall inside one of the burial chambers, which read, "Any man shall do evil or wickedness to this coffin, Amun shall not accept any goods he offers, and may his heir not inherit".

Again, Caesarion calmed his men down and persuaded them to continue moving out the treasures to the carts which were waiting outside.

Caesarion himself felt a sudden fear rise up inside him when he read another engraving on one of the sarcophaguses which read, "Cursed be those who disturb the rest of the Pharaoh. They that shall break the seal of this tomb shall meet death by a disease that no healer can cure."

There was no one there to ease down the fear inside Caesarion, so he did his best to comfort himself, telling himself that everything was going to be OK and they were going to safely get out of there. And they did, once he got warned that the Terrifying Ones and the mummies felt of their presence in the tombs and that they were coming back in a rush, he and his men immediately evacuated the tombs with tons of treasures.

Although the Terrifying Ones had the chance to chase the looters and kill them all, Caesarion saw with his own eyes that the mummies and their beasts had preferred to get back to their tombs and protect the remaining treasures. Once the Terrifying Ones arrived at the tomb, the mummies of Senu III and his brother jumped off. Then, the dreadful beast turned around and looked at Caesarion and his men, who were retreating with tons of stolen treasures. A deafening, shuddering, and grinding roar vibrated through the air challenging the looters to attempt to come back and promising them that they were going to pay for this with their lives.

After hiding the treasures in a secret location, Caesarion paid for his men well and dismissed them. Then, he went to Nebet, she was hiding in a humble house in the heart of Thebes. He told her about what had happened, and she assured him that everything was going to be just fine. However, the next morning, the bad news started to pour in from all directions.

Kneeling before the throne of Upper Egypt, Nebet had recounted to Hamees several stories of those who helped her to loot the tombs and how they had faced their death in strange incidents. It was all started when Nebet and her secret lover received some bad news that one of the looters had betrayed them by stealing some of the treasures and embarked on a sea journey with the stolen treasures in the cargo hold. In the middle of the sea, a storm hit the boat, and the boat started shaking. Meanwhile, the traveler was so alarmed by recurring visions of two spirits that beckoned him to throw the treasure overboard. The stormy sea did not abate until the stolen treasures were thrown overboard. Later, the traveler threw himself after the treasure, but first he tied a big rock in his leg.

Nebet also told Queen Hamees about another man whose four sons died on the looting day, his wife died the next morning, and on the third day, he died. Another looter told Nebet before he died that he read this in Senu III's tomb: "All people who do evil against this tomb may the crocodile be against them in water, and snakes against them on land. May the hippopotamus be against them in water, the scorpion against them on land." A few days later, Nebet was shocked hearing that this very man was eaten by an angry hippopotamus.

More looters had reported to Nebet that they were haunted by dead people in their dreams. The phenomena did not stop until every one of them was killed. One died from a mysterious illness, another died after he developed a fever, three of them died after mosquito bites which became infected, another man died from arsenic poisoning, seven of them died from malaria, another looter died of a suspected smothering, one more threw himself off the high building of Hatshepsut temple.

Nebet was shocked when she found Caesarion dead in a small pool of his own blood. He had slit his wrists open and let himself bleed to death after days of seeing demons everywhere. He even was screaming every time he looked into Nebet's face. He swore that he saw a demon in her. Nebet did not believe him and accused him that he was making all this up because he had enough of her and that he was planning to leave her for a younger and more beautiful girl. She did not believe him until it was her turn.

Once it was her alone, Nebet felt the death creeping on her. She first reported how one of her servants heard a "faint, almost human cry." Upon reaching his mistress' chamber, he saw a bird cage occupied by a cobra. Nebet's canary had died in its mouth, and this fueled rumors among her servants that the death of their lady was just a matter of time now.

Nebet finally believed that Caesarion was telling the truth about his demons when she began to see them herself. Just last night, she was getting ready to sleep when she saw what appeared as no more than a chill in the air or a shimmer of mist, but shortly it congealed into a form. Before her eyes stood a man dressed in luxurious, royal cloth and the red and white double crown on his head. He held a golden shepherd's crook and flail, both crossed over his chest. On his feet were leather sandals. For a moment, all was silent, then the ghost spoke, and not with the voice of human but with the rasping tones of a beast, "We are coming for you."

Sitting on the throne of Upper Egypt now, Hamees did not doubt any of the stores which Nebet had just recited. She had heard a lot about the pharaoh's curse. She even took this into consideration when her father gave her, and her brother, the quest of finding the kairemi for him.

158

Hamees knew that her brother grudgingly accepted to travel to the north and try to extract the kairemi from the royal tombs only to prove that he was worthy of being his father's successor. Meanwhile, Keya convinced her to stay in the capital of Upper Egypt and not to worry about her father's quest. On the one hand, Keya had confirmed for her that Varis was going to select her as his successor regardless of who was going to bring the kairemi to him first. On the other hand, she knew the price which she might pay for looting a royal tomb.

Yet, I don't trust this woman, Hamees thought to herself, doubtfully looking at Nebet who was still kneeling before her.

"And how in the world would I trust the person who attempted to murder my father?" Hamees asked, angrily.

"No, my lady," Nebet pleaded. "I had nothing to do with that."

"Liar," the Queen of the South shouted in a fury.

According to the reports which Hamees received from the Medjay soldiers, a suspicious meeting had occurred between Roma and Nebet a few months ago. In this meeting, Nebet, her son, and a former military general, named Zannanza, had offered Roma all the money he needed to form, train, and equip an army of insurgents capable of fighting the Kushite mercenaries and overthrowing Varis from power.

After the failed attempt to murder Varis, Hamees ordered the Medjay soldiers to raid Nebet's palace to arrest her, Sharek, and Zannanza, for conspiring against the Pharaoh. However, the palace was empty. They had already fled to an unknown destination. Ever since then no one had seen Nebet until this morning when she showed up at the palace gate begging to see the queen.

"I'm not lying," Nebet said. "I swear. I had nothing to do with the failed attempt to assassin our king."

"But you and your son financed the insurgency against our dynasty," Hamees challenged her.

"I can explain," Nebet tried to say, but the queen cut her off by clapping her hands twice. It was clapping which Nebet knew precisely what it meant. The sound of her clapping echoed through the hall.

"You'll have a chance to explain," the queen said, sarcastically. "Not to me. You will explain it to her."

The noblewoman's eyes widened as she noticed that the clapping sound had woken up something that was crouching behind the throne. She quickly stood up and began to recoil in fear, but the tips of the spears that were held by the Kushite mercenaries poked into her from behind, forcing her to stay there, right in the middle of the hall. With wide-open eyes, Nebet stood there frozen like a pillar of salt, but not for so long. Soon enough, her legs failed to support her weight, and she collapsed to her knees.

Coming out from behind the throne was a giant grey spider, which her body was the size of a chubby twelve-year-old girl. On its way to the middle of the hall, the creature hissed venomously. Its eyes locked on the noblewoman.

"I'm sure you've heard of Hairy," Hamees introduced her beast to the noblewoman. "Who hasn't?" She chuckled, loudly, and the sound of her deep chuckle echoed around the stone walls of the hall.

"Please, my queen," Nebet pleaded again, her voice quivering with the intensity of the situation. "Things aren't merely as they appear. Believe me."

"You need to convince Hairy," the queen said, ironically, "not me."

At the queen's signal, the Kushite mercenaries backed out, allowing the giant spider to clamber easily around the noblewoman with its spindly legs. Its feelers were waving in her direction. Hairy shuffled around Nebet a couple of times. As the beast was getting ready to immobilize the old woman with a paralyzing sting, Nebet threw her last pitch.

"I have a good offer for you, My Lady," she talked fast to the queen before Hairy would attack her. "I have something in which you might be interested."

The beast had to stop short when the queen clapped her hands one more time.

"What are you talking about?" Hamees demanded snappishly.

Nebet first did not respond. She just carefully and slowly motioned her head to the beast behind her, in a way that meant, please, my queen.

When the queen clapped her hands one more time, the beast paused circling his victim.

"Now, tell me what the hell you're talking about?" Hamees ordered.

"Thank you, My Lady," Nebet said in a thankful tone, swallowing hard, not believing that she had survived this beast. Her eyes followed the beast as it stood between her and the throne. At the same time, her hands were taking a necklace off her neck. Once the necklace was off, she held it in her right hand and extended it toward the throne, saying, "I'm talking about this."

"And what is that?" Hamees demanded.

"I will share all treasures with you, My Lady," Nebet offered. "This necklace is just a retainer to prove my good intention."

"No way I would accept that," Hamees said, scoffing.

"Why, My Queen?" Nebet was losing hope.

"Because I don't want to be killed by the pharaoh's curse," Hamees answered. "But here is a better offer. Tell me where you hid the stolen treasures, and I might let you live."

After a moment of hesitation, Nebet told the queen about the secret location where Caesarion and his men had hidden the looted treasures. However, once Nebet was done, Hamees clapped her hands to Hairy to finished what it had started.

"My Lady, you promised me that you will let me live if I speak of the treasures whereabouts?" Nebet reminded her, seeing the giant spider coming back to her.

"I did not promise you anything," Hamees corrected her. "I said, I might let you live if you tell me."

At the queen's signal, the giant spider immobilized the noblewoman with a paralyzing sting to the back of her neck. When the old woman's body toppled backward, crashing unconscious to the marble floor, the spider's fangs chopped her head off. Then, it picked the head up from the floor using two of its legs and began wrapping it in webbing. When a white web completely covered the head, Hairy dropped it, and the head rolled across the floor and stopped at the foot of the throne. Then, the beast walked back and crouched behind the throne.

"Go find out if she was telling the truth," Hamees ordered the Kushites who were standing in the great hall.

***

As Hamees was ordering the Kushites to head to the secret location where the stolen treasures were hidden, no one noticed or even felt the presence of Roma. He was standing inside the wall behind the throne, listening and watching what was going on in the great hall through a tiny hole. A couple of hours earlier, he had snuck into the royal palace, the same way he did when he freed Amasis. Again, he came back searching for some answers. Mixed feelings were running through his heart, and confused expressions were on his face because his mission would never have gone any smoother, yet it would not get any harder. He knew where Nebet had hidden the stolen treasures, but he now was going to face the Ra Nt-Ka.

I know who can help me with this, he thought to himself. *She helped once before, and I'm sure she would do it again. I know where I'm heading next, Memphis. I have to talk to the high oracle.*

Chapter 15
Triple-Sevens

"This's the closest I can get," spoke a frail old man with sparse grey hair to Moeris. "You have to walk the rest of the way." The man was talking in a shaky tone, riding a white donkey with the soulful eyes and a bell around its neck.

"Don't freak out. I was one of them," Moeris responded, chewing one more petal from the blue lotus which he held in his left hand, then he washed it down with a sip of wine from a leather bottle made of goatskin. He was riding on a gray donkey, which he rented from the old man next to him, heading to the most dangerous place in Upper Egypt.

"But, but," the old man stuttered, "but you have said not anymore, which means that we're going to get killed if we get any closer. If you want to take the risk, it's your choice. I have to take my donkey and head back before they spot us." The man pulled the reins, and his donkey came to a halt.

"I think we still can get closer," Moeris said, chewing the last petal of his flower. "Don't worry. It's very safe. I know their tactics very well."

The old man did not argue with Moeris. He just whistled to the gray donkey, which immediately stopped and did not budge until the unwanted passenger got off.

"Fine," Moeris said in an annoyed tone, getting off the donkey. "However, I guarantee you that it's very safe as long as you are with me."

"If you say so, son," the old man mockingly said. "I've lived in the area pretty well all my life, and I've never seen or heard of them welcoming the uninvited guests with anything other than poisoned spears in their hearts." He whistled one more time, and the gray donkey headed back to his owner.

"If you think that this is my fate, why did you help me then?" Moeris wondered.

"Because I need your money," the old man responded without any kind of hesitation, grabbing the reins of the gray donkey and getting ready to head back. Yet, he first motioned at Moeris's belt, reminding him that he still needed to be paid. "I have five mouths to feed at home."

After releasing a scoff that sounded too much like a chuckle, Moeris tossed a deben of copper to the man.

"See you in the afterlife," the old man said as he was turning his donkey around and leaving.

"I've been there once before," Moeris shouted back at the old man. "Believe me, it's not fun. So, I wish I don't see you down there."

***

A few years ago, the arrival of Moeris to the Kingdom of the Dead, or the afterlife as the Egyptian used to call it, was not a demanding ordeal like all other dead people who had arrived there the same day.

All the other dead people stood before the Egyptian Gods. With a falcon's head sat Ra in the middle of the gods who gathered for the final judgment for those who died that day. Amun was there too, wearing his golden, double crown. Sitting next to them was Horus, a falcon-headed man wearing the pschent. The jackal headed Anubis also was there, along with several other gods and goddess who sat behind the judgement table.

Shortly, Moeris' ba - a set of spiritual characteristics unique to each individual - was just released from his body and traveled to the afterlife to join the other dead people standing before the gods of Egypt for their final judgment.

One by one, the deceased's' hearts were weighed against the feather of truth and justice. It was a feather which was taken from the headdress of the goddess Ma'at. If the heart was lighter than the feather, they could pass on to the realm of Osiris, which was a lush and pleasant land in the underworld. If the heart were heavier, the dead person would be devoured by the demon, Ammit, and then they were thrown in the lake of the unquenchable fire.

That day, the only dead person who was not devoured by Ammit was Moeris. His sin-free heart was lighter than the feather. After hearing the gods' ultimate ruling, light spirit ushered Moeris to the realm of Osiris.

"Hey, young man," the voice stopped Moeris before proceeding into the realm of Osiris.

When Moeris looked behind at the Gods of Egypt, he found out that Anubis was the one who was talking to him. Anubis or the god of mummification and the afterlife was sitting the third to the left.

"Do you think you have got a fair trial?" Anubis asked.

"I would never doubt your justice and wisdom, my lord," Moeris replied, a clear sorrow in his eyes.

"I don't mean here, son," the god of the afterlife said, his voice resounded over the whole place. "I mean your trial in life."

"It doesn't matter now," Moeris sadly spoke in a bitter tone of voice. "I'm already here, dead."

"No, it does matter," Anubis objected.

Moeris was confused. What difference would it make if I had a fair trial in my life or not?

"I can give you a second chance if you would like," the god of the mummification surprised him.

"A chance!" Moeris was stunned.

"Yes, a chance to correct what had gone wrong," the god replied. His words reverberated down Moeris' spine.

"But I didn't do anything wrong," Moeris defended. "Or at least, that is what I think." He remembered that he was standing before the gods of Egypt. He did not want to say something not accurate.

"We all here know that," Anubis said.

"What I'm supposed to correct then?" Moeris demanded.

"The injustice you have received," the god of the afterlife answered him.

Although Moeris liked the idea, thinking in avenging this man who sent him to the afterlife, he did not reply.

"How about I take you on a tour of the afterlife to show you the fate of this man?" Anubis offered. "Maybe this would help you make up your mind."

Anubis bowed his head to the other gods. When he received a bow back from them, he walked forward to Moeris.

"Follow me," the god ordered, and Moeris silently followed, not believing what was happening.

They boarded a small boat which was floating in the air. The boat had two oars on each side and was made entirely of wood. No nails were used in the construction of the boat. It was tied firmly together with papyrus reeds. Even though there were no oarsmen on board, some kind of invisible power started pumping and baling, sending the boat across the afterlife.

Moeris heard a lot about the lake of unquenchable fire before his death, yet he was shocked to see it with his own eyes. Apparently, Ammit's devouring of the dead people who had arrived earlier that day was just a warming party for those who were the unrighteous in life and those who were destined to be cast and eternally tormented in the lake of unquenchable fire.

Before Moeris's eyes, there was a big lake with flame-red lines as well as fire demons. He saw hundreds, maybe thousands if not millions, of dead people who were infinitely being tortured for their sins in their lifetime. For a moment, Moeris imagined the man who sent him to the afterlife was there in the middle of the lake of unquenchable fire burning forever.

"What do you think, Moeris?" Anubis asked, and his voice brought the passenger back to the boat, which was hovering now above the burning lake.

"I'm not sure," Moeris tried to be honest.

"Justice will be served with or without you," the god of the afterlife made it clear. "I'm just giving you a chance to avenge your murder."

"Can I do that?" Moeris wanted to make sure.

"I would not offer it if you can't," the god answered.

"I mean do you do this for everyone who came here with an unfair trial in their life," Moeris asked.

"Not really," Anubis replied, then explained. "We do it only for those whose mission in life was not done yet."

"Does this mean that I still have a role to play in life?" Moeris was confused.

"Maybe," the god of the mummification said, smiling.

***

As Moeris was walking in the desert toward his destination, two fighters, dressed entirely in black, appeared in the distance, guarding the gate for the training camp of the most

167

famous paramilitary force in the entire kingdom, the Three-Sevens Battalion.

Once the two guards glimpsed Moeris in the distance, one of them skillfully threw a warning spear in the air in his direction, which struck in the ground, precisely between his legs, a few inches from his manhood.

Moeris knew that this spear was called "The Greeting Spear," and it meant that the legendary military force did not invite this person to their camp and that he or she had to head back before "The Goodbye Spear" would pierce the unwelcomed guest's heart, giving him or her a free pass to the afterlife.

Although the warning spear succeeded in making Moeris halt, it did not stop him from sending his counter-greeting spear back to the guards. When he pulled "The Greeting Spear" from the ground, the second guard brought "The Goodbye Spear" in position to throw it the direction of Moeris' heart. As the guard threw the spear in the air, Moeris instantly and skillfully threw the one in his hand in the two guards' direction at the same time.

The two guards at the gate watched in awe as "The Greeting Spear" traveled through the air and met "The Goodbye Spear" in the middle, shattering each other into pieces. Realizing that only one of them was capable of skillfully throwing a spear that way, one of the two guards froze in place. Meanwhile, the other guard pulled a horn from his belt and blew out a single loud blast, especially when he saw the uninvited guest proceeded on in their direction.

***

If anyone ever found himself surrounded by dozens of spears, all of them pointed at him, at least he would try not to move, hoping not to get hurt or killed. However, the guards who surrounded Moeris, whose brain was on fire as a result of chewing too much of the blue lotus, were trying to keep their sharp weapons away from his face and body, at least for now, until they would figure out who was this person who dared to approach their camp.

"Moeris!" One of the guards exclaimed. It seemed that he recognized this man who was swaying like weeds in the bottom of a lake before him. "Is it you?"

Although Moeris did not respond, more soldiers began to ease down.

"Yes, it's him," another soldier confirmed that it was Moeris.

"How in the world are you still alive?" An angry fighter hissed between his teeth, pointing his spear at Moeris's face. "And why did you come back?"

However, Moeris did not respond.

"We don't have the right to ask him these questions," the soldier who recognized Moeris first pushed the spear away from Moeris's face and confronted the other soldier. "Only Odion has the authority to ask a former member of the Triple-Sevens."

***

Hundreds of years ago, three former military generals, who happened to be close friends, after fighting in many wars against the kingdoms' enemies, decided to form an independent, elite paramilitary unit to defend the land of Egypt if needed.

On the same day of the agreement, the three generals managed to recruit seven powerful men as the basis for the unit. Three founding leaders and seven recruited soldiers formed the base of what was going to be the most skillful and fearless military band in the entire kingdom.

Believing that the numbers "Three" and "Seven" were significant numbers in the Egyptians religion, the founding fathers of this legion had decided a long time ago that their troops must be related to these numbers. Number "Three" was the symbol of plurality, and figure "Seven" was the

169

symbol of perfection, effectiveness, and completeness. That was why the founding generals decided that the battalion must consist of seven-hundred seventy-seven soldiers or three-sevens fighters.

To guarantee the effectiveness of the battalion, the three generals agreed that all the chosen warriors must swear a sacred oath that they would take no wife nor father a child in this life or the afterlife.

***

"Nah, this is not Moeris," a man with a muscular body talked in a dismissive tone of voice after his gaze suspiciously scanned Moeris from head to toe. "Moeris was a legendary warrior, but you ...you're not Moeris." He turned his eyes back to the map which laid on top of a table by which he sat. Before him, two powerful fighters of the triple-sevens unit had just herded an intruder to his tent to decide what they should do to him, but first, they told him that many fighters outside believed that this trespasser was a former soldier of their elite band.

"I've never claimed that honor," Moeris mockingly responded, as he was trying to release himself of the hands of the two fighters.

"Which honor are you talking about?" The huge man, who appeared to be the commander of the unit, questioned his captive; still, his eyes fixed on the map before him.

"Being a legendary warrior," Moeris answered in a way that meant he accepted playing this game of words. "But, it's me, Moeris, and you know that very well. Right, Odion?"

Only when Moeris called Odion by name, he finally raised his eyes up and looked back at his captive. He narrowed his eyes suspiciously. Obviously, the way his prisoner answered him made him uneasy.

"So, you are telling me you're Moeris, huh?" Odion questioned. "I don't think so. I executed Moeris myself after a fair trial."

Moeris first scoffed, staring at Odion directly in the eye. Then he challenged his captor, "Is this what you tell yourself every morning, so you feel good?" Then he mimicked him, "Fair trial."

"Yes, you were sentenced to death because you messed around with a whore," even before Odion would be able to finish the sentence, Moeris' leg traveled through the air quicker than a lightning and kicked a plank in the table, which happened to be loose from the table, and which violently tipped Odion's chin and instantly threw him backward.

"How dare you?" Odion cried out as he was struggling to stand up. At the same time, the other two fighters were trying to seize Moeris before he would attack their leader again.

"I'll kill you," Odion continued. Although the hit did not knock him down, it made him dizzy enough to try to sit down.

"As if I wasn't killed once before," Moeris confronted him, "but here I am." He scoffed.

"Why did you come back?" Odion angrily grilled, trying to stand up. He was still dizzy.

"I'm here to demand the triple-sevens' protection for Princess Merit," Moeris responded in a firm tone.

"You have no voice in our unit," Odion responded, furiously. "You aren't one of us anymore after what you have done."

"Well, I've come to reclaim my title and position," Moeris's response left everyone in the tent in shock.

After getting over his shock and disbelief, Odion approached Moeris slowly, suspiciously studying him.

"Listen, Moeris," Odion spoke between his teeth. "I don't know what you are trying to do, but I've to warn you. Things have changed a lot since you left."

"The rules never change," Moeris argued, "and that's what matters most. I know that I have to fight the best of you to reclaim my title."

"Alright, Moeris," Odion responded, staring at him. Then, he directed his speech to one of the fighters who was holding Moeris. "Take him away and make sure he gets no food, or drink, especially anything that would intoxicate him. No blue lotus, no wine, no beer. Tomorrow, he will fight me." Then, he returned his head back to Moeris, talking to him with a mocking tone, "He will fight me sober. Let's see how the legendary Moeris will fight while he is sober."

***

Later that night, Moeris sat on the ground inside a small tent which was supposed to be his cell until morning. He was not in chains. They just put him in the tent with two guards outside. He was famished and dehydrated. And above all, he began to sober up. The effect of the blue lotus which he chewed and the wine he drank on his way began to withdraw.

Could I beat him while I'm sober? Moeris could not tell. An uncertain look appeared on his face. When Moeris remembered what a skilled fighter Odion was, he felt even worse, especially when his mind decided to take a journey through his memories. He recollected the competition between him and Odion over succeeding the former commander of the triple-sevens who was killed a week ago fighting a lion. The competition was intense, and Odion was a dirty player. A few days before the election, Odion spread rumors across the camp that Moeris had a secret wife, named Shani, who worked as a prostitute in a small, nearby brothel.

A quick and secret trial was held. Moeris tried to explain that he indeed snuck out a few times from the camp and went to the inn only to enjoy a few drinks, sing, and dance, but he never had sex nor had a wife. He requested to call Shane to testify that he never slept with her, but the judges refused to have someone not a member of triple-sevens to be a witness for an internal matter of the medallion.

Moeris did not give up. He requested that Donkor, a soldier who used to secretly sneak with Moeris to the inn, to testify. He hoped that his friend would prove that he never slept with any whore over there. However, Moeris was in shock when Donkor testified that they indeed went to the inn with Moeris a few times. Yet, when Donkor was directly asked if Moeris had slept with Shani, he said he was drunk and couldn't recall if this happened or not. The court, which was consisted of Odion and another two elderly fighters took that as proof that Moeris was guilty and sentenced him to death.

Knowing that Moeris was a skillful fighter and that he might request a trial by combat, Odion quickly convinced the other two elderlies to execute the sentence immediately. In return, the two elderly soldiers were promoted to advisory positions once Moeris was killed and Odion became the new commander of the Triple-Sevens. Once the sentence was pronounced, Odion stood up and stabbed Moeris in the belly using his dagger. Then, he quickly sent another stab to Moeris's chest. When Moeris fell to his knees, the same blade was pushed inside his heart.

Moeris also recalled that after Anubis made a deal with him, he woke up in his former black uniform of the triple-sevens. The uniform was drenched in blood, yet he found no trace of his injuries in his chest that were caused by being stabbed by a dagger three times.

Despite his deal with the God of the afterlife, Moeris decided not to avenge the man who killed him after an unfair trial. He remembered his mother's words about vengeance, "Sometimes the best revenge is to smile and move on." The words kept ringing inside Moeris head when he headed to the Nile, took off his bloody uniform, and washed himself up. Then, he burned his uniform, deciding not to go back to the Triple-Sevens. Instead, he traveled north and joined the pharaohs' guards, believing that the best way to serve the gods and thank them for bringing him back to life was to protect the legal ruler of Egypt.

In Thebes, Moeris sought a new beginning, putting all the injustice he received in the past behind him. However, the God of Death was not happy about Moeris not avenging his unfair trial. He was brought back to life specifically for this reason. On the same night when Moeris was selected to join the Pharaoh's guards, Anubis appeared to him in his dream.

"You didn't go back to the Triple-Sevens," The angry voice of the God of the afterlife and mummification was deafening in the silence of Moeris' dream. "You didn't avenge this man who killed you after an unfair trial. You broke your deal with a Divine Embalmer. There's a price for that." Moeris knew in advance that there were going to be ramifications for his decision. He did not know exactly what this price would be, yet he was ready for it. He was done with revenge, the triple-sevens, and his old life.

Sitting in the tent, waiting for his combat with Odion in the morning, Anubis's voice continued to ring in Moeris' head, "Since you refused to send Odion to the afterlife, you're punished by not being allowed to kill anyone else. The day you kill someone is your last day in your life."

Knowing that the day he would kill anyone was going the day he would face the God of Death, Moeris lived his life ever since in fear. Anubis had taken the courage of his heart. Fear always gripped him quickly. He was still a skillful fighter; but every time he fought, he had to find his audacity first. Accidentally, he discovered his bravery in being intoxicated. A glass of wine, a jug of beer, or a blue lotus could turn him into a different person; he was brave, bold, fearless, and a skillful and meritorious fighter.

However, Moeris was now sitting in this small tent waiting for a combat with Odion. He was famished and dehydrated. And above all, he was sober.

***

174

The next morning, Moeris was brought to an arena where all the seven hundred seventy-seven elite warriors gathered to watch the combat between their commander and the legendary Moeris who, somehow, came back from the afterlife.

"Are you sure you want to do this, Odion?" Moeris asked once Odion violently emerged from the audience, amid cheers from his supporters. His voice was shaky, and his legs felt wobbly.

"I have to send you back to where you belong, Moeris," Odion hissed at him. "Your presence here is undesirable." He was wearing the formal black uniform of the triple-sevens and holding a long sword and round shield made of solid wood. He motioned to a man who stood nearby who immediately threw a sword before Moeris' feet.

Moeris looked at the sword and swallowed hard. He hated Odion so much, and he wanted to kill him so bad. Yet, he remembered Anubis' words, "The day you kill someone, is your last day in your life." The ruling of the god of the afterlife instantly made Moeris's breathing become rapid and shallow. He was breathing all wrong, gasping like a fish out of water.

"Pick up your sword, Moeris," Odion challenged him, "and let's put an end to this play."

A ghostly surge of adrenaline pierced Moeris' heart and made it race faster. His eyes scanned his surroundings as the panic grew inside him. He seemed to look for something; something in the air; something in the sky.

"Fine," Moeris finally said when he heard a sound which he immediately recognized. It was a sound of flapping wings. He bent down and picked up the sword.

As Odion was getting ready to strike Moeris using his long sword, a loud roar of the One who Tears into Pieces made every one of the triple-sevens freeze in fear, including their commander. Before anyone could recognize the roar, the griffin appeared in the sky heading directly to where Moeris was standing. On the back of the king of all the creatures rode Princess Merit who decided to make a quick stop at the camp of Triple-Sevens before heading to the land of Kush.

The griffin landed right behind Moeris and roared one more time; his wings still spread out and flapping. With every flap, the sand beneath him danced chaotically in the air.

"Moeris," the princess called out, and he looked backward at her, "It's your chance to redeem yourself and appease the God of Death."

Moeris did not say a word. He just narrowed his eyes for a moment, thinking. It did not take him too long to comprehend what Merit had just said. Anubis prohibited him from killing anyone, but he had sent to back to life specifically to avenge his death at the hands of Odion. If he killed the man who gave him an unfair trial and sent him to eternally burn in the lake of fire, the lord of the death might forgive him.

Moeris slowly turned his head back to Odion, feeling his courage return even while he was sober, and instantly charged with a high-pitched war scream.

Chapter 16
Ra Nt-Ka

When Roma arrived on top of the high eminence, he reined his tired horse to a stop. Behind Roma were almost a hundred men and women, most of them were members of the Free Army, riding on the back of carts which pulled by sturdy oxen. Roma could feel that his followers were scared. Most of them were turning their head from side to side, anxiously scanning their surroundings.

No one will be excited to be here, Roma thought to himself, making an excuse to raise his hand in the air, so all the carts came to a halt. *After all, it's the Valley of the Bones.* The words sent a chill down his spine.

Knowing that his horse and the oxen behind him were exhausted, Roma decided to give them a brief chance to catch their breath before proceeding into one of the most dangerous places in the entire kingdom. Not only this, but he also needed a moment to collect his thoughts before confronting the last Ra Nt-Ka that living in the land of

Egypt. He was excited yet scared to death. He knew that he was going to meet a deadly beast, yet he trusted the high oracle who encouraged him to proceed in his mission.

Two days ago, Roma traveled to the temple of the cat goddess, Bastet. The temple erected south of Memphis on a small peninsula jutting out from the east bank of the Nile. An elderly oracle, named Mau, delivered the answers in this temple. Roma knew that the gods had forbidden this oracle to ever have intercourse with men; and in return, they gave her great power. He also knew that every day, at sunset, Mau would martyr an animal that a cat would eat, such as a mouse, rat, or bird. After tasting the blood of the prey, she would immediately be seized with a divine frenzy to see Bastet. Having entered the presence of the cat goddess, she could reveal the past and future of anyone who sought her help.

As Roma passed the temple's gate, he stood there for a moment, eager to speak to the high oracle. He was wondering what she would reveal to him this time. This was not the first time Roma met the high oracle. He met her once before right after Varis' false rebellion. He traveled with Moeris who backed out at the last moment, and Roma had to proceed inside the temple by himself to receive the most crucial prophecy that circled the land of Egypt in the last few decades, "The short age of the illegal dynasty is drawing to a fast close, and the age of the legitimate heiress is dawning."

Feeling much better this time, Roma proceeded inside the temple. Even though he could see no one in the hall, no oracle, no people, no one at all, he did not back out. He knew where he could find what he was after. He headed directly to the sanctuary or the Holy-of-Holies as the Egyptians used to call it, which was located at the far end of the temple.

Knowing that he was entering a holy chamber, he voluntarily took off his shoes and placed them next to the door. Also, he knew that no weapons were allowed inside the Holy-of-Holies, so he voluntarily took off his belt and put it with his shoes next to the sanctuary entrance, and then he stooped through the low door.

The room was totally dark inside, and the stone floor was cold beneath his feet. He remembered how his heartbeat roared out of control when he entered this room a few months ago, but now he was not scared because he knew what was inside. He even had to shield his eye in advance before a very bright light suddenly illuminated the sanctuary.

Here they come, Roma watched seven black cats coming out from behind the statue and walking toward him. He stood there, and the cats began swirling around his legs, meowing and growling. Then, they eventually started walking behind each other, forming a circle around him.

Roma remembered how he freaked out the first time this happened to him, especially when the cats continued to circle, accelerating their speed. Gradually, the cats' walking turned into running, faster and faster. Eventually, Roma could no longer make out individual cats, as they were spinning around him so quickly. He even felt the heat rising from the stone ground beneath him, and he saw smoke emanating from the fast-moving cats.

Roma blinked several times when the spinning cats began to form a wall of smoke about him. The more he blinked, the thicker the smoke got until he could not see his surroundings anymore. All he could see now was a wall of smoke, and he felt as if he was trapped inside the eye of a tornado. He could not see the statue and the sanctuary walls anymore. Everything had disappeared behind the thick smoke.

As the smoke and the black cats began to disappear, Roma was ready to lead himself to the high oracle to make him relive certain stages of his past life or show him glimpses of the future like she did once before. However, this time, the high oracle allowed him to see, not something from the past or the future, but something that was happening right that moment, the Valley of The Bones.

Roma watched in awe, the valley was covered the bones of hundreds of dead dinosaurs, or the Ra- Nt-Kas as the Egyptians used to call them. The name meant the "beastly creatures" of "enormous size." Dinosaurs lived in the land of Egypt for centuries, and the Egyptians mated them and used them to carry and drag the massive rocks which were used in constructing the pyramids. Unfortunately, these giant beasts gradually began to extinct due to many factors. For another unidentified reason, the dying dinosaurs traveled to a valley in the desert west of Memphis to die. Eventually, the Egyptians began to call this area the Valley of the Dead or the Valley of the Bones because the entire area was covered in bones of hundreds of dead dinosaurs.

Back to Roma's vision, he saw five Kushites entering the valley. They were the mercenaries which Queen Hamees had ordered them to travel to the Valley of the Dead to verify Nebet's story that the stolen treasures were hidden in this dangerous place.

Roma watched the five mercenaries walking between the giant bones, holding their weapons and ready to strike if anyone or anything tried to stop them. Shortly, Roma saw a monster erecting from the middle of the bones. It was over 50 feet tall, and it had scaly gray skin, an anthropomorphic torso with muscular arms, spikes on its back and tail. It had long-necked which reached out to the sky; and when its long tail lashed, it could kill an army of men.

First, the Ra Nt-Ka produced an angry roar. It was very distinctive. It was deep and threating, expressing the fury of the monster. Then, he attacked the five Kushites who dared to enter his domain. Roma screwed up his face with disgust as he saw the dinosaurs devouring two of the men, one of his paws smashing another two, then kicking the fifth making him fly for a while before crashing dead to the ground.

At that instant, the black cats came out of nowhere and began circling around him, and the smoke started to form the wall around, moving him back to the Holy-of-Holies. The seven cats began slowing down, and the thick smoke started to vanish. He saw that he was back finally inside the sanctuary. Before him, stood an old woman. She was totally naked.

And here is Mau, a voice rang inside Roma's head.

The high oracle was a very old woman. Her body was flat, sagging, and ruined. She had lost her eyeballs years ago when she upset the Goddess Bastet for some unknown sin, and her eyes were sewn shut. Her scalp was nothing but tufts and stubble. Her skin was wrinkled, spotted, and so papery thin than Roma could see the web of veins and the shape of the bones beneath. Her loose breasts were dangling there. Long stretch marks covered her saggy abdomen, and bumps of cellulite covered her thighs.

"Welcome back," the high oracle spoke with a feeble voice.

"You took me to the point this time," Roma told Mau. "No memoirs, no past, or anything like that."

Mau first scoffed, then talked, "You know what to do now."

"But how I'm gonna survive this beast," Roma wondered.

Mau leaned forward and whispered how he could survive the Ra Nt-Ka. He had to recoil a little when her smell wafted to him. It was rancid and overwhelming. It was like the smell of a lifeless animal which had been sitting on the side of the street for a few days in the scorching summer sun.

"We should move on before it gets dark," the voice brought Roma back to reality, on top of the high eminence where his men were taking a break. The voice was for one of his men.

"You're right," Roma answered. "Wait here. I will go first."

Even before the man would get a chance to remind Roma that the plan was that they must stick together, Roma spurred his tired horse to a gallop downhill. When he was surrounded with dinosaur bones from all sides, he dismounted his horse.

181

Roma's eyes warily scanned around. His right hand holding the horse's rein, while his other hand was on his short sword, ready for anything. Slowly and carefully, he moved forward toward a group of palm trees huddled together on a slight elevation.

I'm being watched, he knew, swallowing hard. Quietly, he tied his horse to one of the trees, intending to stay there for a while to watch what was happening. *Is it him?* He wondered, gulping, and feeling unseen eyes following him. He was not sure.

Although Roma could see no one or anything, the place was alive with the chittering sounds of unseen beings around him. Hyperalert, his head nervously scanned his surroundings, his hands touching the handles of his swords.

A sudden monstrous roar rose from behind the bones, and Roma almost leaped out of his skin. When he heard thuds of massive, gigantic paws padding toward him, the ground began to shake and move beneath his feet. Suddenly, Roma felt something rising up behind him. When he heard a guttural snarl and his horse nickered in fear, he quickly spun to see a Ra Nt-Ka. Before his eyes, it was the largest predator Egypt had ever conceived. That thing could eat Roma's horse for lunch and have Roma himself for dessert.

I don't know if I can do that, Roma talked to himself, *but I have too. I have no other option.* He decided, his heart pounding like a hammer in his chest. He slowly took the defensive position for which he was famous. Also, he wore a blank look on his face for which he was well-known too. Then, he raised his head a little to be able to look in the eyes of the angry monster before him, ready to either take this beast, or the creature was going to take him.

The ground shook when the beast stepped forward; and in a blink of an eye, it snatched the horse using his sharp teeth, and then the horse was gone inside its colossal mouth. Roma's eyes shot open. Things happened so fast that his mind could not wholly comprehend that this monster had just swallowed his horse and that he was going to be next.

When the Ra Nt-Ka twisted itself, turning to face Roma, and emitted an earsplitting roar, Roma realized that his death was inventible, especially when the beast bared its fangs with a lethal hiss.

I think I should run, he thought, quivering in fear, but he had no chance to go anywhere. In a blink of an eye, the enormous, violent, prehistoric monster came charging and pounced upon him, biting and scratching. Luckily, Roma was aware of the attack, so he, faster than the beast, ducked down to avoid the monster's sharp teeth, and he then jumped high in the air to avoid the beast's colossal paws.

Run, you idiot! A feeble voice shrieked inside his head. It was the high oracle's voice. *What the..? Is she watching me now through one of her visions?* He wanted to think inside his head, but he had no time. Immediately, he bolted as the Ra Nt-Ka leaped after him. Roma launched himself between two enormous dinosaurs' skulls, the smallest was still higher than him, forcing the beast to claw its way around to the side. Meanwhile, Roma scrambled up, around, and over a pile of bones. The beast's claws slashed the air behind him, exploding bark off a skull as Roma willed himself forward in a frenzy. With rippling muscles, the creature was airborne for a moment, blacking out the sun, but Roma dived inside one of the two skulls. It was like a crash when the beast tore into the skull above him, its claws slashed down next to him as he rolled and crawled.

The monster's glistening jaws smashed and snapped against the skull, sending chunks of it flying. Roma rolled onto his back, swinging his left sword widely, faster and faster. When the sword hits the Ra Nt-Ka in the face, it screeched an ungodly wail of pain and rage, and then it snatched the sword out of his hand. As the beast was ripping the entire skull away, Roma scrambled to escape. Yet, he did not get anywhere because the glinting jaws of the monster lunged downward and snapped shut.

The Ra Nt-Ka ripped Roma out of the skull, shaking him like a dog with a rabbit. As the monster's teeth were pushing against Roma's body, he heard the high oracle's voice again ringing through his skull, "Now. Say it now." Again, he wanted to wonder how Mau was able to communicate with him, but he had no time. Instantly, he screamed something. It was not clear what he was saying at first, so he had to repeat over and over, "Your mom is sending her regards." It was the high oracle's advice to ease down the beast.

"Wow, it worked?" Roma was in awe as the beast suddenly stopped shaking him and gently put him to the ground. Roma immediately jumped to his feet and was getting ready to run for his life, but he realized that the beast was not angry anymore. When he cautiously extended his arm toward the Ra Nt-Ka, the beast approached him and sat, next to him, as if it was his pet. The ground beneath Roma's feet was shaking with every move the monster took. Roma extended his right arm even further toward the beast, trying to pet him, but the creature at first snarled. Yet, it leaned its colossal head down so Roma could reach him. Roma's eyes also shot up when his hand touched the beast's cheek. Shockingly, the Ra Nt-Ka stopped snarling and closed its eyes, in a way that meant that it was enjoying the touch.

Chapter 17
Face-To-Face

Although Gapi did not speak Kushite, he could make out some of what he was hearing.

"Bar the main gates," he heard men shouting orders outside the door. "Ring the bells. We're under attack." They were angry orders, punctuated by the sound of men fighting and dying.

"We're all dead," a shaking voice came from Gapi's right. It was the commander of those men who escorted Gapi on this mission. It was, Gebal, an old man, six-four, lean and muscular, with a shaved head, and huge arms.

Gapi first glared at the commander, then he shook his head violently, in a way that meant, *No, we aren't.* Then, he raised his sword high in the air, in a way that said, *We're going to fight. We're going to release them.* His eyes quickly shifted to the seven kidnapped Celestials who were gagged and bound in the cell behind him.

Even if we're really going to die, Gapi thought to himself. *It really doesn't matter. We're dead in the Egyptians' eyes anyway, especially after betraying them.* He could not forgive himself, his sister, and his late father for what they had done to the kingdom.

The treaty of Thebes was the revealing moment for Gapi. After this moment, he realized how foolish was Varis, and his children after him, to trust Keya. He always warned his father that his new wife was going to ruin all their lives. He was sure that she had a motive of her own behind inciting her husband to rebel against Senu's reign. He was not sure what the purpose was exactly, but he never felt good for her having his father's ear.

I was an idiot myself, Gapi reminded himself. *How in the world could I trust the Libyans?* It was a shocking moment for him when he figured out that he was a victim of a big scheme. On the day of the treaty, he could not believe his eyes or ears that day when he discovered that everything was planned in advance between King Alara of Kush and King Fazzaz of Libya. Two of the traditional enemies of Egypt had finally found their way to invade the lands of Egypt without spilling a lot of blood. After decades of trying, the Libyans and Kushites armies were finally in the heart of Egypt, thanks to Varis bloody rebellion and his idiot children.

It's all because of us, Gapi had concluded a few days ago. He was explaining to Bek, the vizier of Lower Egypt, why he must go himself on a mission to rescue the kidnapped Celestials. He was using sign language to communicate with the vizier. Finally, they had a chance to speak alone without the presence of the High Commissioner of Lower Egypt, who was assigned by king Fazzaz of Libya. Lastly, they were able to make a decision without the intervention of the High Commissioner who obstructed almost every single decision that was made lately by the Pharaoh of the North.

186

And because of that, Gapi had continued explaining to Bek, *I have to lead my men myself to Kush and release the kidnaped People from the Sky. If we succeed in safely delivering them, I'm sure the floating pyramid will stop their attack.*

When Bek inquired about how he was going to explain the absence of the Pharaoh of the North, especially to the High Commissioner, they decided that the best way was claiming that Gapi had traveled west to negotiate the high prices of grain and wheat imported from Canaan.

Meanwhile, Gapi ordered Gebal to assemble twenty-four well-trained warriors and prepare them for the rescue mission. Instead of heading west, they traveled south. They had to use rough roads through the eastern desert to avoid being seen or caught by Hamees's forces in the south. It was a long and rough trip, yet their chariots had made it to the land of Kush in less than two weeks. They traveled only through the night, and every night, until they finally arrived in Napata, the capital of the Kingdom of Kush.

Over a high eminence outside of Napata, they quietly camped to rest before taking the next move. They silently watched the city, thinking of a way to sneak into the royal palace and release the kidnapped heralds. It took Gapi two full nights to think of a plan.

On the third night, and on Gebal's signal, his twenty-four soldiers, along with Gapi, descended the eminence and approached the city. One by one, they quietly managed to sneak up on the city watch and kill all the guards who were securing the eastern gate. After sneaking into the city walls, they noiselessly accomplished their next goal. They arrived at the royal palace. They skillfully and quietly threw their ropes over the high walls and began to climb up. In no time, they all were inside the royal palace. They expected to find more Kushites on the palace's wall, but thankfully there were only a few whom Gapi's men easily handled.

"Let's get them and get out of here as soon as possible," Gebal whispered to his men. Immediately, they moved forward to the dungeons where King Alara kept the kidnaped celestials. Nothing was more straightforward than reaching the cells where only one Kushite was. The loud snoring of the sleeping Kushite led Gapi's men to his location, and they quietly broke his neck.

However, right before they broke into the cell where the Kushites kept the celestials, sudden noises erupted outside.

"It's a trap," one of Gapi's men suggested. "It was all a trap."

Probably it's the truth, Gapi wanted to respond, but he could not.

"Shut the door," Gebal ordered his men, and they immediately did, taking defense formation behind the closed door.

However, Gapi's focus distracted by a thundered roar of a monstrous bird which, it seemed, had just flown above the palace. His eyes scanned around and exchanged a stunned look with his men, especially when they could not identify the roar. It was a mix between the high-pitched whistling of an eagle and the deep rumble of a vicious and gigantic lion.

"It's the One who Tears into Pieces," one of Gebal's soldiers shakily implied.

"No way," another man responded, his frightened eyes scanning around.

Is this true? Gapi asked himself, feeling his adrenaline kick in.

The noises outside the door were getting louder, and he could feel his men getting edgy. Fear was hovering among them, especially when cries outside turned into pounding at the door.

"Keep this damn door shut," Gebal ordered his men who formed a protective circle, around him and Gapi, in the middle of the room. "Do you understand?"

Eventually, the shouting outside and the pounding on the door turned into breaking in. Gapi's eyes shot wide when he saw pieces of the wooden door flying in the air. He could see now axes and swords piercing through the broken door. At a certain point, the door could not hold, and it flew open.

"Attack," Gebal cried out, charging forward with a high-pitched war scream, followed by his men. The air reverberated with the clash of hard steel against steel for a moment, covering on the voices of some of his men who was trying to say, "They aren't Kushite. They're Egyptians."

When Gapi realized himself that the man whom he was swinging his sword at was an Egyptian, he eased down himself, and eventually, they both stopped fighting, staring at each other.

"Stop," Gebal finally ordered his men, and eventually the clashes of steel against steel which filled the dungeons a moment ago turned into silent.

The Triple-Sevens! Gapi thought to himself, startled. He recognized the uniform of the men who stood before him.

"Who are you?" Moeris required. "And what are you doing here?" Even though he was sober as a judge, he was bold and brave as a lion. Murdering Odion in single combat and delivering him to the afterlife had finally redeemed Moeris and appeased the God of Death. That night, Anubis appeared to Moeris in a dream and released him from his curse. Moeris finally gained his courage back.

Before anyone could produce an answer to Moeris's question, a female voice came from outside the room, "Did you find them?"

The Triple-Sevens instantly made sure to secure the whole place for an important person coming in.

Gapi's jaw dropped to the floor when he saw Princess Merit entering the room. He had heard a lot about her, yet he never met her in person.

"Drop your weapons," she commanded as she entered the room. Some of the Triple-Sevens quickly lined up to separate her from Gapi and his men. "No Egyptians should die tonight."

"Who are you?" Moeris inquired again. "And what are you doing here?"

"You must speak with manners to the Pharaoh of the North," Gebal objected. "You are all in the presence of King Gapi. You also need to introduce yourselves."

All of a sudden, the eased down soldiers, on both sides, raised their swords in the air.

"We're the Triple-Sevens," the same soldiers introduced themselves, "and you are in the presence of Princess Merit, the only legal heiress to the Egyptian throne. So, you better drop your weapons before you all die."

"I said no Egyptian should die tonight," Merits voice came sharp and firm. "Prince Gapi, what are you doing here?" She looked him in the eyes. It was a challenging look.

"You need to learn how to address a king, you little girl," Gebal snapped at her, but he had to recoil when six sharp spears came out of nowhere, and all were pointed at his face.

Gapi had to intervene, first by dropping his sword and then by carefully pushing the spears away from the commander's face, in a way that meant, She's right. No Egyptian should die tonight.

After that, he requested Gebal's help to interpret to the princess what he was trying to say.

"His Grace wanted you to know that he lost his tongue when he objected the treaty of Thebes," Gebal explained. "And that we're here to release the kidnapped celestials. His Grace wants to safely deliver the heralds back to save his people from the Celestials' attacks."

When they heard another thunderous roar from a monstrous bird had just flown above the palace, they all, Gapi's men and the Triple-Sevens men, turned their weapon to the door.

"We don't have much time here," Princess Merit commanded them. "We have to release them and get out of here immediately." Then, she turned her head to Gapi. "Prince Gapi, I believe that we aren't really enemies to one another. Evidently, we're here for the same reason." She

190

gestured at the kidnapped celestials behind Gapi. "Our real enemy is outside that door." Her head snapped at the door, and all the men in the room turned, not to face each other anymore, but all to face the mutual enemies. Sounds of running footsteps were rushing on the stairs and corridors. Shouting and clacking weapons filled the air.

"Boys," Gebal cried out, addressing his men who responded with a loud shout, "let's show the princess and the Triple-Sevens how the north fights." When he received an affirmative nod from Gapi, he charged with a high-pitched cry, followed by his men.

Chapter 18
The Truce

When Zannanza met Amasis for the first time, he wondered in his head, *how in the world King Senu IV thought of appointing this man successor for Ramose?*

Amasis was moonstruck and did not know what he was talking about.

This man is beginning to get looney, Zannanza thought, yet he soon learned that the young priest had lost his joy when the woman he loved suddenly disappeared during the battle of Badari.

Thank the gods, the old man said in his mind when some good news finally arrived to cheer the priest and stop him from going nuts.

A few moments ago, Zannanza was relaxing on a straw bed in his hideout north of Thebes. He was dressed in a fine white garment made of silk with a blue headpiece. On the floor, next to the bed, was a pair of sandals made of goatskin. It seemed that he was working earlier on some kind of a military plan, evident in the large papyrus scroll which was lying next to him and partly unfolded showing a map of Egypt.

A few feet away, Amasis was sitting on a low cushion made of reed, holding a papyrus scroll in his hands on which his eyes were fixed. More scrolls were scattered everywhere around him. He seemed exhausted from reading, trying to figure out how he could reach a truce with the Adorians.

All of a sudden, the old man's heart fell to his waist when the door flew open. For a moment, he thought that Kushite mercenaries were storming the house and going to arrest them for conspiring against the Queen of the South. However, he released a sigh of relief when he saw a child of no more than seven run in, out of breath and sweating profusely, and hand Amasis a papyrus scroll.

"Who sent this?" Amasis questioned, yet the boy shrugged his shoulders, then he flew out.

"Open it, Amasis," Zannanza said as he was sitting on the bed and pulling his sandals onto his feet.

Zannanza noticed that the young priest seemed lost. Obviously, he was not sure what was happening and if it was a good idea to open the message. The old man nodded his head to Amasis, encouraging him to go ahead, but the young priest seemed hesitant. Not comprehending why Amasis was so frightened of a message, he first rolled his eyes and then stood up and snatched the scroll from the young priest's hand.

"From Nefer to Amasis," Zannanza began to read the message; yet immediately, he had to stop when he noticed that Amasis' face had changed with the shock. From a dreamy person, the young priest all of a sudden snapped to full attention. He even stood up and snatched the scroll back, so he could read it himself.

Zannanza rolled his eyes again and hoped that Amasis would be kind enough to share with him what was happening, but he waited too long watching the young priest's eyes devouring the words without saying a word.

When he was done, he dropped on his cushion like a sack of potato.

"What's happening?" Zannanza had to ask.

"Thank the Gods," Amasis sounded relieved. "She is alive." He leaned his head back, close his eyes, and exhaled a sigh of relief.

"Well, I guess I can figure that out on my own," Zannanza sounded irritated on the other hand. "Nobody is going to write to you from the afterlife. She has to be alive. I'm wondering what is going on. Did she say where she is? And what had happened to her? Is she ok?"

Amasis did not reply. He just handed him the scroll again, so he can figure out himself.

"From Nefer to Amasis," the old man began to read in his mind. He did not have to read it aloud anymore. Amasis had already known what was there. "I'm alive and ok. So sorry for leaving that day without saying anything. Believe me, I have my reasons, and I'm sure you will forgive me once you listen to them soon. For now, there is something much more important to take care of. The Adorians..."

All of a sudden, Amasis stood up and snatched the scroll from the old man's hand.

"Wait, what?" The young priest exclaimed as if he had just now realized that Nefer was talking about something much more important than that she was still alive. "How did she contact the Adorians?"

Zannanza grunted in anger as he got tired of this game of snatching and handing out the scroll which Amasis had played multiple times so far.

"Well, at least read aloud if you don't mind," the old man requested when he realized that Amasis was reading in his mind.

"Yeah, sure. Sorry," Amasis said and then continued reading Nefer's message. "The Adorians know that Princess Merit headed to the land of Kush to retrieve the kidnapped heralds. They know that the princess has good intentions to return them safely. Thus, they need you to arrange for the

195

delivery. They need this to happen in a safe location and as soon as possible. I guess you know how to contact them. See you soon, love. Nefer."

Although Zannanza was irritated because of Amasis's childish behavior, he was half-shocked half-titillated by the news.

"Do you know what this means?" Amasis wondered, putting the scroll down and looking at the old man directly in the eyes.

"Yes," Zannanza finally blurted out after a moment of contemplating. "The Adorians are on our side."

"No, not really," Amasis quickly corrected him. "This means that they are aware of everything we are trying to do to end this war and that they are trying to help us in return." He seemed so excited. Finally, he got his joy back, not only because Nefer was still alive but also because his mission would never have gone any smoother. Instead of figuring out a way to contact the celestials for a truce, they reached him first willing to end their attack on the land of Egypt.

"All we need to do is to arrange for the delivery," Amasis continued. "Would you help me, Zannanza?"

"Of course, I will help you," the old man instantly and firmly confirmed. "I would do anything to end this war." He indeed sounded like a former general.

"But what about the Free Army?" The young priest wondered, knowing that Roma had commissioned his military advisor to regroup whatever was left of the Free Army and recruit new warriors to fight the next battle. "Don't you have work to do? I don't want to distract you."

"The Free Army is almost ready," Zannanza responded. "The old members are already in the training phase. Recruiters are traveling across the country, inciting people to join us. Thousands of new rebels are already pouring in our secret training camp. As you see, there is not much to do at the moment. So definitely, I can help you with this."

"Great," the young priest exclaimed. "This day wouldn't get any better. Actually, this is the best day of my life."

***

In addition to monitoring the preparation of the Free Army, Zannanza spent the whole next week helping Amasis to prepare for the delivery of the heralds. First, it took them too long to decide where the gathering should take place. They thought of a neutral location, maybe outside of the kingdom of Egypt, but they quickly dismissed the idea. Then, Zannanza came up with a plan.

"Why don't we meet the Adorians in Badari?" He suggested. He was talking about the borderline area which separated Upper and Lower Egypt where the battle had taken place. "At least, we won't be at either of Hamees nor Gapi's territories."

At first, Amasis agreed with the old man about Badari as a neutral location, but later he changed his mind, especially when he received another note from Nefer.

"The Adorians are requesting one more thing," Nefer said in her letter. "They need all the Egyptian noblemen and noblewoman to attend the delivery of the heralds, especially those who are involved in the tussle over the Egyptian throne."

"Well, that's bizarre," Zannanza commented.

"True that," the young priest agreed.

"But you know what?" The old man quickly realized. "I think I know why they wanted this way."

"Why do you think?" Amasis wondered, seeming a little bit confused.

"I think they are trying to help Princess Merit," Zannanza explained. "If she delivered the heralds to the Adorians safe in front of everyone, she will prove for them that she is the one who deserves to wear the crown of Egypt, not only because she is the legal and rightful heiress to the throne but also because she earned it after saving the whole kingdom from inevitable destruction."

197

"Good point," Amasis not only agreed, he even added, "and I think the Celestials might gift her more kairemi before everyone as their blessing for the future Queen of Egypt."

"I'm not sure about the kairemi," it seemed the old man disagreed with Amasis regarding this part. "I have a feeling that the People from the Sky would never agree to provide us with more kairemi after what had happened to their heralds and pyramid." Then, it seemed that he quickly realized that he was talking to a priest. "I don't know. I might be wrong. You are a priest and know the Adorians much better than me."

"To be honest, I'm not sure at this point," Amasis responded. "The good news is that the People from the Sky are aware of what everything is happening, including Princess Merit. That's a good sign."

"True that," Zannanza agreed. "So, let's get back to the delivery location."

"Yes, let's talk about that," the young priest realized that they have much more important things to discuss. "I have an idea. I think Thebes is the perfect location to invite everyone to this highly anticipated event." Then, Amasis went ahead, explaining why he chose the capital of Upper Egypt. His point of view was that if the Celestials indeed intended to help the rightful heiress to the throne there was no other place would be better than Thebes, the city that was the capital of the great kingdom of Egypt before the separation of the north. Over the ages, Thebes symbolized the unification of Upper and Lower Egypt.

At first, Zannanza seemed not convinced of the idea, yet the more he listened, the more his eyes widened in admiration of the young, brilliant priest before him.

I can't believe that he is the same person, Zannanza thought as he was listening to Amasis' logic, feeling bad that he once believed that this man was looney and was not worthy to succeed the former high priest of Egypt.

Although Zannanza was a very close friend to Sheamay's family, he never felt bad when he killed Sheamay's only son, Sharek, who tried to kill Princess Merit during the battle of Badari. After all, the young nobleman proved that he had funded the insurgency just because he desired to sit on the throne of Egypt. Zannanza also never got sad when he heard about what happened to Nebet. He didn't know about nor participated in her plan of looting the tombs' treasures. He believed that she got what she deserved. If it were not about her, the mummies and the Terrifying Once would have brought an easy victory to the Free Army during the battle of Badari.

However, Zannanza had always appreciated knowing Sheamay's family for two reasons. First, through this house, he was able to reach for Roma and join his insurgency against Varis and the Kushites. Second, through this family, he knew and connected with the most influential noblemen and noblewomen across the kingdom. The thing that was going to help him to implement his part of preparing for the delivery of the heralds.

Through his connections across the kingdom, Zannanza was able to contact everyone who was invited to meet with the Adorians.

First, he sent a messenger to the Queen of the South telling her about their efforts to secure a safe return of the heralds to the Adorians. He also requested that Hamees would host the meeting, since it was going to be in her territory, specifically in Thebes. The old man was shocked when the messenger returned with a papyrus scroll sealed with the Queen's signet ring. He briefly exchanged a hesitant look with the priest, then he broke the seal in a rush.

"From the Queen of the South to Lord Zannanza," Hamees wrote in her message. "Only to stop this war and spare thousands of innocent lives, I agree, not only to attend this event but also host it. Feel free to arrange all the other

199

details with my advisors. Just to let you know, the high commissioner of the South will join me at the meeting."

It was great news for the old man and Amasis. However, he and Amasis felt ashamed that the woman that called herself the Queen of the South and sat on the throne of Upper Egypt could not make any decision without getting back to a foreigner. They thought about sending her another message to tell her that the presence of the Kushite high commissioner was not desirable, but they had to suck it up because they did not want to risk everything.

In the same day, Zannanza sent another courier to the north with a message to the Pharaoh of Lower Egypt. The messenger took almost forever, and Zannanza thought for a moment that he sent this young man to his death. He believed that Gapi had executed him and that he was going to receive the messenger's head soon with the refusal from the king of the north to attend the meeting. However, the old man released a sigh of relief when the messenger finally came back to Thebes. It turned out that when the messenger found out that Gapi was not in Memphis, he decided to follow him to the land of Kush. The messenger knew the importance of the message he carried, and he was ready to deliver it to Gapi even to the afterlife if he had to.

"From the Pharaoh of the North to Lord Zannanza," the old man listened to Amasis who was reading Gapi's message. "The north will be glad to end this war." Again, the old man cheered the excellent news with Amasis, yet they both did not fully comprehend the next part of the message, "And we are happy to help in retrieving the kidnapped heralds." Unfathomed, both looked at each other at first, then shrugged.

"I bet you the high commissioner of the north will invite himself, too," Zannanza, however, managed to tell the young priest.

"I don't have any doubt about it," Amasis commented.

Zannanza then sent more and more messengers with papyrus scrolls written by Amasis inviting dozens of noblemen and noblewomen across the country. For the next few days, the messengers returned, confirming that all the invited people accepted their invitation. The only exceptions were a nobleman who was just killed two days ago by the green beam of one of the celestials' spaceships and another old noblewoman who politely apologized that her health would not allow her two travel from Memphis to Thebes.

"Now what?" Zannanza asked about their next move.

"Now, we have to inform the princess that everything is being taken care of," the young priest said, "and that we are ready for her return."

Zannanza watched in awe when Amasis held his father staff and walked outside the house. When he muttered something to the staff and pointed it at a palm tree before the house, all the birds who were resting on the tree magically flew toward them and landed at their feet. Then, the young priest leaned forward, picked one of the birds, and whispered something in its ear. The bird had beautiful yellow and black feathers. Zannanza's eyes shot wide when he saw the bird first nodded its head to Amasis, then it flew away. A few days later, the old man was shocked when the same bird came back and stood on the priest's shoulder.

"I swear by the Gods I heard the bird softly whispered something in Amasis's ear," Zannanza would later tell everyone he knew about this outlandish trick which he saw with his own eyes.

"What is it saying?" Zannanza asked the young priest, he could not wait any longer.

The priest didn't answer. He just held up his hand, *Wait*.

When the bird was done, a big smile appeared on Amasis's face. Then, he reported, "She is on her way back with two precious cargos." Both men instantly believed that the two loads must contain the freed heralds.

"Well, I think we are ready then," Zannanza exclaimed. His role was over.

Chapter 19
The Arrival

A few days later, a blare of a trumpet sounded, announcing the departure of a small boat, carrying Queen of the South, from the royal palace in Thebes heading to the meeting location which was going to take place on board of the 140-foot-long royal boat, in the middle of the Nile. The boat had twelve oars on each side and was built completely of wood. No spikes were used in the assembly of the boat. It was tied securely together with papyrus reeds.

As the host for this event, Hamees carefully picked the time of her arrival. She wanted to board the royal boat after the coming of all the Egyptian noblemen and noblewomen, yet before the influx of the high-profile guests who were expected.

It was a sunny afternoon, not extremely warm because the breeze was picking up and a few clouds were thinly distributed over the sky. Birds were flying around, singing and chittering in the trees.

When Hamees arrived at the royal boat and was on board, dozens of men and women stood up and bowed to their queen. Even those who came from Lower Egypt still got to their knees for the Queen of the South, showing respect to their host. Hamees walked and sat on a luxurious chair which faced lines of seats which were assigned to the nobles. Next to her chair was another one who supposed to receive the high commissioner of the south. On her left hand was another chair on which Gapi was supposed to sit. Facing Gapi's chair was another one which was assigned to Princess Merit. Between the three chairs, there were another two on which the Libyan and Kushite commissioners were supposed to be seated.

Sitting on her chair, Hamees was offering polite and very brief smiles here and there to people she knew and others she never saw in her life. She was dressed in beautiful clothes and sparkling jewels. On her head, she wore the Hedjet crown of Lower Egypt. She was nervous and restless, wishing that her step-mother would have been there next to her.

***

Shortly, another blare of a trumpet sounded, announcing the arrival of Princess Merit. At first, she was seen riding her griffin, flying over dozens of small boats traveling north toward the meeting location. The boats were carrying Moeris and the Triple-Sevens troops who were guarding two covered boats which seemed carrying precious loads.

The One who Tears into Pieces first roared as he flew over the royal boat from where the nobles' shrieks filled the air. After two full circles about the boat, the king of all the creatures landed on the far end of the boat, causing hubbub among the soldiers who guarded the boat and causing the boat to plunge more than it usually did. Princess Merit jumped off the king of the creature and walked toward Hamees. The griffin then took off, however, every few moments, he would fly above the boat to make sure that his princess was safe.

Again, the nobleman and noblewomen on the boat stood up and bowed to their princess. After all, she was the rightful heiress to the throne even though she was not crowned. Merit was elegantly dressed in an Egyptian blue leather corset and skirt. Her swords on her back, and her bow was on her right arm.

"Welcome to Thebes," Hamees courteously greeted her guest, ushering her to her chair.

"Don't welcome me on my land and on my boat," Merit reminded her, and she could tell that her words made Hamees fume inwardly. She ignored her host and headed to her chair. Before she sat, she looked at the nobles with a charming smile and a little bow with her head.

The two foes restlessly sat, each of them recalling how the other one either killed her father or helped in killing her father. Hamees recalled the reports that described how the princess had brutally murdered Varis; meanwhile, Merit imagined how the father of the woman sitting near her now had mercilessly beheaded King Senu.

"You're much more beautiful than the last time we met," Hamees said, swallowing her pride and trying to ease the tension and sitting back on her chair.

"And you're still the same," Merit replied, with a dry voice and constrained smile.

They both were trying to speak as low as they could, so no one could hear them.

The last time Merit and Hamees saw each other was during the coronation of King Senu IV. Varis' daughter instantly liked the princess so much and tried to flirt with her through appraising her beauty. However, Merit was aware of her intention, and politely was able to not end up in her bed that night. That was why when Hamees today was making a compliment about the princess's beauty, Merit immediately said what she said in a way that meant that she was still not interested.

"I thought Gapi was supposed to come with you from the south," Hamees said, getting angry. She was trying to appear like she was aware of what was happening.

"We got separated once we left Napata," Merit revoltingly explained. "He insisted on taking a different route. I thought that he should be here by now."

"Well, he likes to show up last," Hamees replied. "He likes people to wait on him. He doesn't do any waiting."

"I'm sure it's something that runs in the family," Merit said in a mocking tone of voice, scoffing and looking away.

Only then, one more blare of a trumpet sounded, announcing the arrival of the high commissioner of the South, followed by his equivalent in the north. The Libyan commissioner in Lower Egypt was a large man with a strong-featured face and bushy eyebrows. Aged around forty, he seemed the type who would be too stubborn.

Merit angrily looked at Hamees and spoke under her breath in disgust, "That's what you and your brother have brought on us. Foreigners intervene in our internal affairs."

Hamees fired back with a silent, angry look.

"Well, at least your step-mother or whatever is left of her isn't here," Merit said.

"Nobody saw the Queen-Regent ever since you attacked the palace," Hamees responded.

"The Queen Regent!" Merit mocked, then she proudly spoke, looking upward at the griffin who was passing over head now. "The One who Tears into Pieces taught her a good lesson. She will think twice before she would get near us again."

Again, Hamees fired back with a silent, angry look.

When one more blare of a trumpet sounded, Hamees and Merit exchanged a look which meant, it must be him. And indeed, it was Gapi. Coming from the south was an elegant boat rowed by two strong men with oars. On board, Gapi stood next to Hent. He was dressed in the same military attire he wore during the liberation of the celestial heralds, yet he was now wearing the crown of the north.

"I heard that it was you who freed my brother's secret lover," Hamees whispered with a faint chuckle.

"Yes, it was me," Merit proudly whispered back. "And very soon, I will free the whole kingdom from this foreign invasion," she gave a disgusting look to the two commissioners who were sitting now on their seats, "and from all the domestic traitors." She returned her eyes with a challenging look.

"Do you really think that I, or my brother, would abandon our thrones for you?" Hamees wondered in a mocking tone, scoffing and lightly shaking her head; a big smile on her face.

"No, I never said it would be that easy," Merit fired back. "But I know for sure that I'm going to force you to do so. Not only this, but I will also unify this kingdom that your house has divided"

"You think you can do all that?" Hamees said in a doubting tone, scoffing, and her eyes scanning her guest from head to toe.

"Yes, I think so," Merit gave her another constrained smile.

"We shall see," Hamees challenged.

"We shall see." Merit dared back.

The royal boat rocked a little when Gapi boarded accompanied with Hent who instantly headed to Princess Merit and appreciatively bowed her head. It was the first time for Hent to meet the princess since she was freed. Once she was free from the dungeon, Hent was asked if she would like to join the princess, but she preferred to travel to protect her love. She went to the north, but he was not there. When she knew from the vizier of Lower Egypt the whereabouts of Gapi, she immediately traveled south and met him somewhere past the borderline area between Egypt and Kush.

After bowing to the princess of Egypt, Hent went back and stood next to her lover who was having now a heated argument with the Libyan high commissioner of Lower

Egypt. It was apparent, for everyone on the boat, that the Libyan man was giving grilling Gapi for traveling to Kush without consulting him. Gapi was angry, and his sign language became impatient, explaining himself.

"What a true ruler!" Merit mockingly whispered to Hamees.

"We had no other chance," Hamees defended between her teeth. "As you see, he lost his tongue for objecting to the treaty."

They both were still trying to speak as low as they can, so no one could hear them. They did not care about the two commissioners, one of them was sitting now between them, because they did not speak Egyptian.

"No, you had other options," Merit firmly objected. "You just preferred the easy one."

"What are we waiting for now?" Hamees tried to change the subject. She spoke loudly this time.

"Waiting for them," Merit replied, gesturing at their guests; a natural smile on her face.

In awe, everyone on the royal boat, Princess Merit, the Pharaoh of the North, the Queen of the South, the two commissioners, all the noblemen and noblewomen, even the soldiers who guarded the boat, looked to the north. They all watched in admiration the Adorian mothership, Colossal, which was escorted by twelve smaller ships, three on each side. Behind them came a fleet consisting of more ships; hundreds of them, following the mothership to the delivery place.

The arrival of the Adorians was marked with the most extraordinary respect from Gapi, Hamees, Merit, and all the other Egyptian nobles. Even the commissioners welcomed the Celestials with silence; faces down. It was natural respect for a much more advanced civilization coming to meet a relatively primitive nation.

As all the eyes were on the coming Adorian fleet, no one paid attention to what was approaching from the other direction, except for one. The king of all the creatures, who was still flying and hovering above the boat ever since he dropped the princess, suddenly roared and flew away to the opposite side.

Involuntarily, all eyes shifted from the celestials floating pyramids to the One who Tears into Pieces. Screams instantly filled the air, and hubbub buzzed around the whole place.

"No," Princess Merit screamed, running to the end of the boat and trying to get to her griffin before it was too late. She pushed against the tide of fleeing noblemen. She instantly realized that the One who Tears into Pieces roared, trying to alert her of the danger coming from the south. Meanwhile, he flew off to confront the threat himself.

Another dreadful roar caused more chaos on the boat. This time the cry was not from the griffin. It was Keya's who was coming now from the opposite side of the Adorian fleet, along with hundreds of parudas heading to the meeting location. The collective roars of these winged creatures struck fear in everyone were in the royal boat.

Chapter 20
The Parudas Army

Coming from the south was Keya who was leading an army of winged women, or parudas like the Kushites used to call. No one around was aware of the intention of this airborne army. They were heading to the delivery location and the Adorian fleet; but first, they had to confront the One who Tears into Pieces.

Hamees was not lying earlier when she told Merit that no one had seen the Queen-Regent ever since the princess attacked the royal palace to free Roma. After the second defeat of Keya at the claws of the king of all the creatures, the Queen of the South sent several Kushites bands after her step-mother to make sure she was ok. All the bands came back with one single report, "No trace of her could be found."

However, rumors swirled around like a wildfire that the winged creature had traveled to the land of Kush, seeking the help of her father's priests to be able to defeat the griffin.

When she arrived at Napata, she was shocked by the news that Princess Merit, along with the Pharaoh of North, had attacked King Alara's palace. She was even more dazed when she heard of what the Egyptians had done to her father.

The rumors continued to grow and fly that Keya, out of rage, and with the help of the Kushite priests, ordered to gather hundreds of skillful, female Kushite fighters. She lined them up in rows and had them all drink from the kairemi, the same way she did during the battle of Badari, just a very tiny bit of it. Then, the Kushite priests murmured a magical spell, closing their eyes and raising their arms in the air.

The stories continued to describe how these women felt pain in their muscles. Eventually, they began to groan, louder, and louder. At a certain point, their groanings turned into screams. As they were twisting and writhing in pain, they felt small objects protrude out of the back of their shoulders. They tried to look over their shoulders, but these things were too small to be seen. Gradually, they could see little wings, which were growing bigger and bigger by the moment, until they became as big as the griffin's wings.

Apparently, these rumors were not just rumors. They were the truth, and Keya was now coming to fight the One who Tears into Pieces, Princess Merit, and everyone who dared to attack her home kingdom. She even had the intention to attack the Adorians as well. Not only her but a whole army of Parudas.

Easily, one could distinguish Keya from the other parudas by her appearance. She was the only one on whom the kairemi had taken full effect. Anyone could tell that the other parudas had drunk this magical substance just a day or two ago. Tiny black feathers began to cover their entire body. Their eyes were turning into bloody smaller reddish eyes. Small fangs started to protrude from their shrunken gums, and their wrinkled lips commenced to leer horribly.

Their nails turned into short, yellow, and deadly claws. Their wings were like bat's with sharp hooks on them.

Not only this, anyone could effortlessly differentiate Keya from the rest because she was the only one who was dressed in fine chainmail, which barely covered her female parts. All the other parudas were completely naked, some of them held swords, others carried spears, most of them had axes, and a few held bows and arrows.

Everyone on the royal boat shivered to the marrow of their bones when the parudas army collectively roared, heading directly at the One who Tears into Pieces.

Princess Merit almost lost her mind when she saw the griffin roar one more time before dozens of these winged creatures swarm upon him from every side. For a moment, she looked around, and she found out that the royal boat was filled with screams, cries, panic, and chaos. The nobles were running for their lives. They ran in various directions, shrieking. When Merit turned her head back to the sky, she could not see the king of all the creatures anymore as dozens of the parudas overwhelmed him. Using their weapons, claws, and teeth, they were attacking him from all sides.

"No," the princess cried out and raised her arms at the air at the griffin's direction. She hoped that she could reach and help him. "No," she cried again when she heard his roars turn into shrieks and whimpering. She immediately pulled two arrows from the quiver and shot them together, killing two of the parudas. Faster than a light beam through space, she drew another three arrows and killed the next three of the winged creatures. She had to lean to the left to avoid being hit by one of the parudas which were attacking the royal boat now. Then, she quickly pulled two more arrows and killed two more of them.

Merit saw some heads, feet, limbs, hands, wings and other parts of the parudas fly in the air, and blood splash everywhere, amid of anguish screams of those monsters who were attacking the One who Tears into Pieces. However, the griffin's shrieks and whimpers were growing louder and louder; until at a certain point, it was a brief silence. Merit felt her heart stop, and her eyes instantly watered when she saw the substantial, bloody body of the king of all the creatures falling free from the sky and then disappeared into the Nile river in a huge splash.

Not believing her eyes, Merit stood there for a moment, staring at the water which had just swallowed her griffin. There was a brief moment of silence. Inside Merit's mind, all the shrieks and noise around her stopped all at once. Yet, she quickly had to get back to reality when a nobleman, who was running for his life, pushed her hard that she was about to fell off the boat. She barely caught the rail and steadied herself.

Merit looked around to find out that a lot of the Egyptian nobles were already killed by the parudas. The winged creatures were freely flying around, using their swords, spears, and axes to slash at and pierce people randomly. People were trying to escape the massacre, but there was nowhere else to go. They were in the middle of the water. When Merit looked for the small boat which brought Gapi a few moments ago, it was not there. When she turned her head to the right, she found Hamees, the Kushite high commissioner in Upper Egypt and the Libyan high commissioner in Lower Egypt had taken the boat and were fleeing to the royal palace.

Faster than a speeding cheetah, Merit cried out, "Jump into the water." Then, she kept repeating her instruction to the people around her.

"But I can't swim," objected a noblewoman dressed in a fancy canary-yellow dress.

"Trust me," Merit said. "Just jump." She even helped the lady by a gentle push, sending her flying into the water, screaming as loud as she could for help, and followed by other few nobles who flounced off into the water, screaming profanities.

""I, Merit, the daughter of Senu IV," Merit rushed to the boat's rail, closed her eyes and muttered, "and the legal heiress to the Egyptian throne, command The One Who Chews and The One Who Smashes to come out and help me."

Once she opened her eyes, two clumps of bubbles broke from the water's surface.

They're coming, she told herself. "Into the water," she cried out even louder, full of confidence now. "Trust me. To the water."

At first, the nobles around her exchanged hesitant looks, then they jumped off the boat. Some did it because they trusted their princess. Other jumped because they did not have any other option. A few needed more encouragement from Merit who helped them by gentle pushes.

As dozens of the Egyptian nobles were in the water, some of them screamed when they felt their feet hit something in the water; something which began to push them up.

Although Princess Merit was shocked of what had just happened and the death of her griffin, she felt a little comfort as she saw the heads of "The One Who Chews" and "The one who Smashes" emerging from under the water.

"Go, now," she screamed, and the two giant crocodiles instantly took the nobles away from the massacre which was taking place on the royal boat.

When the princess turned around, she found the parudas were killing those noblemen and noblewomen who did not trust their princess or did not get a chance to escape. She quickly pulled her two short swords and planted them deep between the rips of one of the parudas which was attacking a young lady next to her. She did not wait to see the outcome. Faster than a deer, she pulled her swords and swung one of them to decapitating another winged woman who happened to be flying nearby. By only a couple inches, Merit's sword missed one of the parudas who grabbed a nobleman by the waist and flew away, carrying him for a brief moment before dropping him in the water with a big splash.

The cargo, the princess suddenly remembered.

She had to stop fighting for a second and looked backward at the boats which she was flying over earlier. She released a sigh of relief when she saw Moeris and his Triple-Sevens force were proving for once and for all that they were the most legendary military battalion on the land of Egypt, or maybe in the entire known world.

Merit's eyes shone in admiration as she watched the Triple-Sevens had already gotten all their boat together, including the two covered boats; as close as they could get. Then, they had raised up their shield together in the air, forming one massive shield above their heads. The shields prevented the attacking parudas from reaching them or the cargo which they were guarding. Now, the princess watched in awe Moeris and his men shooting their arrows through holes in their shield at the winged creatures who were going down like dying flies.

Princess Merit's attention was brought back to the massacre taking place on the royal boat when one of the parudas attacked her from behind. She screamed in pain as claws tore into her shoulders. Right before the winged woman behind her could close her jaw about her neck, Merit violently recoiled against the boat's rail. The paruda shrieked in agony as her back crushed against the railing, giving the princess a brief a chance to release herself from the claws. She quickly turned around and send her right foot into the winged creature's chest, sending her off the boat. The paruda happened to fall right on top of the head of "The One Who Chews." The crocodile, who had over a dozen people on his back now, raised his head and received the winged women between his sharp teeth.

Knowing that she had no time to waste, Princess Merit quickly spun and started swinging her swords in a counterattack and stabbing the parudas who were flying

216

around her like bats. Only a few nobles were still there facing their death.

Merit felt her body flying in the air when something powerfully hit her from behind. Without looking back, she knew that it was Keya who attacked her. She had seen her doing the same to Roma during the battle of Badari. When the princess violently landed on the boat's wooden deck, she felt something brake inside. Through the overwhelming pain, she turned around and laid on her back for a moment to see Keya before her, flapping her wings and giving her a smirk, in a way that meant, *You're mine now after killing your stupid griffin.*

Keya was facing Merit, holding a bow at full draw, ready to end her life with one single shot in her heart. However, it was like a second, a split of a second, which separated the death of Merit from Hent's violent hit which knocked Keya out with a crashing thud. The hit was so forceful that Keya missed her target and threw her to the boat's deck. The arrow pierced the wooden floor only one inch away from Merit's face.

For a short moment, Merit eyes stared at the arrow that was still rattling next to her face, then she shifted her sight to Hent who was violently swinging her long sword at the flying parudas around her. Behind Hent, Merit saw Gapi fighting for his life too. Knowing that Hent's hit did not kill Keya and that she must be getting ready now to attack her from behind again, she quickly jumped to her feet and turned around. As Keya was angrily getting to her feet, Merit kicked her leg, sending her trembling across the boat. Grunting in pain and anger, Keya began to clamber to her feet, but the princess did not give her any chance, as she brought her elbow down hard on the winged woman's back sending her to the ground again.

Merit got distracted for a moment by two parudas who attacked her from above. She had to shift her focus from Keya to the direct danger above her head. It did not take her too long to pierce the sword in her right hand into one of the paruda's heart and to cut off the head of the other flying creature using the sword in her left. However, this brief period was enough to give Keya a chance to get back to her feet.

When Princess Merit turned around, she found out that it was only her, Gapi and Hent still alive on the boat. Everyone who did not escape on the back of the two crocodiles had been cruelly killed. She quickly spun to face the Kushite queen, and she found Gapi angrily swinging his sword at his step-mother. She heard a lot about how Keya and her step-son hated each other a great deal, evident in the fierce combat between them now.

Keya was using her bow to block Gapi's sword strikes; meanwhile, Merit noticed that Keya stretched her right arm out, with her hand held flat in step-son's direction. Then she muttered some mysterious words under her breath. As she was curling her hand slowly into a fist, Gapi suddenly stopped attacking her and opened his mouth in panic, gasping for air. He shuddered for a moment before collapsing to the floor, almost dead.

Merit had heard once before that Keya had some kind of magical power. When she curled her hand into a fist, she had actually squeezed Gapi's heart for real, crushing it, even though she was standing far away from him. Knowing that Keya's magical power was over men, and only men, and knowing that Gapi was still alive and that there was a chance to save him, Merit didn't hesitate for a moment to plunge into Keya, sending her off the boat.

As Merit was helping Gapi to stand to his feet, Keya came back faster than a rabbit being chased by a dog and slammed both the princess and her step-son and throw them away. The hit was so powerful that it was a shock to Merit that she and Gapi were still breathing afterward. As they were getting back on their feet, Hent came out of nowhere and jumped up, grabbing Keya by the feet and violently slamming her to the boat's wooden floor. Merit had known by Hent after freeing her how much she hated Keya who scammed her and made her the number one suspect in the failed attempt to assassinate Varis.

Without any kind of coordination, the three of them, Merit, Gapi and Hent, faster than cheetahs, they jumped over Keya as she laid sprawling face down. After a moment of struggling, Gapi and Hent were capable of holding Keya by the arms forcing her to stay down. Meanwhile, Princess Merit stood up, towering over Keya, and pulled her two swords. As a picture of the dead body of the One Who Tears into Pieces falling free into the river and another picture of the two now-orphan, baby griffins unfolded before the princess's eyes, she did not find any kind of hesitation to swing her two shorts swords, together, cutting off her two wings.

When a loud, long shriek came out of Keya's mouth, Merit, Gapi and Hent found themselves under attack by all the other parudas. They had to release Keya and duck down, their arms shielded their heads from the weapons, claws, and teeth of the attacking winged women.

For a moment, Merit thought that her death was imminent. No one was there to help. Her griffin was gone. Roma was not there to protect her. Moeris was far away, and not much he could do. The Free Army was not there to defend her. It was only her, along with Gapi and Hent, against hundreds of airborne monsters.

However, all of a sudden, the princess heard a boom, and she immediately felt that the parudas paused their attack. When she opened her eyes, she could tell that the crashing sound which she had just heard was a result of the green beam which one of the floating pyramids had launched next to the royal boat. It was like the People from the Sky - even though they were not supposed to intervene - had decided to distract the flying monsters who were attacking the legal heiress to the Egyptian throne.

Following the crashing sound of the Adorian green beam, Merit heard dreadful shrieks from some of the parudas. When she shifted her eyes up to see what was happening, she saw all the parudas leaving them alone and heading to attack the Adorian fleet. The Celestials not only succeeded in distracting the parudas army, but they also provoked them to attack.

At the same moment, Merit felt something hit the side of the boat and made it violently rock. She quickly ran to the boat's rail and looked downward to find "The One Who Smashes" down there. The giant crocodiles had already delivered the Egyptians nobles safely to the eastern bank of the Nile; and now, they were coming back to save the princess and whoever was left on the boat.

"Let's go," Merit cried out, jumping off the boat onto the back of "The One who Smashes," followed by Gapi and Hent who jumped onto the back of "The One who Chews."

As they were heading to the Nile bank, Merit crouched on the back of the crocodile. Worried about the precious cargo which she had brought from the land of Kush, she quickly turned her head toward the south. She found out that Moeris and the Triple-Sevens were breaking their massive shield after defeating the parudas who were trying to reach the precious cargo. Moeris himself, along with a few other fighters, was now checking the two covered boats to make sure that everything was alright.

Only then, Merit shifted her sight upward and to the North to find hundreds of parudas attacking Colossal and the other floating pyramids.

Chapter 21

Adorian Fangs

Even though the first commander of the Adorian fleet, Azan Zalga, had strict orders from the Supreme Council of Planet Adoria to not intervene in the tussle over the Egyptian throne, he could not stand idle and do nothing when the parudas army was about to finish the legal heiress to the Egyptian throne. Especially when he recognized the attackers; Kushites who had screwed up the whole situation from the very beginning.

There was a price for this, Azan knew. A price that the supreme council was going to make him pay for defying its orders. He had never done something like that before, he never disobeyed his leader; yet, he had to save Merit. He could not do nothing while the civilization which he personally nurtured to existence was going to hell because of some hating neighbors.

Inside Colossal, Azan stood in the middle of the hologram screen surrounded by his subordinates. The screen showed what was happening on the ground. Just a few moments ago, and as the Adorian first commander was watching dozens of winged creatures attacking Princess Merit on the deck of the royal boat, he ordered one of the floating pyramids to launch a distracting green beam, not at the boat, but next to it.

Now, Azan was standing in the middle of the screen, he was watching hundreds of parudas flying toward the mothership with no good intention. Before the winged creatures could reach the floating pyramids, the commander wiped the air with his tiny hands in a virtual explosion, then he watched the result on the screen.

Coming out of Colossal, a short burst of energy shielded the mothership and the entire Adorian fleet. The disruptive and damaging pulse was powerful enough that it wiped out hundreds of parudas in a blink of an eye. They just vanished like a puff of smoke in the wind. The rest of winged creature paused for a short moment, astonished and pondering their options; yet, they quickly flapped their wings, heading to the Adorian fleet.

When Azan saw that the warning shot did not scare off the aggressors, he instantly wiped the air again with his tiny hands. This time, his arms stretched away wider in a bigger simulated explosion. Another pulse of energy came out of the mothership and traveled faster than light, setting everything in its path on fire. The whole parudas army instantly was engulfed in fire, and its winged monsters were falling down burning like miniature comets before they hit the river in splashes and whooshing sounds.

***

Not believing his eyes, Amasis stood at the main dock of Thebes. He was half-troubled, half astonished. He stood there with mixed feelings inside him and diverse expressions on his face. He was fuming because of the massacre which had just taken place on the royal boat, yet he was in awe seeing one of the Adorians' advanced weapons. It was not like anything else. The Celestials had just destroyed a whole army of flying monsters in a blink of an eye like this. The People from the Sky had just viciously bared their fangs to those who dared to assault them.

"Amasis," a female voice drew his attention.

When he turned around, he recoiled in surprise. Before his eyes stood the first female priest in the kingdom of Egypt. Instantly, he felt butterflies in his stomach and his heart as he saw his junior priest walking toward him. He could not believe it and thought it was no more than a dream.

"Amasis," Nefer's voice came again to wake him from his daydream.

"Nefer," he could not help it. He ran to her and hugged her with all his might. "I can't believe it. I can't believe that I have you again." He held her in the way soldiers held their loved ones when they returned from war. "I missed you so much."

"I missed you too," she said with watery eyes.

"Where have you been?" He quickly asked, releasing her. "And why did you leave me in the first place? Did I hurt you? Did I say anything you didn't like? Why? I can't understand. How did you reach the Adorians? And how..." The questions did not stop until she approached him, her breasts touched his chest, and gently put her soft index finger on his lips with a shush.

"You will know everything," she quietly said, looking directly at his eyes. "Don't worry, I will tell you about it all. But first, we have something more important to do. We have to deliver the heralds before it's too late. Amasis, do you understand?"

Since his lips were blocked by her finger, Amasis responded with only a hesitant, gentle nod. However, his eyes exposed how strongly the sense of curiosity was eating at him.

As they were talking, suddenly their attention was arrested by the sound of the two giant crocodiles who were carrying on their backs Princess Merit and the last two survivors from the royal boat's massacre.

"My lady," the young priest cried out, running toward the "One who Smashes" who just came out of the water, followed by his brother.

He watched the princess jump off the crocodile, shocked, dripping wet and out of breath, and saying, "We have to get this done. Any Ideas, Amasis?"

Amasis could tell that Merit was using all her strength to hold her tears after witnessing the murder of dozens of her people and the death of the One who Tears into Pieces.

"My Lady," Nefer called out as Hent was helping her love to jump off the "One Who Chews." "I think I know what we should do."

Amasis noticed that the princess did not recognize the person who was talking to her. He was getting ready to introduce Nefer to the future-queen of Egypt, but Merit did not give him a chance.

"Nefer?" She wondered, tilting her head and narrowing her eyes.

"Yes, My Lady," Nefer surely answered.

"I know that you have already played a critical role in arranging for the delivery," Merit said in a rush. There was no time for a proper introduction, or wondering where Nefer had been, neither how she managed to contact the Celestials. "You really know how we could save the day?"

Nefer did not answer. She just looked at the princess directly in the eyes, nodded her head confidently, and then shifted her sight toward Amasis.

Shortly, the Triple-Sevens arrived. The young priest watched Moeris signaling to his men, who immediately uncovered the first boat, revealing its content. Inside the boat, there were the seven Adorian heralds whom the Kushites had kidnapped and Princess Merit had recently freed. When Moeris and his soldiers uncovered the second boat, Amasis recoiled in shock. Before his eyes was King Alara of Kush, gagged and bounded from behind.

Princess Merit took a moment to explain to Amasis that after freeing the heralds, she, with the help of Gapi and his men, and of course the Triple-Sevens, was able to storm the royal bedchamber and arrest the king of Kush with intention to deliver him, along with the free celestials, to the Adorians for his crimes.

"Now what?" Merit then wondered, addressing Nefer.

As Nefer continued telling them how to deliver the heralds to the Adorians, everyone there suddenly shivered to the marrow of their bones, and their head immediately scanned around, when they heard screams of anguish mixed with angry shouts.

***

With sad eyes, Azan continued watching through the hologram screen what was happening out there. The screen was not focused on the royal boat anymore. Instead, it moved to the east a little to the city of Thebes, where the first commander of the Adorian fleet, along with his subordinates, was watching live pictures of what was happening in the capital of Upper Egypt.

A few moments ago, the Kushites mercenaries who guarded the city's gates had betrayed Queen Hamees and opened the gates to the Kushite Army which followed Keya to attack Egypt after kidnaping King Alara of Kush.

Thousands of huge, bare-footed men with dark skin, dressed in simple kilts and feathers in their hair, were running in Thebes' streets, randomly killing and wounding civilians; women, children, and elderlies; as well as detaining scores of people. They were setting everything they can reach on fire; houses, markets, temples, and stables. Burning animals ran off, screeching, killing innocent people under their hooves and causing more fire.

When the hologram screen zoomed in at the royal palace, he saw the Kushite high commissioner in Upper Egypt standing in the window of appearance, giving orders to more Kushite soldiers to kill as many innocents as they could reach, torch as many buildings as they could, rob as many treasures as they pleased, and seize as many Egyptians as possible. Meanwhile, the Queen of the South stood next to him, ashamed and her eyes were constantly fixed on the ground, not able to defy Shubba's orders.

***

Later that night, and as the Kushites soldiers continued burning the city of Thebes and killing its innocent, civilian residents, Nefer stood next to Amasis at the main dock. Even though she still could hear the sound of screams, sobs, cries, and terror coming from the city, she tried to stay focused. She must help the young priest to deliver the heralds to the Adorians before it was too late. She knew that Azan Zalga was not going to wait forever. The deadline was within reach. If the heralds were not delivered by dawn, the Egyptian civilization was going to meet the same destiny of Planet Loki.

Before Nefer's eyes, Colossal, and the entire Adorian fleet hovered over the Nile, waiting for the signal to approach. She looked at Amasis and encouraged him by a nod. He first responded with a small nod, then he tapped his right index finger twice on his staff's handle and muttered something under his breath. Emanating from the staff's handle, a pillar of light rose into the sky which he directed to Colossal. It was the signal for the Adorians that they were ready for the delivery.

Behind Amasis and Nefer nervously stood Princess Merit who obviously wanted to run to save the innocent people of the burning city of Thebes, yet she had to stay to deliver the freed messengers. Gapi was there too, along with Hent. Moeris and dozens of soldiers from the Triple-Sevens guarded the site.

Shortly, Nefer saw Colossal approach the dock and hover nearby. When the door of the mothership opened, everyone on the pier had to shield their eyes as the interior of the mothership was lit by blinding light. When Nefer's eyes adapted to the bright light, she could see silhouettes of six Adorians coming out of the ship. They were Azan and his five subordinates who mysteriously were moving forward; their feet not touching the floor and their wings not flapping. When the Celestials arrived at the dock, everyone there slightly bowed their head in respect for their guests.

In advance, Nefer knew that she was going to play a critical role in this meeting. She was going to be the interpreter.

"Welcome to Egypt," Merit said in a sad tone, and Nefer translated to Azan what was being said into Adorian. "I'm Princess Merit, the rightful heiress to the Egyptian throne after my father, Senu IV."

Azan replied with only a small nod.

"Thank you for saving my life," Merit continued, and Nefer interpreted. "Without your help, I would not be alive."

"Yes, without your help, we all would be dead by now," Gapi intervened using sign language, but Azan cut him off.

"Don't talk to me unless you are sitting on the Egyptian throne," Nefer translated.

"But I'm the Pharaoh of the Lower Egypt," Gapi irritably objected.

Azan did not say anything to him, he just looked at Merit and continued, "I'll pay a high price for helping you out."

Merit did not have any words to offer, so Nefer singled to her to move on in the conversation.

"We can't fix your destructed floating pyramid," Merit continued, and Nefer helped her with the interpretation, "but we were happy to release the heralds from the Kushites' hands."

When Merit looked behind, the seven freed messengers moved forward and joined their first commander and his subordinates.

"Not only this," Merit said, "we also managed to capture the person who was behind the attack on your ship." Again, she looked behind, and two soldiers of the Triple-Sevens came forward; each was holding King of Kush by the arm. Alara was angrily muttering some profanities behind his gag.

Azan first appreciatively nodded his head to Merit, then he raised his hands in the air. Mysteriously, King Alara was raised to the air, and his body was moved inside the ship; still mumbling vulgarities.

"What are you going to do with him?" Gapi wondered using sign language, and Nefer interpreted.

Azan replied that there was going to be a trial for King Alara of Kush before the Supreme Council of Adoria who would decide his fate.

"Please help us," Merit suddenly pleaded, as the sound of screams, sobs, cries, and terror kept coming from the burning city behind them.

"I truly can't," Azan made it clear.

"But we need your help," the princess' eyes watered. "Right now, my innocent people are paying the price of arresting the king of Kush. The Kushites are killing everyone in their way and burning everything which they can reach. Please help us."

Azan sadly shook his head, then explained, "I already did too much, and I will pay a high price for it." After a moment of silence, he added, "But I can help him to be the next pilgrim." He looked at Amasis whose mouth fell agape in surprise.

Nefer continued to translate Azan's words, yet she cast her eyes proudly toward the young priest. She looked at him like any proud woman would look at her special man.

"We appreciate that," Nefer said, yet she was disappointed.

Chapter 22

The Ruins of Thebes

The next morning, outside the walls of the ruined city of Thebes, Princess Merit stepped into a pavilion which was situated at the extremity of a beautiful garden. The pavilion was overlooking the ruins of the city where smoke and ashes were so thick that no one could see the buildings nor the sun. Over two dozen Kushites guarded the high-profile parley to which Princess Merit was invited.

Inside the pavilion sat Shubba, for the first time, on a higher chair than Hamees' who sat next to him, her head to the ground. On the other side, Gapi and the Libyan high commissioner in Lower Egypt sat next to each other. Hent stood behind her lover.

Escorting Princess Merit to the Meeting was Zannanza and Moeris, along with four warriors from the Triple-Sevens, two before them and two behind.

"We demand the immediate release of King Alara of Kush," Shubba said in Kushite, and Zannanza quietly translated to the princess. The Kushite high commissioner did not even invite them to sit down. "Thebes was just a start. This morning I ordered the Kushite army to do the same to Dendera. Tomorrow, they will attack Abydos. And on and on until King Alara is safely released."

"I'm afraid we don't have King Alara anymore," Princess Merit replied, anger boiling inside her. "If you need your king, you have to talk to the People from the Sky."

"Why would I talk to them if you are the one who attacked our lands and kidnapped our king?" The high commissioner said, scoffing.

"You should be appreciated for what I have done," she lost her temper. "If it's not for me, our planet would be burning by now."

Zannanza tried to hold the princess' hand to calm her down, but she quickly pushed him away.

"My lady," Moeris hissed, putting his hand on the handle of his sword. "Give me the order, and I will gladly send every one of them to have dinner with Anubis tonight."

"The Celestials never attacked the land of Kush," Shubba spoke with the same mocking tone. "We have no business with them."

"You don't understand," Merit responded, even angrier. "The destruction of both Egypt and Kush was inevitable if I didn't deliver the heralds along with your stupid king who got us all in this mess."

Even before the princess could finish her sentence, the spears of the Kushite fighters who guarded the pavilion were raised in the air to Merit's face. Moeris and his men did not need an order to protect their future-queen; their swords instantly were pulled and pointed at the Kushites.

"How dare you?" The Kushite high commissioner yelled, standing up.

"You are talking to the rightful heiress to the Egyptian throne," Zannanza reminded the Kushites.

"What throne?" Shubba derided. "Which one?" His mocking eyes sending his cold, cruel look toward Hamees and then toward her brother; both of them ashamed and looking at the ground.

"There's only one throne in the Kingdom," she challenged. "It's the one on which my father sat."

"In your dream," the Kushite sarcastically said.

"Be careful of my dreams," Merit warned him, "because they come true. I've dreamt once of my return to claim my father's crown, and here I am. I also have dreamed of delivering the heralds safe to the Celestials, and I did it. Moreover, I've dreamed of arresting your king, and it is done. And now, I'm dreaming of beheading you." She scoffed.

"I'm warning you, little girl," Shubba lost his temper. "If King Alara is not here by tonight, tomorrow morning the Kushite Army will burn the next city on its path."

"And I'm warning you, little boy," she challenged. "Keep your army here to protect you because my army will be here at dawn to kick out all the foreigners from the city and the kingdom. Tomorrow, all the Egyptians will unite to fight you."

"All the Egyptians!" The Kushite echoed, chuckling. "I told you. You're a dreamer."

"Yes, all the Egyptians," the princess confirmed.

"As far as I know the army of the north," he looked at Gapi, "and the army of Upper Egypt," he turned his head to Hamees, "are going to stay neutral in this fight."

With eyes full of disgust, Merit looked at Gapi and said, "Prince Gapi, is this true?"

He did not respond, his eyes fixed at the ground beneath him.

"After all we went through?" She demanded, "And after I saved your life. I thought you cared about the Egyptians, especially after helping me to retrieve the heralds."

Yet, Gapi never responded.

Angrily, the princess shifted her eyes to Hamees, giving her a contemptuous look.

"I'm not going to ask you the same," Merit talked to her, disgustingly, "because I know that you would do anything to stay on the throne."

Then, she addressed both the siblings, "I've already given you a chance to fix your mistakes, yet you turned it down. For your betrayal, you both are going to die tonight."

***

"We tripled the guards around your bedchamber, My Queen," Hamees' advisor told her. "Not even a fly would come in or out without my personal approval. Please, go to bed, My Lady. You need to get some rest. We need you sharp tomorrow."

Nervously, Hamees was sitting on a luxurious chair next to her bed, biting her nails. Princess Merit's threat flashed through her mind every time she tried to close her eyes.

"Not enough," she yelled at the old man before her. "Add another dozen. I don't feel safe."

"There's over a hundred guards on duty tonight," the man tried to soothe her, "most of them are already around your room."

"Just do what I told you to do," she screamed, "or I will find someone to do it."

Not fathoming what was happening, the man nodded his head to his queen and then left.

"I need to relax," Hamees told herself. "There is no need for all that." She tried to calm herself down. "The One who Tears into Pieces is dead. The Free Army won't be here till morning. So, there is no need to worry. This bitch can't come here alone. Just relax. Just breathe. Breathe. Breathe."

Hamees desperate efforts to relax herself were suddenly broken by a faint meow. When she looked at her bed, she saw her magical cat, looking at her and giving her a wink.

"I think you're right," she spoke to her pet; a natural smile appeared on her face. "I need to focus on something else." She finished with a clap from her hands. "I need some sex. I need a release."

As Hamees was standing up and removing her see-through rope, the cat turned into a striking, naked woman ready to satisfy her queen in whatever way she thought would gratify. Instantly, Hamees walked to the bed, but the woman quickly jumped off and met her in the middle.

"You know what to do," the queen said in a naughty tone, throwing herself in the woman's arms. Their lips met, and their breaths mingled like a soft breeze before they deepened their kiss. It was a soft, passionate kiss which instantly made Hamees melt. She pulled the woman's right hand and put it on her breast, inviting her to touch her. The woman replied by violently turning her around and fondling her left breast from behind while kissing her neck, up and down. Hamees felt a shiver run through her body when the woman's tongue touched her ear.

When Hamees looked at their reflection on the highly-polished bronze mirror next to the bed, she thought that this was precisely what she needed to get through this horrible night. However, her eyes suddenly shot wide open when she saw, in the mirror, the woman was holding a knife against her throat. Even before Hamees could say or do anything, the blade sliced across her throat; instantly made her feel her warm blood on her chest.

"The Queen of Egypt sends her regards," the woman whispered in Hamees' ears who held one hand over her throat trying to stop the flow of blood, and then she sank to the ground.

The sound of Hamees' body thudding on the floor instantly forced the guards at the door to check on her. When they came in, they stopped short in horror, seeing the Queen of the South laid naked on the floor in the middle of a small pool of blood, drawing her last breath. When they looked around for the killer, they found no one. They just found the knife that sliced their queen' throat lying next to her dead body.

"Meow," they only heard the cat which was laying on the bed saying.

***

At the exact same moment, Gapi entered his tent, stumbling over his own feet and falling against the nearby wall. He was drunk like a fish. Intentionally, he drank himself to a state of unconsciousness, trying to forget how he betrayed, not only Princess Merit, but all the Egyptians.

A few minutes later, when the guards on his tent heard a thud of a body striking the floor, they rushed inside to see the Pharaoh of the North take his last breath and close his eyes forever.

"Meow," was the only thing the guards heard when they searched for the assassin who killed their king. Sitting on a chair made of reed and wood was Gapi's cat getting ready to take a nap.

Epilogue

At dawn, Merit stood with watery eyes; her arms crossed over her chest; two men in uniform kneeling before her. The first was Lagus, the commander of the southern army; and the other was Gebal, the leader of Lower Egypt's military. Just a little bit ago, the two generals arrived at the old temple of Amun, outside the city of Thebes, which was highly secured by the Triple-Sevens. The temple was no more than an abandoned wreckage after moving all the religious ceremonies to the new Amun temple in the Karnak Complex.

After learning about the death of the Queen of the South and the Pharaoh of Lower Egypt, Lagus and Gebal, came to Merit, kneeled before her, and pledged loyalty to their new queen, believing that their troops must join the Free Army and that all the Egyptians must unify to defeat the Kushites who had turned Thebes into a no more than ashes and ruin.

As the two generals stood up and stepped back, the Egyptian High Priest, Perneb, started a symbolic coronation ceremony for the queen of Egypt in the presence of a couple of hundreds of Thebans who survived the Kushites' attack on their beloved city. With grim and weary expressions on their faces, the old men and small children, barefoot girls and bare-chested women, huge men and little men, and poor folks and rich nobles stood in lines witnessing the crowning ceremony for their legal queen.

The coronation ceremony started with the Pschent being carried on a raspberry-colored pillow in a procession around the gathered people. After the murder of Gapi and his sister, Perneb came out of the royal palace carrying the red and white double crown that symbolized the unification of Upper and Lower Egypt. Secured by over two dozen of loyal veterans who believed in Merit's right to the Egyptian throne, he walked through the streets of the ruined and still burning Thebes in a venerable scene which made the survived Thebans leave their dead and injured relatives and beloved ones and follow him to the old temple of Amun to witness a moment they all waited so long for it. The Pschent was followed by another pillow on which was placed shepherd's crook and flail.

After blessing the new queen of Egypt, the high priest placed the Pschent upon her head. Merit could not hold her tears, remembering that her father was murdered because of this crown and recalling what had happened to Thebes and its people. Then, Merit carried the shepherd's crook and flail and crossed her arms over her chest again.

When the high priest turned around to face the people, he hailed, "Long live Queen Merit," followed by a lusty cry from the crowd, "Long live Queen Merit." Meanwhile, the queen stood there trying to appear stronger than she was at that moment. More tears rolled down Merit's cheek when the high priest, the two generals, the soldiers of the Triple-Sevens and the entire crowd kneeled before their new queen.

A little bit after the coronation, the Free Army appeared in the horizon, marching west to the burning city of Thebes. Ten thousand insurgents; lines of cavalry, archery, and infantry, came from their secret training camp in Wadi Hammamat and were heading now to liberate the Capital of Egypt from the Kushites' hand. Zannanza was leading the Free Army now. He had traveled very early that morning to meet the rebels somewhere in the Eastern Desert.

As the Free Army was approaching Thebes, Queen Merit was riding on a white horse, dressed in her military gear and wearing the blue war crown. Behind her rode Lagus and Gebal.

When Queen Merit looked over her shoulder, she saw a mixture of the army of the north and the southern troops. Ten thousand infantry deployed in the center, five thousand cavalries on the flanks and five thousand chariots on the wings. They were waiting for the arrival of the Free Army to form a united army consisting of thirty thousand Egyptians capable of crushing the Kushites who separated them from Thebes.

Not only this, But Moeris was also there, along with his Triple-Sevens battalion. The legendary band stood on top of a high eminence, waiting to intervene in this battle if needed. For a moment, Moeris looked at the blue lotus which he held in his left hand, then he smiled, throwing the flower away. Then he turned his sight to the queen of Egypt, waiting for her command and knowing that he had already redeemed himself and that he was in no need to be intoxicated anymore to be able to fight.

When Merit looked forward, she saw a massive army of the Kushites consisting of chariots, cavalry, and footmen, lined up in front of the walls of Thebes. Shubba was leading the Kushites, not knowing that regardless of this battle's results, King Alara was not coming back.

237

The cutest smile in the worlds spread on Princess Merit's face, and she felt butterflies in her heart when she heard a loud roar of a monster approaching. She even felt the ground beneath her horse's hooves shaking with every move the monster took.

***

Coming from the North was Roma riding on the back of the Ra-Nt-Ka. Proudly, he sat on the back of the dinosaur, looking forward to seeing the look on his lover's face. He did not only succeed in locating and retrieving the looted treasures, but he also was able to tame the last Ra-Nt-Ka that walked on the land of Egypt. And now, he was heading to boost the army of his queen with the most colossal monster was known in the kingdom.

When the Ra-Nt-Ka roared one more time, Roma could see the hubbub instantly take place in the enemy's lines.

***

At the same instant, Amasis was boarding a small Adorian pyramid which landed north of Thebes. After the safe delivering of the heralds, Azan fulfilled his promise to the queen of Egypt that he was going to help this young priest to be the next pilgrim. Amasis now was entering the Adorian spaceship, ready to travel across the galaxy to be the Adorians' guest on their planet for at least twelve moons to learn as much of their magic as possible. Thinking of how much his father would be proud of him, he proceeded in, promising himself that he was going to come back to help Merit when she set on the Egyptian throne.

***

In a fabulous location on the Red Sea coastline, the high priest of Egypt, Perneb, entered a small cave at the foot of a great hill by the sea with giant cliffs looming above. He was accompanied by a small military band which Princess Merit had assigned for him a few hours ago for this mission. After the death of Gapi and Hamees, Perneb kneeled before Merit, declaring his loyalty to the only rightful heiress to the Egyptian throne.

To forgive Perneb for serving an illegitimate king and queen, the princess ordered him to stay in his position for now, but he was going to step down once Amasis returned from Planet Adoria. Also, Merit commissioned him to lead a rescue duty for the two orphan, baby griffins. As soon the high priest entered the cave, he cast a magical spell which made the two babies sleep peacefully, and the soldiers who accompanied him were able to quietly move them to Thebes, where Queen Merit was going to name them the new guards for her future-husband and herself. "The Queen of all Creatures," for her, and "The King of all the Creatures" for Roma.

***

Back in Thebes, and on top of a high peak on the left hand of Merit's army, stood Nefer dressed in leopard-skin. She was reading from "The Great Ones of Egypt" book which was held by another old priest; meanwhile, she held in her right hand Amasis' staff, which every time she read a name, it spontaneously moved into the air, pointing in the direction where this Pharaoh's tomb was located; exactly like Amasis had instructed her before his departure to Adoria.

***

In that instant, hundreds of miles away, at the Valley of the Kings, the circular stone which blocked the tomb's door moved to the side as if some mysterious power had pushed it away. The wax seal on the tomb's door abruptly exploded, and the door flew open. As the mummies of Senu III and his brother, Senu IV, were leaving the tomb, the Terrifying One came back to life, got to his paws, and roared loudly.

The two mummies did not climb onto the back of the Terrifying One like they did in the battle of Badari. Instead, the beast roared and stayed there to protect the deceased Pharaohs' tombs and treasures. Meanwhile, the pharaoh mummies, along with other dozens of mummies across the kingdom, walked forward into the deserts, then they all suddenly stopped. When they all, in synchronization, raised their arms a little, a dry, sand wind blew violently, and small whirlwind began to form beneath each one of them. As the twisters got stronger and stronger, the mummies magically flew in the air, still trapped inside the eye of the whirlwinds, and began traveling in high speed, answering Nefer's call and heading to Thebes to help the Queen of Egypt.

To be continued...

The Demi-Goddess of Egypt

A Sneak Peek

Even though the Adorians made sure that Amasis memorized the magical spell which he was trying to cast now, he stood speechless in the doorway of Senu's burial chamber. He was not able to utter a single word or intelligent sound. It appeared like the words suddenly vanished from his mind when he tried to summon them.

Dressed only in a leopard-skin sash, he just stood there, frozen and hardly breathing. He was staring at Queen Merit, who was in the middle of the chamber; her sad, teary eyes were looking down at her father's monumental stone sarcophagus.

As Amasis was trying to remember the words, he felt his heart ache for the queen because she could not yet ascend her father's throne even though she won the battle of Thebes. He felt waves of sadness since she had no other option now but to descend to the underworld and ask for the help of the gods, especially after losing the man whom she loved.

241

"I'm sure it starts with Anubis," Amasis tried to stay focused, rubbing his head hard to remember the spell. "Yes, yes, it starts with Anubis." And it seemed like the words unexpectedly flashed in his mind and rushed to his mouth. "Anubis, Anubis, the lord of the underworld, please accept our offerings and permit our queen the honor of entering the realm of the dead."

According to what the new high priest of Egypt had learned on his pilgrim journey across the galaxy to planet Adoria, the only way the queen could cross to the afterlife, or Duat as the Egyptians used to call it, was through a touching-point between the world of the living and the underworld. It has to be a burial chamber or a tomb where dead people could cross to Duat. Earlier that day, when Amasis outlined his plan to save Egypt to Queen Merit, she elected using her father's tomb, in the Valley of the Kings, as her gateway to the afterlife.

Amasis had to repeat the call when he received no response, "Anubis, Anubis, the lord of the underworld, please accept our offerings and permit our queen the honor of entering the realm of the dead." This time louder and with a rising edge to his voice. He also pointed his father's magical staff at the cold, rocky floor, where earlier that day, he had cut his hand, poured blood, and drawn the symbol of Duat, a star-in-circle, not too far from the doorway.

Amasis flinched when his dried blood on the floor suddenly and magically began to glow with a mystical blue color. Also, he almost leaped out of his skin because of the weird noises which suddenly emanated from the symbol. At first, it sounded like a rambling gibberish of a madman mixed with distant thunder, but as soon as Amasis' ear was in tune, he could make out the words. It was the lord of the underworld responding to his call.

"Only dead may cross the gateway," the voice was so powerful that Amasis felt the hair on the back of his neck bristled with the thought that a god had just talked back to him.

242

Most probably, Anubis is going to refuse to help a living person even if it is the queen herself, the high priest recalled the instructions of his mentor on planet Adoria. *If this happened, Queen Merit has no other option but to confront Apep.*

Please, gods, Amasis prayed in his mind, *don't let this be happening. Please, don't force her to face such a dreadful beast.*

One more time, he pleaded to the lord of the afterlife with fading hope, "Anubis, Anubis, the lord of the underworld, please accept our offerings and permit our queen the honor of entering the..."

Before Amasis could finish the sentence, a terrifying roar filled the air. His heart raced wildly with anticipation of what was coming next. He knew that Anubis did not produce this frightful roar that rumbled both the world and the underworld. He knew it was the gatekeeper, Apep, who was coming out now to prevent Queen Merit from entering the underworld.

When tiny beams of light began to make their way out of the glowing blood on the floor, Amasis shifted his focus back to the symbol of Duat. He took a deep breath and willed his heart to slow, focusing the handle of his father's staff toward the illuminating star-in-circle.

As Amasis continued casting the spell, cracks began to form in the ground, within and around the symbol. The faster he muttered, the wider the cracks grew. More blinding light broke through the cracks accompanied by intense sounds of something trying to make its way out of the ground, causing the ground beneath their feet first shook violently. Then, it was like a thousand claps of thunder occurred simultaneously.

"Watch out," he screamed, warning the queen, and Merit rapidly held onto her father's sarcophagus so she would not fall. That was right before the symbol of Duat exploded, showering the chamber with debris and letting a giant serpent rush out with a terrifying roar.

For a brief moment, the new high priest of Egypt felt his legs give way, and he almost slumped to the ground. He instantly recalled what he had learned about the giant snake which was coming out of the underworld now. It was Apep, the lord of darkness, and the greatest enemy of the bringer of light, Ra. In addition to the endless battle between Ra and Apep in the afterlife, the lord of darkness also guarded the gate to the underworld and permitted only dead people to cross to the other side. Amasis knew that this monster was coming out now to defend the gate which he had just opened and to prevent Queen Merit from passing through Duat.

The body of the giant serpent was very long, over 50 feet, and thicker than a tree trunk and covered with glittering scales. Once Apep was halfway through the gate, he turned around to face the pretty young woman who was standing before the sarcophagus. He looked at her with his gloomy eyes and hissed at her menacingly. With wild expectation, Merit challenged him with a glare which made Apep attack even faster.

"Now," Amasis instructed in a rushed tone; and immediately, Merit fell backward before Apep's teeth could tear into her flesh. The giant snake had to pause for a brief moment, not fathoming what his eyes were seeing, especially when the queen's body violently hit the floor and mysteriously transformed into a flock of white birds flying everywhere at once. In his surprise, the lord of darkness momentarily froze, not knowing which bird to attack.

"Here," Amasis quickly hollered before the snake would hurt any of the birds. "Over here." He was trying to distract Apep, so the queen would be able to use the opportunity. He wanted to clear the way for her, so she could sneak into the underworld through the gate which he had just opened and from which this monster had just come out.

... to be continued

244

OTHER EXQUISITE SPECULATIVE FICTION FROM D. X. VAROS, LTD.

THE HEIRESS OF EGYPT
Samuel Ebeid

THE PRISONER OF THE
CASTLE OF ENLIGHTENMENT
(coming February 2020)
Therese Doucet

BATTERED
SMOTHERED
(coming May 2020)
G. P. Gottlieb

A STORM BEFORE THE WAR
THE SOUL OF A STRANGER
(coming July 2020)
Phillip Otts

THE INQUISITOR'S NIECE
Erika Rummel

INTO THE FAIRY FOREST
J. M. Stephen

WHERE THE ALLEGHENY MEETS
THE MONONGAHELA
WE HAVE MET THE ENEMY
SPOOKY ACTION AT A DISTANCE
(coming March 2020)
Felicia Watson

IMMORTAL BETRAYAL
IMMORTAL DUPLICITY
IMMORTAL REVELATION
PROPHECY OF THE AWAKENING
Daniel A. Willis

CPSIA information can be obtained
at www.ICGtesting.com
Printed in the USA
FSHW021847151019
63023FS

9 781941 072608